M000101984

AN INCONVENIENT WIFE

A MODERN TUDOR MYSTERY

KAREN E. OLSON

PEGASUS CRIME

NEW YORK LONDON

AN INCONVENIENT WIFE

Pegasus Crime is an imprint of
Pegasus Books, Ltd.
148 West 37th Street, 13th Floor
New York, NY 10018

Copyright © 2024 by Karen E. Olson

First Pegasus Books cloth edition April 2024

Interior design by Maria Fernandez

All rights reserved. No part of this book may be reproduced in whole or in part without
written permission from the publisher, except by reviewers who may quote brief excerpts
in connection with a review in a newspaper, magazine, or electronic publication; nor may
any part of this book be reproduced, stored in a retrieval system, or transmitted in any
form or by any means electronic, mechanical, photocopying, recording, or other, without
written permission from the publisher.

Library of Congress Cataloging-in-Publication Data is available.

ISBN: 978-1-63936-565-4

10 9 8 7 6 5 4 3 2 1

Printed in the United States of America
Distributed by Simon & Schuster
www.pegasusbooks.com

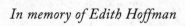

In memory of Edith Hoffman

Oh, how many torments lie in the small circle of a wedding ring!

—Colley Cibber, *The Double Gallant*

PROLOGUE

They came in the early morning. The police cars, sirens blaring, lights flashing against the cattails, a bright red strobe, like blood splatter. Voices drifted across the lawn, unintelligible, swallowed by the humid summer air.

The six-bedroom wood-and-stone Craftsman house on the other side of the marsh had been freshly painted robin's-egg blue with white trim and had the air of a girl waiting for her prom date who was late. The shutters still covered the windows; it hadn't been opened for the season, even though it was already June. It sat on a rare secluded spot with a cobblestone driveway about a quarter of a mile from the main road. The only ones who'd been there so far this summer—until today—were the ubiquitous landscapers who mowed and weeded and tended to the gardens of the rich and comfortable all over town.

It was understated, considering who owned it. A man who had amassed massive wealth, owned several international companies, and yet was still most known for his weakness for wives.

The reporters would arrive next. They'd hear about this on the police scanners, climb into their vans with the satellite dishes on top, each hoping to be the one who'd get the exclusive. They wouldn't stick to the crime scene. They'd come here, asking their questions, probing into their lives.

It was bad enough that they skulked at the edges already, always watching. But this would give them permission, under the guise of journalism, a bona fide news story, to take it further.

The porch door squeaked as it opened behind her. She didn't turn around, her eyes still trained on the activity at their neighbor's.

"What's going on?"

"Looks like trouble." She took the coffee cup that was offered. "Thanks."

"Break-in?"

She shrugged. "Maybe."

They stood quietly, sipping their coffee.

"I think it's more than a break-in."

She didn't answer. She didn't have to. The police were spread out along the marsh. No one was near the house.

She'd made the phone call. The one she was expected to make. Her job was done now. She could hold off the police and their questions. She had a lot of experience doing that. It was why she was here. It was how she'd survived.

The crunch of gravel announced the arrival of the first cruiser. The car door slammed, and a young cop climbed out, adjusting his hat. The gesture didn't mask the paleness of his skin as he bit the corner of his lip, blinking against the sun. It wasn't until he got closer that she saw the fear etched in his eyes.

Neither of them moved as the officer came up the steps onto the porch. He touched the rim of his hat as he approached.

"What's happened?"

His gaze skittered across the lawn to the scene he'd just escaped. "A body was found. In the marsh." The words caught in his throat, and he coughed to try to hide it.

"Body?"

"Kayakers found her."

"Her?"

"I have to ask you if you've seen anything. Over there." He added the last bit as though they might misunderstand.

"You found a dead woman?"

He nodded, his jaw clenching and unclenching. She could smell it on him now, the faint odor of sick.

"Coffee?"

He looked so grateful, she almost felt sorry for him.

They settled him in a white wicker chair facing the tennis court on the other side of the porch. His hands trembled as he held the cup to his lips, letting the scent seep into his nose and throat, eradicating the scene.

"How did she die?"

His eyes met hers. "She was killed."

"Murdered?"

It was barely a whisper, but his words settled between them, and there was no mistaking them.

"She had no head."

She turned away, her own coffee cold, and went back into the house.

PART I

1

Kate Parker's fingers found the ring on her left hand and twisted it slightly. Hank had slipped it on as they stood before the judge at city hall only two weeks ago. He hadn't wanted to wait, promised her a lavish reception and honeymoon later in the summer at the house in Tuscany. She'd worn a light-blue taffeta dress—something blue—and a pair of dazzling sapphire earrings that he'd given her the day before—something new. She wasn't so superstitious as to seek out anything old or borrowed; anyway, Hank was all about looking forward, not backward. His suit was charcoal gray; his tie matched the color of her dress. The paparazzi captured them as they emerged, just before climbing into the limo. His arm was around her waist, pulling her toward him; she leaned into him, allowing him to lead the way. After an elegant dinner of oysters, caviar, and filet mignon, they'd gone alone to the penthouse. No one would believe it was the first time they'd slept together as the headline screamed: BILLIONAIRE MOGUL HANK TUDOR MARRIES ASSISTANT AT CITY HALL. She knew what everyone was thinking. It was a far cry from his last wedding, which was why he'd wanted it this way. Or so he'd told her. Still, there was no reason to act as though this was the first time for either of them. She was in her mid-thirties and had been married twice before, so she couldn't exactly fault Hank for his previous five marriages. Sometimes it worked out, sometimes it didn't.

As the limo moved swiftly along the highway toward Hank's Greenwich cottage—and the questions about the body found in the marsh between his house and the inn run by his fourth wife, Anna Klein—Kate studied her husband's profile: the long patrician nose, thin lips, pointed chin. The skin sagged slightly along his jaw when he wasn't smiling, like now. But the rest of his face belied his age. He didn't know Kate knew about the facelift he'd had before he married his last wife, Caitlyn Howard. He didn't know Kate knew about a lot of things that were supposed to be secret.

She wasn't sure what she'd gotten herself into by marrying Hank Tudor. A first wife who still made his shirts by hand while she imprisoned herself in a mansion, growing more bitter and older every day; a second who'd held his heart and his passion and then abandoned him; a third who'd died too soon; a fourth who was content running a small business and taking care of his children; and a fifth who was, well, how to describe Caitlyn? Impetuous, moody, sexy, young—an actress but also a drug addict and a drunk. Hank's midlife crisis.

What role did he want her, Kate, to play in his life? Was she the last in the long line of wives? Would his marriage to her satisfy his itch for all women? Hard to say. All she knew for sure was that she loved him, despite his flaws, despite his money. She'd been working for him for a little more than two years, the whole time he'd been with Caitlyn. He had loved the girl until she betrayed him. Kate dried his tears, listened to him, kept the media at bay so he could grieve. He allowed his work to swallow him whole—until that night in London when he looked at her and she couldn't look away. He'd kissed her then, and it wasn't the kiss of a man on the rebound, but a tender, passionate kiss that held hope for the future.

Everyone told her to stay away from him. If she hadn't known him so well, she would have. She believed that he loved her as much as she loved him.

Kate watched her husband, his expression dark, his cell phone stuck to his ear. The company stocks had plummeted after the news that a body had been found on his property. He was going to have to placate the shareholders, but he was still trying to grasp the severity of the situation.

Her own phone pinged. Tom Cromwell, Hank's lawyer, who was sitting across from her, looked up.

"Is it the police?" Cromwell's deep, gravelly voice was too loud for the limo.

Kate didn't like him or his tactics. They'd butted heads over how to handle Caitlyn's indiscretions before Hank divorced her. If it had been up to Tom, Caitlyn would have been destroyed personally and professionally. Fortunately, Hank still had a soft spot for the girl, even though she didn't deserve it, and allowed Kate to take the reins. Tom didn't take well to that but grudgingly conceded.

She shook her head. The number on the screen was a familiar one. She answered the call. "Yes, Anna?"

"I tried to reach Hank but got voicemail."

"He's on the phone."

"I figured. How far out are you?"

"Another twenty minutes, give or take, I'd say."

"You can't get to the house because of the police and the media. Come here instead." Anna Klein's voice was smooth, soft, stress-free. Kate bit down an irrational irritation.

"Let the police know when we'll be there," she instructed. "They'll have a lot of questions, and we have to show them that Hank will do everything to cooperate in their investigation." She shook off the impulse to do damage control the way she was used to. It wasn't her job anymore. She glanced at Hank's new assistant, Lindsey, who sat across from her, recognizing herself in the young woman. Eager to please, an eye always on Hank Tudor, making sure he always had his eye on her.

And he did, Kate realized now. Even though he was on the phone, even though it looked like he was looking out the window, his gaze had settled on his new assistant's legs.

Should she be surprised? Yet, almost as though he could read her mind, his eyes suddenly met hers and he gave her a wink and the small intimate smile she had come to know so well. She felt her cheeks flush.

"Kate?" Anna's voice brought her back to the moment.

"Yes?"

"It was a woman's body. She was beheaded." Anna's tone was matter-of-fact, as though she said such things all the time. "You have to warn Hank."

Kate tightened her grip on the phone and took a deep breath, the scent of the new leather in the limo rushing into her nose. She absently worried the soft seat with the side of her thumb. This particular piece of information would be a game changer as far as the police—and the media—were concerned.

"Do you know more than that?"

"No. And I only know that because a couple of local officers were here and told us. They asked if we'd seen anything, but we hadn't. It wasn't until the police cars arrived that we noticed anything at all."

"So that's not public information yet?"

Anna knew what she was asking: Did anyone else know the body was decapitated? "Not that I'm aware."

Someone was going to leak it. Maybe the local officers who told Anna. Kate stole a glance at her husband, still glued to his phone, no longer looking at her—or Lindsey. She had to tell him, prepare him for the inevitable.

"They were asking about Mary," Anna continued.

Mary Brandon, Hank's sister, had planned to spend several weeks at the house. Kate wasn't surprised the police knew about her sister-in-law. Hank's life and family had been in the spotlight—and a topic of gossip—in the community ever since he bought that house for his first wife, Catherine, all those years ago.

"Isn't she there?" Kate asked.

A second or two of hesitation, then, "No. I left a message on her voice-mail. She was here two days ago, but only briefly. She hasn't been back. At least not that I've seen. The police wanted to know how to reach her. I didn't tell them anything except that Hank would have to give them her information."

"Thanks, Anna. I'll see if I can find her." *I hope I can find her*—the ominous thought pushed its way into her head, but she wasn't about to say it out loud. "What about the press? I mean, I know they're at the house, but are they bothering you, too?" It wasn't a secret that Klein's Bed and Breakfast was owned by Hank Tudor's ex-wife.

"I've got security keeping them off the property."

It wasn't merely Anna's status but that of her guests that would call for top-notch security, and not only at times like this.

Anna was still talking. "I've sent the children out with Joan. They'll spend the day with friends. There's too much going on, and I don't like the idea of them here with the police milling about, not to mention being this close to a crime scene."

Right. Hank's children. Lizzie, who was almost twelve, was his daughter from his marriage to Nan, his second wife, and Ted, seven, was his son with Jeanne, his third wife. Anna had brought them to the city hall wedding and to the dinner afterward, but then they'd gone back with her and her wife, Joan. Kate had met them only a handful of times. Hank wasn't too concerned about that, said that there was plenty of time to "get acquainted." But in retrospect, she began to wonder if it wasn't a mistake. She was Hank's wife now. Anna wouldn't possibly want to continue in her role as surrogate mother, would she?

"We'll see you in a little bit, then, right?" Anna's voice interrupted her thoughts.

"Yes." Kate ended the call.

Hank reached over and touched the top of her hand, a soft caress.

"How are you holding up?" he asked.

Kate took a deep breath. "I'm as fine as I can be. How are you?"

"That was Anna? Did she say anything else about this, um, incident?"

"It was a woman." She hesitated a second. "She was beheaded."

Hank's fingers danced along hers before turning her hand over, tracing her palm lightly. She shivered.

"Was she?" he asked softly.

2

A couple of media vans were lying in wait, reporters standing outside in front of cameras, microphones in their hands, and when they spotted the limo, they sprinted toward it. The gate that was usually open and welcoming during the day was closed but swung wide as soon as the limo approached. Kate twisted in her seat to look out the back as they entered the drive. A security guard had his arms spread out, herding the reporters back toward their vans, fending them off as the gate barricaded the property once again.

A tall state trooper stopped pacing the front porch when the car pulled up and came to a stop; another trooper came around from the back. Kate reached for the door, but Tom put his hand up.

"Make them wait," he said, indicating the police, his voice low, deep.

She glanced at Hank, who gave her a short nod to tell her she should do as told.

As Hank's personal assistant, Kate had been barraged with questions from reporters, politicians, anyone who wanted to bend his ear for a few minutes about his empire and what kind of arrangement they might be able to make between them. She had smoothly kept them at bay, knowing who to keep out and who to let in. She had handled Hank's schedule, rearranging when necessary, always in control.

As his wife, she didn't have the same power.

Ironic, really.

She settled back in the leather seat as the driver got out and came around to open the door for them.

Tom was first, then he reached for Lindsey's hand. Once she was out of the limo, he leaned down and gave Kate a nod, indicating that she was next. When she stepped onto the driveway, her heel caught on a cobblestone. She stumbled slightly but recovered quickly as her husband—it still seemed so strange to think of him as her *husband*—emerged from the car. The rest of them parted like the sea as he straightened up, tall and confident, striding toward the two police troopers who had come to greet them.

Hank held out his hand with a loud, gregarious, "Hank Tudor, welcome."

The troopers seemed a little taken aback but shook his hand as offered. They had no other choice.

Hank didn't stop, kept walking toward the inn, with the troopers, Kate, Lindsey, and Tom following.

Anna met them on the steps, her long hair plaited in a thick braid down her back. She wore a crisp white sleeveless cotton blouse over beige linen cropped pants, a pair of Birkenstocks on her feet. She was hardly stylish, but she had a quiet sophistication and gracefulness despite herself. Kate was aware of her own white cotton shift dress and heels that were highly impractical, but Hank liked her to wear them. She'd never seen Anna in heels.

Hank bounded up the steps and stopped to give Anna a peck on the cheek. "How's my favorite girl?" he asked with a wide grin.

Anna smiled warmly at him. "Very well," she said, then turned to everyone else. "Please follow me," she said, taking Hank's arm, indicating that they should go around the porch to the back.

As soon as they rounded the house, Kate's eyes settled on the light-blue water of the swimming pool, still and glistening as the sun beat down on it. Chaise lounges were lined up like little soldiers on the stone patio, umbrellas closed. Beyond the pool, the lush green lawn spread out and disappeared over a rock wall and continued down to a sandy beach with the iridescent water of Long Island Sound beyond. The tennis courts were to the far left; a croquet game was set up and waiting for players to the right. It was serene, and Kate could almost forget about the activity at the house next door and along the marsh: the flashing cruiser lights, media vans parked on the lawn, the police and investigators combing what was no longer a summer retreat but a crime scene.

She turned away to focus on her immediate surroundings. Anna had set up a table with cheese and crackers and fruit; crystal glasses and bottles of wine, champagne, and liquor stocked a small bar. "Can I get anyone anything?" she asked, ever the hostess.

Anna didn't wait for Hank to answer, poured a short glass of bourbon, and handed it to him. Hank took it without a word, then turned and raised his eyebrows at the troopers.

They shook their heads, uncertain how to react. They were here for a reason, an interrogation, but Hank Tudor wasn't the type of man who was going to let anyone else run a meeting.

Kate felt herself smiling at him. He met her eyes and nodded slightly, as if telling her everything would be okay.

She had no choice but to believe him.

The taller trooper cleared his throat. "I'm Trooper Pawlik, and this is Trooper Lawson," he said after a second, indicating his partner.

Lawson was the younger of the two, by at least ten years. He looked like he was still in his twenties, a roguish, boyish look to him. Pawlik, on the other hand, was good looking, too, but not in that pretty boy, vain way. His nose was a little crooked, his mouth wide and full, and his stiff jacket more than hinted at the muscular build beneath it. He had an aura of authority; he wasn't used to being controlled. He might not have Hank's money, but Kate could see the similarities between them: powerful men who would stop at nothing to get what they wanted.

"I'd like to know what happened on my property," Hank said, his voice measured and calm.

Pawlik leveled his stare at Hank, and Kate admired his nerve. Not many people could hold their own with Hank, but it was clear that her husband may have met his match. She was curious how this was going to go.

"A body was found," Pawlik said.

Tom stepped in front of him before he could continue. "I'm Thomas Cromwell, Mr. Tudor's attorney. We are happy to cooperate to the best of our ability, but as you know, Mr. Tudor hasn't been out to that house since last summer." His words belied his tone and the threat beneath them.

Tom was full of threats. It was what made him so good at his job—and what made Hank keep him on all these years. He'd been Hank's lawyer since his first divorce, and Hank didn't trust anyone more than he trusted Tom, although Kate had heard there was a rift after the situation with Anna.

"Has there been an ID made on the body?" Cromwell asked when Pawlik didn't respond.

Pawlik cocked his head slightly and let his eyes move from Tom to Hank, whose posture was perfectly still, like a cat just before it goes in for the kill.

"The victim was a woman," Pawlik said without answering the question. "We've already gotten confirmation that all of Ms. Klein's female guests in the past couple of weeks are accounted for." He turned to Hank. "Have you had any problems with trespassers on your property, sir?" he asked.

The "sir" was a nice touch.

Hank shook his head. "I'm rarely at that house, Detective. Anna probably knows more about what goes on there than I do." He glanced at her, but her expression was neutral.

"Does she ever take care of the house when you're not there?" Pawlik spoke as though Anna wasn't standing right next to him.

"No. She's busy with her own house; I can't ask her to do that. I have a local company that takes care of the lawn and landscaping. If I plan to spend any time there, I have someone go in before I arrive to get the rooms ready. My sister is there more than I am, to be honest. She likes to have a reprieve from the city." His tone was measured, as though Pawlik would have a hard time understanding him otherwise.

"That would be Mrs. Brandon?" Pawlik asked.

Hank nodded. "Yes. She should be there now, but something must have come up."

Pawlik turned to Anna. "You haven't seen her?"

Anna laced her fingers together. "She was here a couple of days ago but didn't stay long. I must've lost track of time, because I didn't notice that she hadn't come around again." Kate recognized that she was repeating what she'd already told the local police.

"You didn't speak to her?"

"No. We don't socialize when she's here."

Kate suppressed an urge to chuckle. The idea of Mary Brandon and Anna Klein "socializing" would be akin to a lion accepting an elk into its pride.

Pawlik waited a second, then turned back to Hank. "We'd like to talk to Mrs. Brandon. Is there a way to reach her?"

Without mentioning that he'd already tried to reach Mary from the limo but hadn't been able to, Hank turned to Lindsey. "Get Mary on the phone."

As Lindsey pulled her cell phone out of her black leather tote, Pawlik held up his hand. "Thank you, but I'd like to have her contact information, please."

Hank hesitated a moment, took a sip of his bourbon, then nodded solemnly. "Certainly," he said. "Lindsey will give you everything you need." He turned to her and said, "Give him Charlie's number, too, in London." Charlie Brandon, Mary's husband. None of this would matter anyway. If the police tried to get in touch with her, Mary would talk to Hank first. That's just the way it was. But they had to make it look good.

Hank's eyes flickered over to Cromwell, who shifted slightly, lifting a hand to smooth an imaginary flyaway hair at his temple.

"Excuse me, Mr. Cromwell," Pawlik said. "How did you get all those scratches on your hands?"

3

Tom didn't miss a beat. "I've been pruning rosebushes without gloves." He gave a short shrug and an apologetic smile as if to say, *Yes, I know that's stupid.*

Kate envied how casual he was in the face of interrogation. But he was a lawyer, so he was used to it. And he was *Tom*. So far no one had asked *her* anything, yet she absently looked at her hands to make sure there wasn't anything that could be considered suspect.

Hank sidled over to her and handed her a glass of wine. She hadn't even noticed that he'd poured it. His fingers brushed hers as she took the glass, and an electric spark rushed through her. He locked eyes with her; he'd felt it, too. She smiled at him, but his attention had already moved elsewhere.

"Lindsey has all the information," he told Pawlik, as though he'd never been interrupted by something as menial as rosebush scratches on his attorney's hands. "The landscaping crew, my sister, anyone else you feel you need to speak to. We will cooperate fully." He cocked his head at Lindsey. "Can you give Trooper Lawson everything he needs?"

She nodded, her smile bright. She'd already retrieved her tablet from her bag, and as she touched it, it sprang to life.

Hank put his hand up. "Why don't you take him into the house?" He turned to Pawlik. "It's more comfortable there."

Kate wondered what he was up to.

Lawson glanced at Pawlik, who frowned but nodded his consent. He was curious why Hank was sending them inside, too.

Kate watched as the trooper and Lindsey went toward the French doors that led into the house, but then Hank surprised her by saying, "Kate, perhaps you and Anna should go with them."

She'd heard that tone before. It was the one that told her he was about to try to cut a deal and he didn't want any witnesses, save for Tom.

Still, Kate clutched the wineglass as she bristled at being dismissed. She was tempted to look back, see what was going on behind her, but she forced herself not to. That trooper wasn't going to buy into Hank's line, whatever it was. He wasn't the type.

She put the wineglass on the cocktail trolley as she passed it, following Anna across the porch.

"Everything okay?" Anna whispered, leaning in toward Kate when they stepped over the threshold into the foyer. A stairway led upstairs, and on the other side, a great room was dominated by a large stone fireplace and an original Rothko.

"I don't know," Kate said.

"He's not going to get anything out of that trooper," Anna said, confirming Kate's intuition about Pawlik. "He has a look about him."

"Who do you think the body is?" Kate wanted to know what Anna thought. Anna had a good head on her shoulders. She knew when to keep her mouth shut and listen. Because of that, Hank trusted her and made sure that her life was comfortable, although it was more the legalities that surrounded both their marriage and their divorce that guaranteed Anna's silence and Hank's generosity.

"I have no idea," Anna said, but something in her expression told Kate that she might have an opinion on this.

Kate and Anna turned the corner around the staircase just as Lindsey giggled at something the trooper said. Kate cleared her throat loudly. A smile tugged on Lawson's lips as his fingers played along the top of the gun at his hip. Kate had dated men like him, men who tickled and teased and touched her in the right places but without meaning any of it. Lindsey was buying into the line—Kate had to admit the trooper was good looking—but she'd get hurt if she took it much further than this. And very possibly lose her job.

"Is Lindsey getting you everything you need, Trooper Lawson?" she asked with her public relations voice.

The smile faded. Lindsey giggled again—a nervous giggle.

Even though there were two plush sofas and chairs in front of the stone fireplace, no one took a seat but remained standing, eyeing one another warily.

"When was the last time you were out here?" Lawson asked Kate after a few seconds, his voice a little too deep and serious.

There was no way Hank couldn't have anticipated an interrogation, but he must have felt it was worth separating them. She would have to tread carefully. "Last summer," Kate offered.

"You and your husband weren't married then, though, right?"

He had to know about their recent wedding, but Kate decided to play along. She leveled her eyes at him. "No. I was his assistant. I've been to the house in a professional capacity only."

The trooper scribbled something on the small notepad in his hand, but Kate was sure it was only a power play. She wasn't telling him anything of any importance.

"How about your husband? Has he been out here without you?"

This time he watched her carefully, even though he must have known she was going to be guarded about any information she'd give him, despite her husband's declaration that they would "cooperate fully." Kate shrugged. "It's his private residence. He's been here without me, yes. But I hardly see how that would be unusual."

"Has he been here without you recently?"

Lindsey should have taken over by now, but she just stood there holding her tablet, making no move to intervene. If the police had started asking

Caitlyn or Anna about anything, Kate would've immediately stepped in. She was going to have to talk to Hank about Lindsey. Too bad if he liked her legs. She wasn't doing her job.

"I don't know," she said. "You should ask *him* that."

"You were just in New York City?"

"That's right. We've been there the past couple of weeks."

Lawson looked at her with a curious expression. "Since your wedding, right?"

He was playing games with her, or so he thought. She wasn't about to give anything away, though. "Yes," she said. "That's right."

"No exotic honeymoon anywhere?"

"No." Not that it was any of his business.

"So you've been in the city this entire time." He again scribbled something on the little pad. "Your husband has been with you?"

"Of course. Where else would he be?" Kate stiffened. Despite expecting him to badger her, it didn't make it any less uncomfortable.

He studied her face a moment, then said, "He wasn't divorced too long when you snagged him. What do you think the fifth Mrs. Tudor thought about that?"

Kate snapped her head back and frowned. Her heart beat a little bit faster as the tension crawled between her and Lawson. He was deliberately trying to goad her, get her to say something incriminating.

"Trooper Lawson, I do not see how Hank and Kate's marriage has any relevance in this situation." Anna's voice came from behind her.

Kate silently thanked her but didn't like the fact that she'd been rescued.

Lawson narrowed his eyes at Anna, as though noticing her for the first time. "I didn't mean to step on any toes."

Of course he did, although Kate was uncertain how prying into her personal life was going to get her to reveal anything. It only made her guard her secrets more closely.

"I understand that you are looking for a woman's killer," Anna continued. "I would think that perhaps you'd be more concerned about trying to find out who she is and who killed her than looking for gossip."

Lawson gave a short nod. "Fair enough." He hesitated a second, then asked, "But don't any of you find it more than a coincidence that this is the second time a woman has been found beheaded on your ex-husband's property?"

4

CATHERINE

The first time it happened, it didn't go as planned. Mistakes were made, but in the end, she had to admit, she got what she wanted.

The girl had been her secretary. Administrative assistant, she'd called herself. She came in with all those airs, speaking French, reading French books, wearing all those stylish clothes that made it seem she actually came from money.

The girl *was* pretty, but in an obvious sort of way. She'd heard the rumors, how the girl had flitted around Europe after college, young men seduced by her supposed appeal. Hank wasn't a young man, though. He was middle-aged—but not immune to a pretty girl's charms.

Her husband had never been discreet about his affairs. She knew about Bess, the wife of one of the other vice presidents. And that other secretary who had come into the office one day and turned Hank's head. They didn't worry her. Hank always came home to her. But when *she* entered their lives, it was different. It wasn't only an affair. She closed her eyes to it for a long time, until Hank decided he wanted a divorce. She wouldn't give it to him. Then he fired her, moving her out of Tudor Enterprises so quickly that she didn't even realize what was happening until she was here, in this house, alone, waiting for her husband to see his mistake, to come back to her.

Catherine Alvarez Tudor slipped the thread through the needle, her fingers deftly making a knot. She had only the cuffs left, imagining the silver cuff links that would adorn them. She'd bought them before she started making the dress shirt; she always included a set in the package. He'd never have to make that decision. She made it for him.

In the background, the TV was merely white noise. She'd already gotten what she needed from it. But as the image of the house flashed on the screen, the crawl sliding across the bottom announcing that a body had been found in the marsh next to billionaire Hank Tudor's Greenwich cottage, she paused her sewing, the shirt in her lap.

"Mrs. Catherine?" Lourdes's voice interrupted. She had been with Catherine almost ten years, and she had a kind, ageless face. Catherine loved to watch her in the kitchen, her smooth hands deftly kneading bread dough or wielding paring knives as she effortlessly sliced and diced vegetables and fruits, her movements efficient and graceful.

She looked up from the television. "Yes?"

"If you don't mind, Mrs. Catherine, I'm going to step out to the store. You're almost out of milk."

Catherine felt her heart skip. She kept her expression neutral as she asked, "Do we need anything else?"

"I've got a short list. I thought fish for dinner? I can get fresh at Lenny's."

"That sounds lovely, thank you."

"I won't be but half an hour."

"Take your time. I'm fine here."

Catherine watched Lourdes from the window, the car moving down the driveway, out onto the street, and then out of sight. She waited a few more minutes, making sure that Lourdes wouldn't suddenly come back, having forgotten something. The seconds moved slowly, until Catherine was sure. And then she scurried up the stairs.

She took the key out of her pocket and slipped it in the lock. When she heard it click, she pushed the door open.

No one, especially Hank, could know what she did in here each morning while she still had the house to herself, before Lourdes arrived for the day. Lourdes wasn't allowed in this room; Catherine told her it was merely for storage and didn't need cleaning.

The five large computer monitors lined up on the table were dark. Catherine edged closer, reached out and touched the keyboard. The screens lit up, the graphs bright with colors, stock prices moving in a crawl underneath. She sat in front of the one in the center, her eyes moving across them and back again, taking it all in. She had no idea how much money she'd made today, but from the looks of it, the sell-off had already begun.

Tudor Enterprises's stocks were hemorrhaging.

It was a good thing she'd sold everything this morning before that body got in the news. She resisted the urge to pick up where she'd left off. She couldn't continue; it was possible her shorts had already been flagged. And the stocks would continue to go down, she was sure of that. Tomorrow, she could buy them back at less than half the price she'd sold them for.

Of course, today's bounty wasn't a result of her intelligence or luck. But it was just as sweet.

It wasn't about the money. She had plenty and didn't need more, although this money was hers. She'd earned it, and knowing she was making her own way and didn't have to rely on Hank gave her a sense of independence she hadn't felt in a very long time. But ultimately, it was all about the rush, the strategy of it. The power.

She'd run four Tudor Enterprises companies before Hank forced her out. No one knew that for a couple of hours each morning, as she traded stocks, she became her old self. The woman Hank Tudor had married all those years ago.

They'd met in college, in a Romantic literature class. He came in late, the door slamming shut behind him, and slid into the seat next to her, giving her a wink, as though they were already conspirators. Hank was the most beautiful man she'd ever seen. He'd had a boyish grin, a twinkle in his eye. He stood almost a foot taller than she, his limbs long and lean. His mop of red hair was always a little too perfectly tousled. He had an arrogance in his mannerisms, a sense of entitlement. He'd grown up in affluence, in line to inherit one of the biggest companies in the world. She'd grown up around rich boys—her father's company rivaled Hank's—so she wasn't put off by him. Just the opposite. When they had a picnic lunch on the quad only a week after they'd locked eyes the first time, he joked that they were the Montagues and the Capulets, teasing her that they would kill each other in the end.

He had girls hanging all over him, but it didn't take long for him to have eyes only for her. She couldn't believe her luck. He wooed her, telling her that they could rule the world together—and she believed him. He was careful with her, as though she were made of fine china, honoring her until their wedding night, when they were finally able to release all the passion that had been building for a year. They were young and in love, and when his father died, they bought out her father's company and became richer than she'd ever imagined. In those days, they were happy. When their daughter, Maril, was born, they celebrated the future.

But that was all before *her*. Catherine couldn't even say her name.

Catherine had hoped that once *she* was gone, he would see his mistake. That had been the plan. He'd come back to her, tail between his legs, and they could resume their life together as it had once been, as they'd done after the other affairs. But she hadn't counted on all those wives. Especially Caitlyn Howard. She was Number Five. A twenty-one-year-old actress with a sixty-year-old billionaire. It was so clichéd. Hank was above all that. She'd spent the past two years embarrassed for him, how the girl had made a fool of Hank publicly in the press. That girl turned the tables on him, had affairs, ended up in rehab. Hank had stood by her. Until Alex Culpepper, that singer turned actor, that incredibly handsome boy who stole Hank Tudor's wife. Hank hadn't deserved to be humiliated like that.

It had been almost too easy. Just like the first time.

Headless Body Found Near Tudor Property

MARTHA'S VINEYARD, MASS. (AP)—The headless body of an unidentified woman was discovered by a tourist on a private beach owned by billionaire businessman Hank Tudor in Tisbury on Thursday morning.

Tudor's wife, Nan, had been staying at the house on the property with their daughter, Lizzie, 3, but was reported missing three days ago by Margery Horsman, the housekeeper.

Police Chief Edward Foxe said police have not confirmed if the body is that of Nan Tudor. He said Hank Tudor, who has been in London for the past week, is cooperating with police.

Tudor is owner, president, and CEO of Tudor Enterprises, a multimillion-dollar international communications company.

The tourist, Henry Norris, said he was walking through the dunes with his metal detector when he came upon the body.

Norris called 911 immediately when he realized she was dead. He said he did not touch the body for fear of contaminating the scene, something he knew about from watching TV.

"I didn't notice right away that she was missing her head," he said.

Foxe said the body was taken to the medical examiner's office in Boston for an autopsy. The investigation is ongoing.

5

"M y husband was cleared in that investigation," Kate told Trooper Lawson. She'd done her homework before she accepted Hank's job offer. "You know that. The DNA sample did not match Nan Tudor's. The body was never identified."

Hank had initially been detained, but no charges were ever filed against him. He'd turned a hairbrush of Nan's over to police.

Lawson nodded. "That's right. It's still an unsolved crime." From the tone of his voice, though, Kate could tell he very well suspected Hank, despite the evidence presented that it wasn't Nan. *DNA doesn't lie.* She could still hear the relief in Hank's voice when she'd asked him about it.

"I didn't want anything to happen to her," Hank had said. He'd spent seven years pursuing her, divorcing Catherine. He had loved Nan. She was the mother of his child.

But maybe it was the thrill of the chase, because once they married, it didn't take long for him to wander. There were reports about Nan's very public tantrums, confrontations with other women Hank had taken up with—and even some he hadn't. Hank's infidelities after years of devotion seemed to have unraveled her.

"I'm not going to make excuses for my behavior," Hank told Kate. "Nan and I had been growing apart, and I made mistakes. It became clear that we couldn't put it back together, so we decided to move forward separately with our lives." He made it sound so civilized. Kate wasn't that naïve. Still, it was eight years ago, and having gone through two messy divorces herself, she couldn't judge.

Hank and Nan never got as far as divorce, though. Nan simply vanished. The only clue she left behind was a closed bank account, one hundred thousand dollars missing.

Hank hired several private investigators, trying to find her all over the world. It was highly publicized, overcoming the initial discovery of that body. Nan must have known her husband was looking for her. The missing money left no trail. She'd managed to take it in cash over a period of six months, which was, as Cromwell argued in court, proof that her abandonment was not spur-of-the-moment. After the requisite year, Hank divorced Nan and married Jeanne, who was already pregnant with Ted.

No one had seen nor heard from Nan in all this time. She hadn't even reached out to make sure her daughter was okay.

Standing here, right now, with another body of a headless woman found on Hank's property, Kate grudgingly admitted that if she were investigating the crime, she would look a little more closely at Hank Tudor, too. Yet, as before, he had a rock-solid alibi: he'd been in New York City with his new wife for the past two weeks.

Lindsey should have stepped in by now, but before Kate could nudge her, the door swung open and Trooper Pawlik strode into the room, Hank and Tom behind him.

"Ms. Klein," Pawlik said, ignoring everyone else in the room. "Just a couple more questions, please."

Anna nodded. "Certainly."

He pursed his lips, his eyes never straying from hers, then, "You have a partner?"

"Yes. My wife, Joan Carey."

"I'd like her to join us. Is she home?"

"She won't be able to tell you any more than I have."

He gave her a condescending smile. "I understand. Is she here?"

"She took the children to their friends' houses. We didn't want them to be here during, well, all of this." She waved her hand around.

"Understandable." Pawlik held out a business card. "I put my cell number on there. Please have Ms. Carey contact me as soon as she comes back. And because of the proximity of your houses, I'd like to talk to whoever's in charge of your security detail."

Anna must have been expecting that, because she pulled a card out of her pocket and handed it to him. "His name is Will Stafford. He's on the property, holding back the media. If you call this number, he'll answer."

Kate had to admire Anna. She was calm and collected. No wonder Hank was so generous with her.

"Thank you, Ms. Klein," Pawlik said, tipping his hat slightly. That might have been a bit overdone, but it was a nice gesture all the same. He turned to Hank. "We'll be in touch." He cocked his head at Lawson, who barely gave a side glance at Lindsey as he followed the older trooper to the door.

"We'll walk you out," Hank announced, moving ahead of them, opening the screen door, Tom close on his heels.

From the window, Kate watched her husband and Tom escort the troopers down the steps and across the driveway to the gate before a final handshake. As the troopers made their way down the road, walking back to the crime scene, Hank and Tom stood talking. They were too far away to eavesdrop, not that Kate really wanted to know what they were saying, anyway.

When she turned back to face the room, Lindsey was alone, on the sofa, concentrating on her tablet. A basket containing soft slippers sat by the door, and Kate slipped off her heels as she pulled out a pair and put them on. Anna didn't like shoes on in the house, but they'd been too distracted by the police to change when they first came inside. She shuffled across the room, grudgingly admitting to herself that the slippers made her feel welcome and warm. This was only one of the reasons why Anna was so good at this, running a bed-and-breakfast.

Kate pulled open the French doors and stepped out onto the back porch, the water spread out in the distance, glimmering under the sun. Anna had come out here, too, and she was gazing in the direction of the house next door. The marsh lay between the properties, the small estuary hidden behind the grasses and cattails. The police were still creeping about, gathering their evidence.

"Are you going to be okay here?" Kate asked, a tickle of fear grazing the back of her neck as a breeze rippled through the marsh.

Anna frowned, then she realized what Kate meant and nodded. "We're fine."

"You're not worried? I mean, there's a killer out there. You need extra security. Hank can arrange it. I'll talk to him."

Anna shook her head. "Thank you, but I'll take care of it."

Kate studied the other woman's face for a moment. "Are you sure?"

"I've already talked to Will Stafford about expanding the team temporarily, and I know the local police. They'll keep an eye out, too. That should be more than enough."

Kate wasn't as optimistic. Out of sight, out of mind. At least, that was her experience. She'd talk to Hank. It wouldn't hurt, and Anna didn't have to know. "What about your guests? Where are they?" She realized now that she hadn't seen any other cars in the small parking lot.

Anna sighed. "Joan and I decided after the police showed up here that it would be best to find them other accommodations for now. We gave them a refund and moved them out pretty quickly this morning. We've got good relationships with the other inns in the area, so it wasn't too difficult. So I guess we're shut down. At least until the police finish their investigation next door."

Kate was nodding. "Good idea." While some of Anna's guests were almost as high profile as Hank, they were not immune to curiosity about their hostess and her history with her ex-husband. Having a murder next door and Hank here would start tongues wagging even more. The TV vans were parked out in the street, the reporters eyeing the property, trying to figure out a game plan. They could easily have infiltrated and caught one of Anna's guests off guard, and who knew what they'd say.

Hank and Cromwell came around the side of the house and walked across the yard in the direction of the marsh. Hank was gesturing toward it; Cromwell's hands were shoved in his pockets.

"Penny for their thoughts," Anna whispered.

Kate chuckled nervously. "I don't think we want to know what they're talking about."

"No, but aren't you ever curious?"

Kate considered the question. Yes, she *was* curious, but the less she knew, the better off she was. She shrugged noncommittally.

"Do you think they know we're watching them?" Anna asked.

"What do you think?"

As though they'd heard, Hank and Tom turned around. Hank lifted his hand in a wave; Tom's face was clouded in a frown. Neither seemed surprised to see them.

"What do you think about those scratches on Tom's hands?" Kate asked before she could stop herself.

Anna took a deep breath. "Nothing. They're nothing." But there was definitely something behind her words, and Kate shouldn't have even asked. It was as though she no longer knew the rules. She felt a little off-balance. She didn't like not being in control. Not knowing everything that was going on with Hank.

Neither Tom nor Hank was speaking as they strolled companionably back to the house. Tom squinted into the sun; Hank's sunglasses shielded his eyes. Even though he didn't indicate it, Kate was certain he was watching her. He watched all of them.

Kate was so deep in thought that she didn't hear her husband approach until he was right behind her, his hand slipping around her waist. She stiffened for a moment, then relaxed against him. His other hand slid along her hip, settling there. Anna shifted a little, moved away, turning back into the house. Hank's hand tightened around Kate's waist.

"Are you okay?" he whispered, his breath hot against her neck.

"Yes. But I was thinking Anna might need some more security here."

He pulled away, crossing his arms over his chest as he leaned against the railing. "Did she say something about that?"

"No, it's my idea. She said she would be fine, but considering . . ." Her voice trailed off.

"It's sweet of you to be concerned, but isn't that a little bit of an overreaction?"

Kate frowned. "There's someone out there who's killed a woman. I don't think that's an *overreaction*."

Hank reached over and cupped her cheek in his hand. "Don't worry. She's going to be fine." He stared out over the marsh, the police moving around the crime scene. He gave a short snort. "They're wasting their time. They're not going to find anything," he said.

He sounded so sure.

6

Hank's cell phone pinged. His expression grew dark, and he gave Kate a quick kiss on the cheek before moving into the house to take the call. Kate worried the wood railing with her thumb and forefinger as she watched the activity across the marsh. It felt as though that body had been found right here, instead of next door. She wondered about Mary Brandon, where she might be. Kate didn't want to let her thoughts drift to that other body, the one found on Martha's Vineyard, the one before. She told herself it had nothing to do with this; it was a coincidence. Had to be.

Kate shivered and forced herself to turn away, stepping through the French doors and going back into the great room. She could hear murmurings from the direction of the kitchen. Joan must have come home. Kate felt helpless, uncertain what to do.

The sound of the screen door slapping against its wood frame startled her. She looked up to see her husband's oldest daughter—four years older than she was—step into the room. Maril was petite, even more so than Catherine, and had inherited her mother's thick hair that shimmered with natural auburn highlights. That wasn't the only thing she'd inherited, either. Maril had a stubborn streak, like Catherine, and when she got an idea in her head, she was like a dog with a bone. Neither Catherine nor Maril had accepted the divorce, and to both of them, Hank was still married to

Catherine, and all the other wives were merely distractions until he tired of them and returned to his first wife. Not for the first time, Kate thought how depressing it must be to live with that kind of delusion.

"Hello, Kate," Maril said.

It wasn't a surprise that Maril showed up. Maril was a gossip—and undoubtedly would be reporting everything she witnessed back to her mother. For that reason, Kate knew she shouldn't trust her, but she respected her loyalty and honestly liked her. Early on, when she joined Tudor Enterprises as Hank's assistant, Maril made an effort to help her settle in and feel like part of the team. They'd gone out for drinks a couple of times and commiserated about past relationships—until Hank made a comment that perhaps she should keep the relationship on a professional level. It was casually said, but the underlying tone was serious. Kate got the message and felt guilty about her vague excuses when Maril reached out. And then Maril stopped reaching out. She wasn't stupid. She knew what had happened.

Maril was wasting her life working for her father, relegated to a lower position because of her mother, even though she was smarter than most of the vice presidents and presidents throughout the companies. She should have been running at least one of them by now, and Kate wouldn't be surprised if headhunters were actively trying to recruit her. Yet she hung on, unwilling to be disloyal. Kate could understand that. Maril desperately wanted her father's attention and respect. Maybe Kate could help her. She'd always thought it unfair of Hank to hold the grudge he had against Catherine against his daughter as well. If she approached Hank in the right way at the right time, maybe she could get him to see that Maril's talents were being wasted and she deserved a promotion.

"Hi, Maril. Here to scope out the newest scandal?" Kate asked, aware that she was making light of a woman's death, and instantly regretted her question.

Maril grinned. "Busted. Where's Daddy?"

"He's inside. How have you been?" Kate asked, when she was really wondering, *What do you think about me marrying your father?* It was too late now, but she had a sudden, inexplicable need to have Maril's approval. She didn't want to cause Maril any more pain, and she had an irrational and unrealistic hope that neither she nor her mother would resent her for marrying the man they loved.

"I'm good," Maril said, her tone suddenly wary. "I didn't realize that you and Daddy were going to get married so soon, though. It was a little bit of a shock for me and my mother."

Kate's guilt grew. Hank had said he'd tell Maril about the wedding plans, but when Kate noticed her absence at the dinner, he brushed it off, saying he'd gotten too tied up and hadn't gotten around to it. She should've insisted she take care of it. It wasn't as though she didn't know how Hank could be, but the past weeks had been such a whirlwind. "I apologize for that. It just—"

Maril held up her hand. "Stop. I don't want to hear it." She indicated a bag she was carrying. "I'm going to find my father. My mother made him a couple of new shirts." She pushed the door open, then stopped and turned back to face Kate. "Do you love him?" she asked, her voice too loud against the still summer air.

"Yes," Kate said. It was the only reason she would marry him.

"Kate?" Tom Cromwell's voice came from behind her, and she welcomed the intrusion. He nodded at Maril. He didn't seem surprised to see her, either. "Your father is in the den. Why don't you go say hello?"

Maril scurried away, always so quick to try to please Hank.

"We're leaving in the morning," Cromwell told Kate after a long silence.

"I thought we all had to stay here. In case the police have more questions."

Tom gave her a patronizing smile. "Kate, Kate, Kate. You should know better by now. And anyway, you'll be staying. With Anna and the children."

If Hank wanted to leave, nothing—not even the police—could stop him. He was used to doing what he wanted. But only two weeks ago, she would have gone with him and not been left behind.

"We wouldn't leave if it weren't necessary," Tom continued. "But there's a, um, situation at the office."

It had to be about the stocks falling. If Hank was going back to the city already, it must be even more serious than she realized. It wasn't a surprise, though. The shareholders were running scared. Hank was now connected to a murder, even though he hadn't been here. It was unfair, holding him responsible, but that's the way it was. Eventually someone would report on what had happened on Martha's Vineyard, which would undoubtedly make it worse. She hoped the police could wrap up their investigation quickly, before it got out of control.

She felt her phone vibrate in her pocket. Tom had already disappeared, off to be by Hank's side, his duty to tell her about their departure taken care of. She pulled the phone out and frowned at the caller ID.

"Yes?" she asked curtly.

"Kate? It's Jane Rocheford. It's about Caitlyn."

She really didn't need this right now. Caitlyn Howard, Hank's fifth wife, was in rehab up in Litchfield County. Not for the first time, either. Jane was Caitlyn's publicist, and whenever something went wrong with Caitlyn, she called on Kate to take care of it, not realizing that it was *her* job to keep her client under control. But a tiny part of Kate felt guilty. While Hank hadn't left Caitlyn for her—their attraction had grown over time, but they hadn't even shared a kiss before the divorce—the girl might not see it that way.

"What is Caitlyn up to now?" Kate asked.

"I saw on the news that a woman was found murdered on Hank's property."

Kate pushed down her annoyance. The sooner she could get Jane off the phone, the better. "That's right. The police are investigating. We don't know any more than that. Tell me about Caitlyn."

"You don't get it. It *is* about Caitlyn."

"What is?"

"Cait left rehab three days ago. She told me she was going to see him. Hank."

Kate sighed. "Hank and I have been in the city. We haven't seen her."

"That's the thing. *No one* has seen her. She's missing."

7

Jane was being melodramatic.

"Have you called Alex Culpepper? If anyone would know where she is, he would," Kate suggested, annoyed that Jane was dropping this into her lap. She wasn't Caitlyn's keeper.

"Of course I've called him. He hasn't seen her, either. He's on set, though, so I really couldn't talk to him."

Culpepper was the reason Hank divorced Caitlyn. He was young, movie-star good looking, with a mop of blond hair that always fell across his blue eyes and a wide, sexy grin. He was the latest in the line of James Bonds. He'd been plucked from a boy band for an independent film that became a sleeper hit and caught the eye of Hollywood. When a new director wanted a younger, fresher, more innocent-looking Bond, he thought he'd found him in Alex Culpepper. Too bad the boy couldn't act.

"You're not getting this, Kate," Jane said. "No one has seen Caitlyn, and there's a dead woman."

"I don't see that there's any reason to think that it's Caitlyn. It's not as though she hasn't disappeared before. She does have a habit of taking off and drinking too much, doing too many drugs. If she left rehab, that's probably what's going on."

"True," Jane conceded. "But I'd feel so much better if we could make sure."

Kate sighed. "Okay, let me make a few calls and I'll see what I can find out." She barely hid her resentment.

"Thank you. I've exhausted my sources."

She wanted to press Jane on which sources she'd "exhausted." She was willing to bet that she'd been the second call—after Culpepper. She didn't even say goodbye, merely ended the call. Kate knew she was being unfair. Just as her job had been—and still was—to protect Hank, it was Jane's to protect Caitlyn. Jane was unusually loyal to Caitlyn, who had treated her shabbily the past couple of years. But Caitlyn was also a cash cow for Jane, who'd been struggling until she'd snagged her most famous client. Unfortunately, Caitlyn was more famous as Hank's wife than as an actress.

Kate heard footsteps behind her and expected to see Maril again, but instead it was Anna carrying a glass of white wine; she handed it to Kate. How had she known? Kate smiled gratefully. "Thank you."

"You look like you're ready to rip someone's head off," Anna said.

Kate nodded. "Jane Rocheford. She seems to think that Caitlyn is missing and that I can somehow conjure her up out of thin air." She tried to make her tone light, but the day's stress was getting to her and she heard the tenseness in her voice. She took a sip of the wine.

Anna frowned. "Missing?"

She sighed. "That's what she says. 'No one has seen her,'" she said with air quotes. "Three days now, apparently. She left rehab. She's probably fallen off the wagon and taken up residence in a bar somewhere."

Anna was quiet, but there was something in her expression.

"What is it?" Kate asked. "Do you know something about Caitlyn?"

"Caitlyn was here. A few days ago."

Jane should have called Anna instead, but then she wondered: "What for?"

"She was drunk. Really distraught about something, but she left before I could get anything out of her."

Kate suspected that Anna knew well and good what Caitlyn Howard could have been upset about. The ink on her divorce from Hank had hardly been dry before Kate married him. Not that Caitlyn had any right to be upset, since she was the one who'd been having the affair.

"Do you know where she was heading? Jane said she was going to see Hank, but she didn't show up in the city."

Anna shook her head. "Like I said, she didn't tell me anything. I honestly didn't think much of her visit. Caitlyn can be a bit of a drama queen."

No kidding. But something about this wasn't sitting right. Caitlyn's MO was to be dramatic in public, not private. That way she could end up in the tabloids, on the entertainment news cycle.

"Why would she show up *here*? Were you that close?" Kate hadn't been aware of any kind of special relationship between Anna and Caitlyn, but Anna was the mothering type, so maybe the girl felt comfortable with her, like Hank's children Lizzie and Ted did.

"No. I mean, I tried to be kind to her, although she made that difficult at times."

Kate nodded in agreement. And while Anna said she'd been distraught, it could have been anything with Caitlyn. How many times had Kate seen her like that? Ten, twenty? More times than she could remember. But Jane's concern began to stir up uncomfortable thoughts. Anna's house was next door to the marsh where that woman's body was found.

Caitlyn's disappearance might not be her own choice. Kate shrugged the morbid thought away. It didn't have to be Caitlyn. The brutality of the murder was spooking her. That body could be someone who'd been trespassing, someone who'd been in a boating accident and floated into the marsh on the tide. There were myriad scenarios that were possible; the woman could have been anyone. But then Kate had another thought. What if Caitlyn *had* gone next door? What if she'd seen something over there? Something that would push her into hysteria. Something that might cause her to disappear. Caitlyn, despite her transgressions, was not stupid. If she saw something she wasn't supposed to, she knew what to do. They all did.

She shivered in the heat. A missing woman. No, not just a woman, a missing wife. And an unidentified body in the marsh.

It was like Martha's Vineyard. Nan Tudor hadn't been seen since.

8

ANNA

A nna had said too much. She shouldn't have told Kate that Caitlyn had been here. But the shock of hearing that Caitlyn might be missing caused her to let down her guard. Kate said Caitlyn had told Jane she was heading to see Hank. Anna had a feeling she knew why.

Caitlyn had been drinking. A lot.

Anna prided herself on being a tolerant person, but it had been a long day. Lizzie had been giving her a hard time because she wanted to go to the city with a school friend and her father had said no, and Ted refused to take a bath after a day at the beach. Because she'd had a full house of guests, she'd been going nonstop since five thirty that morning. All she'd wanted to do was take a hot bubble bath and go to bed with Joan, forget about her day, and start over the next.

Will Stafford, head of security, had called her to let her know Caitlyn was at the front gate. "She's insisting on coming in," he said in his usual unflappable tone.

Sensing her hesitation, he added, "She shouldn't be driving."

If something happened to Caitlyn, Anna didn't want to feel accountable. "Okay, let her in," she said reluctantly.

She opened the front door and stood on the porch as the car screeched to a halt in the driveway. The driver's side door opened and Caitlyn stumbled out, tripping over the cobblestones. Will caught her before she fell, lifting her up, his hands under her armpits. She teetered, her ankles seeming unwilling to hold her upright, but finally she managed to stand and shrugged Will off.

"Keep your fucking hands off me," she growled.

Anna cringed inwardly as she forced a deep breath to stay calm.

Will followed Caitlyn to the door—close enough so if she stumbled again he'd be able to keep her from falling—and his eyes met Anna's. She shook her head at him and mouthed, "Thank you," before he disappeared back into the night.

The anger that she'd heard in Caitlyn's tone when she spoke to Will dissolved into tears that streamed down blotchy cheeks, her mascara running. The scent of whiskey was overpowering as the girl lurched toward her. Anna steered her into the great room, toward one of the sofas. When they reached it, Caitlyn pulled Anna down with her, her sobs seemingly uncontrollable.

"What's wrong?" Anna asked, wrenching herself out from under the girl's body and shifting to the cushion next to her. She wondered if Caitlyn would be sick, if she should find a trash bin just in case. "What's happened?"

Caitlyn shook her head, sucking in great bits of air and hiccupping in between sobs.

Could she be upset about Hank and Kate? Anna wondered. The idea seemed far-fetched, but you never knew with Caitlyn. Despite her affair with Culpepper, which had begun before and continued off and on throughout her relationship with Hank, Caitlyn had seemed fond of her ex-husband, sometimes actually seeming as though she truly loved him.

But then, the girl *was* an actress.

Caitlyn's sobs were subsiding slightly.

Coffee. She needed some coffee. Anna got up, moving the tote bag that Caitlyn had dropped on the floor to the side table.

"I'll be right back," she told the girl, who had spread out on the sofa, her arms over her face.

In the kitchen, Anna busied herself with the kettle, and as the water boiled, she scooped coffee into a French press. When she came back out with the mug of black coffee, she realized she shouldn't have left Caitlyn alone so long.

Because she was gone.

"Where did she go?" she asked Will Stafford when he showed up at the door.

"She just got into her car and drove off. I was out back—I'd heard something but it was nothing. Murph told me he ran toward the car, but she sped out of the driveway. We'd left the gate open because the Morgans are on their way back from their evening out."

Anna sighed. She hadn't wanted the gate at all; it didn't seem too welcoming for an inn, but it did provide security and her guests didn't seem to mind. This time she'd wished it had kept someone in—instead of out.

It wasn't until later that she saw the tote bag on the side table next to the sofa, where she'd put it. Caitlyn had left it behind. Anna picked it up by one strap, and it fell open, revealing the only thing inside: a book with a plain brown leather cover. Caitlyn wasn't the literary type, and there was no title on the cover. Before she could think about it, Anna took the book out and opened it.

A handwritten scrawl crossed the pages.

It was a journal.

She didn't want to invade Caitlyn's privacy. She'd make sure the girl got it back. But where had she gone? It didn't matter. She could messenger it to the girl's apartment. She'd show up there eventually.

Anna started to put the book back into the bag, but as she did, the back cover flipped open.

In large block letters, it read:

HE'S GOING TO KILL ME

PART II

October 31

Tonight was my "coming out," like Cinderella at the ball. I've always loved dressing up for Halloween, but this took it to a different level. A masquerade party, straight from the pages of the books I love so much.

I've been working the last several weeks on the arrangements, but I never dreamed that I'd get an invitation.

I've been at Tudor Enterprises for six months. I didn't want to leave Paris, but when one company takes over another and the layoffs start, it's hard to hang on. And then no one wanted to hire an American, even though my French is fluent and I know no one can tell by talking to me that I'm not a native. But my passport can't lie. If I had a job, I might be able to establish permanent residency and maybe become a French citizen. But there I go again. Dreaming of something that won't happen. Especially now. My father pulled some strings and got me into this job. It's not ideal. I was pushing for London, but New York was the best he could do. I'm back to being an assistant, too. Granted, I'm working for Catherine Tudor and she's pretty powerful, but I'd rather work for her husband. That's where the power really is.

She's not so bad, though. She does insist on me calling her Mrs. Tudor. It's a little too 1950s for a woman in her position, but she doesn't want to hear it from me. Anyway, she's the boss. She realized pretty quickly that I'm a quick study and smart, so now I'm organizing and managing her events. I've grown to like it. I get to order people around. My father says it's the perfect job for me. I don't have to run personal errands for her. She's got someone else who does that.

So, tonight's event. It was at The Plaza. I couldn't believe the guest list. Politicians and judges and tech CEOs and venture capitalists. And then there were artists and writers and newspaper columnists. The masquerade idea was mine. I'd read about Truman Capote's black-and-white party in the 1960s, a "masked ball" for Washington Post *publisher Katharine Graham. I mentioned it, left a printout of the* New York Times *story on the desk. Next thing I knew, I was organizing a masquerade ball. That's the way to get things done the way you want them.*

I designed the invitations myself, made sure they were engraved with gold lettering. The calligraphy was especially classy. When I found one on my desk with my name on it, I thought it was a mistake. I took it to Catherine's office to ask her about it.

She told me it wasn't a mistake. She said I deserved it because I put so much work into it.

Granted, I found out that she'd invited all the other assistants and it wasn't exactly a party for us. It was going to be work. We were brought in to make sure everyone had a good time, to strategically make sure that so-and-so was able to talk to so-and-so without it seeming arranged. I should have been upset about it but decided to turn it into an opportunity.

I'm not going to be an assistant forever.

My costume was a white strapless satin dress with a black sash over one shoulder. All the assistants wore the same thing, and we had black lace masks shaped like cats' eyes. Our hair was done up with loose curls around our faces. We were fucking gorgeous, and I knew that we would make a splash.

The ballroom was decorated with torches and a castle at one end, its turrets accented with gold foil that sparkled in the soft light. It was elegant and playful at the same time. Everyone wondered who had come up with the idea, but I kept mum, not wanting to take any attention away from the beauty of the night. There's time enough to let everyone know who was the brains behind it.

I drank champagne and ate caviar, my hair coming loose while I danced, the music swirling around me. I knew I was beautiful; I felt beautiful. At some point I took off the sash. My face was hot with the booze. I had to find a corner to adjust the top of my dress, because I'd felt my breasts start to escape it.

When I turned around, I saw him watching me.

9

ANNA

Anna pulled the diary out of its hiding place in the shoebox in her closet. The large, loopy scrawl was confident and self-assured. She'd recognized it immediately for what it was once she'd read the first entry. Anna knew the stories. The history. The players. This journal belonged to Nan Tudor, Hank's second wife, who disappeared eight years ago, abandoning her daughter and her husband. No one knew why she'd left.

But what if she hadn't?

As Anna flipped to the back of the book again—how many times had she done that in the last couple of days—a chill slid down her spine, settling under her skin, goosebumps rising.

HE'S GOING TO KILL ME

She stared at the words until they began swimming around on the page, her eyes playing tricks on her.

Someone told her once that Nan Tudor was dead. What if these words were a premonition?

Hank had loved Nan, so much so that he waited for her for years. Their affair had been notorious—and not just because he was divorcing his wife and business partner of twenty-seven years but because of how devoted he was to her.

Hank had not wooed Anna the way he had Nan—or even the way he'd wooed Jeanne or Caitlyn or Kate. Theirs had merely been a business transaction, a merger. Anna's father had left her his newspaper business when he died. She'd been working there since she was a teenager, and it was a natural progression to take it over. Whether she'd enjoy it or not was never a question. She'd been relieved when Hank Tudor showed up with his offer to buy it. But what shocked her was that he wanted to include *her* in his acquisition.

In retrospect, she should never have taken him up on it. She should have just sold him the company. But he had lost his third wife—tragically, a complication after giving birth to their son—and Hank Tudor liked being married. Anna was a young woman who was also a publisher, and until he was ready to fold this smaller newspaper into one of the bigger ones he owned—that was the plan even from the beginning—he needed some stability among the staff and advertisers. He convinced Anna that he needed her, too, in a more personal way. He liked how practical she was, how steady. He had two children who'd lost their mothers, and he liked how she was with them.

"Marry me," he'd pleaded, taking her face in his hands, locking his eyes on hers. "You are so beautiful."

No one had ever told her that before. She'd had no idea how desperately she'd wanted to hear it, how she *had* to feel beautiful. And Hank Tudor made her feel that way, despite a distant tugging at the back of her mind that told her it would be a big mistake because it wasn't a sexual feeling, it was more a validation. Her father had always told her she was "pleasant looking," and she should never expect to sweep a man off his feet.

But then Hank Tudor was telling her otherwise, that he wanted her to be his wife, that she would make his life complete.

He swept *her* off her feet.

What he didn't know was that she had just come off a relationship—a bad one that had left her raw. She married him impulsively—she who never acted on impulse.

While they'd had a comfortable rapport, once they found themselves in bed, it was a disaster. Despite his affairs, when he wanted to marry a woman, Hank had a very prudish view of sex. He wouldn't sleep with her until they were married, and by then it was too late. Anna had never been with a man, and by the time she was, she realized she didn't want to be. She'd been fooling herself and should have seen it coming; it wasn't who she was.

Hank was angry, first that he couldn't satisfy her, then later when she admitted she preferred women. He blamed her for not telling him; he blamed Cromwell, who had negotiated the deal. Anna was aware much of his rage came from embarrassment; he'd made a big splash in the press about his new wife. She had been careful to flatter him, to let him know that it was *her* mistake, not his.

"You couldn't have known," she'd told him. "I was wrong not to say anything."

She agreed to stay with him for six months, to keep up appearances and to care for his children. She'd become very fond of Lizzie and Ted, aware that she might never have a child of her own. After the divorce that cited the innocuous irreconcilable differences, he bought her the house in Greenwich and set her up with her business. She didn't really care what type of business she had, but she discovered she was good at this, welcoming people into her home, cooking and cleaning, and being a good hostess. She built a nice life for herself with his help.

Because she didn't ask for anything and had given him his freedom, he gave her everything she wanted.

Nan should have done the same.

Anna ran her hand across the soft leather. She hadn't told Joan about the book. She didn't like keeping secrets from her, but there were things she couldn't tell her, things Joan couldn't be privy to. Hank expected discretion, even in her relationships, and she had to respect that. He was, after all, responsible for her comfortable life, and as easily as it had come, it could disappear. She didn't have any delusions about that.

But while she couldn't tell Joan, she might be able to tell Kate. She'd already told her about Caitlyn's visit. If she gave Kate the diary, then it would be *her* problem and *she* could figure out what to do with it. Kate had spent the past three years doing damage control for Hank, so this was much more in the other woman's wheelhouse than Anna's.

Hank and Tom were still sequestered in the den; Joan had gone to fetch the children. Kate was in the room Anna had given her and Hank for the night. Before she could change her mind, she took the diary and went down the hall.

"Kate?" she asked as she stuck her head inside the door.

Kate was standing at the dresser and turned at the sound of Anna's voice. Not for the first time, Anna felt inferior. Kate's sleek auburn hair was twisted back and up into a loose bun that rested on her long, white neck. Her face was a mass of angles—cheekbones, nose, chin—mirrored by thin shoulders, tiny wrists, and long fingers that hinted at piano lessons. Her beauty combined with the incredible efficiency of her movements, which translated into how well she'd done her job, was something Hank Tudor never could have resisted.

But now Anna noticed the tight lines around Kate's mouth, the furrow in her brow.

"Yes?" Kate asked.

Anna stepped inside the room and softly closed the door behind her. She held out the diary without a word. Kate frowned as she took it, opened it, and began to read. She hadn't gotten too far when she looked up, her eyes wide. "Where did you get this?" She'd recognized it for what it was as well.

"Caitlyn. She left it here." Anna hesitated. "Turn to the last page."

Kate did as she asked, and a gasp escaped her lips. She glanced quickly at the door, as though Hank would come in at any moment.

"Do you think this is why she wanted to see Hank?" Anna asked.

"If it is, then it's a good thing she left it here," Kate said, her voice almost a whisper. "She didn't say anything before she left?"

"No. She just took off." Anna shouldn't have left the girl alone. She should have put her in a room upstairs and kept an eye on her. But she hadn't even considered it. If she was being honest with herself, she was glad when Caitlyn left. It was too much drama—too much drunkenness and crying. "I found this in her tote bag. She left it behind. No one else knows I have it." She'd gone upstairs, tucked it in the shoebox, took a sleeping pill, and crawled into bed. Where did Caitlyn go when she left? What if she had turned right instead of left at the end of the driveway? What if she'd ended up at that house next door?

Anna saw her worry mirrored in the other woman's eyes. "Are you thinking what I am? Do you think something happened to Caitlyn after she left here? Do you think that body might be her?"

"I don't know," Kate admitted.

Anna caught her breath.

"Maybe she saw something she shouldn't have," Kate said. "Something that upset her."

Anna considered that possibility, a more palatable alternative to the worst-case scenario. That Caitlyn may have, for some reason, been over at Hank's house and seen something and that was why she'd been so upset and drunk. If she had, who knew the state she'd be in now—and who knew what she might say to someone? They all knew the rules, but if any of them were to break them, it would be Caitlyn.

Yet . . .

"There's no reason why she would go over to that house," Anna said. "It's not as though Hank was there. Everyone knew he was in New York with you. Except maybe she thought Mary was there and for some reason wanted to see *her*?"

Kate shrugged. "I'm just throwing ideas out there. Until we find her, we don't know anything." She leafed through the pages of the diary. After a few seconds, she closed the book and looked at Anna with a puzzled expression.

"How did Caitlyn get her hands on this?"

10

K ate stepped out of the shower and wrapped herself in a towel. She padded into the bedroom. The wallpaper was dotted with small pink rosebuds, and the white duvet and pile of pillows on the wrought iron bed were inviting. A glass decanter of cognac sat on the dresser, two brandy glasses next to it. Hank should be here soon. He was saying good night to the children, who'd come barreling in before dinner, chattering and laughing, glad to see their father. He was a good distraction to the activities across the marsh. Their half sister, Maril, sat in the background, trying to catch her father's eye. Anna and Joan had their arms around each other, both clearly wanting everyone to leave and get back to their normal, everyday lives. But the shadow of that murdered woman hung over the bed-and-breakfast as everyone tiptoed around it. The police had said they might have more questions, so they were trapped for the time being, a forced togetherness that seeped into their expressions and body language. As long as the police scoured the property next door, until the body was identified, nothing would go back to normal.

Kate tucked her towel in across her chest and poured two short ones. She picked up one of the glasses and sipped, letting the brandy warm her throat, wishing it would ease the tension in her shoulders as she thought about Nan Tudor's journal. She was initially surprised that Anna shared it with her, but after thinking about it, she supposed it made sense. They both understood the consequences if it were exposed. Especially with that damning last page.

"Joan doesn't know," Anna had confided.

It was best she didn't. The fewer people who knew about it, the better. But Caitlyn had gotten it somewhere, so at least one other person was privy to it. Kate was certain, though, that Hank didn't know about it. If he did, it wouldn't have been in Caitlyn's hands.

"I'm keeping it in a shoebox in the closet," Anna had said. "Seemed like the best place right now, until we can figure out what to do with it."

What Kate wanted to do with it was read it. All of it. Discover Nan Tudor's secrets—and why "he" was going to kill her.

He who?

The question hit her hard. Maybe she really didn't want to know after all.

She had given the book back to Anna. "Put it back. We can talk about this later. Sort it out." They had to wait until Hank was gone. The last thing they needed was for Hank—or Tom—to discover them poring over Nan Tudor's life.

Kate's loyalty to Hank had come slowly. She'd been skeptical of him at first, a man who'd had four wives and three children and never seemed to give anything or anyone his full attention except his business. She'd felt sorry for Catherine, didn't blame Nan for leaving. Jeanne, the third wife, died so tragically after Ted's birth. She and Hank had been married less than a year. Kate wondered if that marriage would have lasted had Jeanne lived; a small part of him was still mourning her. But he married Anna and merged businesses, ruthlessly taking over and ordering massive layoffs. That was when Kate had come in, hired to smooth out his image.

It had just been a job. She'd been laid off from the public relations firm—across-the-board cuts "to save money"—and needed to pay her bills. Working for Hank Tudor was temporary, a way to fill the hole in her résumé, and then she'd move on.

If it weren't for Caitlyn, Kate might have done just that.

"I'm going to marry her," he'd told Kate. "Your job might get a little more difficult." He'd known what would happen, the media frenzy, the headlines. While everyone was talking about the May-December relationship, she'd seen how hard he'd fallen for the girl, his vulnerability. This wasn't the billionaire businessman; this was a man who desperately wanted to recapture his youth.

She had wanted to tell him it wouldn't work. Caitlyn Howard was a spoiled child barely out of her teens. A B-level actress whose only asset was her looks. Instead, she had found herself saying, "Congratulations. And I don't mind." She hadn't. She'd deftly handled the press, deflecting Caitlyn's drinking and drug problems.

The tabloids had reported Caitlyn's affair first. That had been easy to dismiss. The tabloids were always wrong, and Hank wasn't tolerant of the fake news that they perpetuated. Caitlyn hadn't neglected him; she'd been his wife in every way. She'd shared his bed, hung on to his arm at all of his business functions, and played the role she'd signed on to without any complaint. But that's what it was: a role. Maybe it was the frustration of that, of having to constantly be "on" as Hank's wife. Because then there were the sightings: Caitlyn and Culpepper on the set of his new movie, out at the clubs at night, going to premieres together. Still, all of that could be dismissed as publicity stunts to get attention.

Until the photo of Caitlyn topless on Culpepper's new yacht off Sanibel Island.

Hank had been two time zones away, so there was a little window of time. Kate had some connections, dangling the Bond gig, guaranteeing it if Culpepper did what she asked. Culpepper was ambitious, and he was smart enough to know that sort of role didn't come along every day. Was Caitlyn worth his career? Kate had asked, explaining how far Hank's reach could be, how Hank could sabotage him but might be persuaded not to if Alex stopped seeing Caitlyn.

It was something Tom Cromwell would do, and she wasn't proud of it. But Culpepper was true to his word: he'd broken it off with Caitlyn, and in return, Kate did what she'd promised. Culpepper was the new James Bond.

What Kate hadn't anticipated was that Hank would divorce Caitlyn anyway.

"I know the truth about her," Hank had told her one night. "I knew, going in. I thought she could change with me. I thought I could make her love me."

He didn't have to make Kate love him.

When she'd told her friends about Hank, about how she was going to marry him, they all asked why. Why would she marry a man who seemed to have no qualms about switching out his wives in quick succession? Sure, he was rich, but would that be enough? Kate had laughed it off, told them yes, it was all about the money. But it wasn't.

No one understood what happened, why she married Hank. It was as though he cast some sort of spell over her the first time she saw him, looking deep into her eyes, searching for something—she didn't know what. But he made her feel like she was the only woman in the room, the only one whose opinion mattered. He listened to her; he talked to her. She hadn't expected much from him sexually when they married. She'd told herself that it didn't matter; she'd been married before and neither of them were teenagers. But he'd proven to be an attentive lover who managed to tap a passion in her that she hadn't known she had.

Loving Hank Tudor was dangerous, but Kate was willing to risk it. She hoped she wouldn't regret it.

⚬—✦—⚬

Kate was still wearing the towel, sipping her cognac as she leaned against the headboard of the bed, when Hank slipped into the room, shutting the door behind him. He gave her an apologetic smile. "Sorry."

She shook her head. "You hardly ever see your children. I don't want to take that time away from you or from them."

He took the second snifter of cognac and settled in next to her. "I was wondering if you might want to get to know them better."

This was a conversation they should have had before they married, a conversation Kate wasn't sure how to broach. "I'd like that," she said, wondering if she meant it. Children had never been part of her life plan, but now she was married to a man who had two—no, three—of them. Maril didn't really count, though.

He brushed her lips tenderly with his, and she could taste the brandy. Kate smiled and leaned against his shoulder, his arm around her, his fingers gently stroking her neck. Suddenly, he stiffened, and she sat up straighter. His gaze had moved toward the window, which overlooked the marsh next door.

"What do you make of that?" he asked her, his eyes now on her. He wanted to know what she thought.

"It's a tragedy. I hope they find out who she is."

He took a sip of his cognac. "They never identified that other woman."

The one on Martha's Vineyard. "They haven't?" she asked, although she already knew the answer.

"No. Poor woman. How someone could do that to another person . . ." He took another swallow of the brandy. His eye twitched; his mouth formed a thin line. He'd been called in to make a possible identification. She'd seen that in one of the news stories.

Kate put her hand on his arm. "I'm sorry you had to see something like that."

Hank gave her a grim smile. "Two headless bodies found near my homes. I know I'm the common denominator, and they'll be back, asking more questions. It will be difficult for you. For Anna. The children."

"For you," Kate said. Should she mention Caitlyn? That the girl had been at the inn? That Jane Rocheford said she'd gone to talk to him? She could do that without mentioning the diary; she still had to figure out how to handle that.

Hank finished his brandy and pulled on her towel, opening it and sliding his hand over her breasts. He leaned over and kissed her, whispering gruffly, "Let's try to forget about all of it. For a little while." And all thoughts of Caitlyn and Nan disappeared.

February 8

He told me today he knows we're meant to be together. It's got to be a line. He can't possibly mean it. I'm his wife's assistant. She's a vice president of his company. She's almost as powerful as he is, might even be just as smart. Maybe smarter. She's certainly as ruthless as any man during a corporate takeover. But then again, it's not like she's doing what she can to keep him. I don't understand how a woman that powerful can let herself go physically like that. Those frumpy pantsuits do nothing to hide her thick waistline, the double chin. Her hair's starting to go gray, making her look even older than she is. She doesn't even bother with highlights or color. She should go to the gym, work out, find a trainer, something. Get a personal shopper to dress her if she doesn't have any fashion sense herself. There are things she could do. Women don't have to look their age.

He doesn't look his age at all. Every time I see him, I'm awestruck. He is tall, tan, muscular. He clearly works out, although with his schedule, I'm not sure where he finds the time. He's mentioned tennis and squash. I'd love to see him on the courts. I like that he's older. He's got a maturity and confidence that the guys my age only dream of. He wears his power and success in his posture, his stride, and it's incredibly sexy. When his eyes catch mine, I can barely stand it. I try to stay cool, act like I don't care. He can't know that when he looks at me like that, I get wet with desire for him.

He started by leaving me voicemails. I found Post-its inside my desk, asking me to meet him. He wanted me to go out for drinks after work. I told him I don't drink. *I'm not stupid. I've heard about the other women around the office. One of them got pregnant and left. She's living somewhere uptown with her son, a new job at one of the company's subsidiaries. He always throws them a bone. People around the office say he keeps buying companies because he needs places to send his women when he's done with them.*

I don't want to be like them.

When he asked me what I do outside work, I told him I read. He wanted to know what kinds of books I like, so I told him eighteenth-century French literature. In French. And two days ago, I found a battered copy of Voltaire's Lettres Philosophiques *on my desk. I gave it back to him and he wanted to know why. He said it was his own copy from college and he wanted me to have it. I can't take gifts from him. It's not right.*

Yesterday, I found a strand of pearls loose inside an interoffice envelope, a red ribbon tied in a perfect bow. There was no note. I'm not an idiot. I knew it was from him. I told him I couldn't accept it. He played stupid, said he didn't know what I was talking about, said I must have an admirer. He said he wanted to see the necklace, wanted me to wear it when he took me out for a drink.

I went. I don't know what I was thinking. I knew what he wanted, what he expected. I wore jeans and a loose cotton top with a scoop neck, nothing too low cut. I didn't want to wear anything too provocative, but the outfit looked better with my heels, and the pearls were so delicate. I couldn't stop fingering them, they were so smooth. And it turned out to be amazing. He's amazing. He spoke to me in French, and we talked about Voltaire. He kissed me where each pearl kissed my neck. He didn't try anything else. Even though I wanted him to. I would have gone down on him right then and there in the bar if he'd asked me. That's how far gone I am.

Then he told me his wife doesn't understand him. Biggest cliché ever. I told him I'd heard that before. But he didn't stop. He said that she was too wrapped up in the business, that she was making a lot of bad decisions and he might have to fire her. I told him I wouldn't be responsible for that, that if he did it, it would be his decision and I couldn't be a part of it. Anyway, if she goes, then I go, because I work for her. What would I do without a job?

I can't tell him that I secretly want her job. I'm afraid what he might say. What he might do. I hear things around the office. There was an incident, Catherine threw something at him because she was taken off one of the merger deals. That's why he travels alone now. He told me he's going to divorce her, but I told him not to make promises he can't keep.

I don't want to be a statistic, one of those #MeToo women who will end up on TV telling my story about the powerful man who seduced me, an innocent woman, taking advantage of me.

The crazy thing is, he's not taking advantage of me. He's not just trying to get me into bed.

He says he wants me more than he's ever wanted any other woman, but he'll wait until we're married because that's the right thing to do. He wants me to keep my reputation. It's almost comical.

11

ANNA

Anna wasn't disappointed that Hank wasn't going to stay longer. It was always too complicated when he was here. The children loved seeing him, but only because they loved the *idea* of him. He was their father, but he'd never spent that much time with them. He'd always had more of a relationship with Maril, because he'd been with her mother longer than he'd been with Nan or Jeanne.

Anna felt sorry for Lizzie and Ted. She did what she could to make them feel the inn was their home as much as hers. But they had little stability, what with being sent away to school and then shuffled from house to house—and wife to wife—during holidays. Maril filled in some gaps, too, but all the money in the world wouldn't give them a normal life. Now that Hank was married to Kate, he might expect her to take over the role of mother. But Anna didn't see Kate as the mothering type any more than Caitlyn had been, for different reasons. Secretly, she was pleased about that. She'd come to love them as her own and didn't want to give up the time she had with them. Joan kept telling her that Hank needed to work this out with her, but Joan really didn't understand. She had a difficult relationship with her own children, nothing at all like the one Anna had with Lizzie and Ted.

Anna opened the dresser drawer and reached around for the basket of clean laundry. Lizzie's T-shirts and shorts were carefully folded, and she put them into the drawer. She'd made sure that she washed Lizzie's dresses, too. Lizzie didn't always want to wear them, but if the girl didn't have something she wanted when she wanted it, she could have a temper about her.

Anna had never met Lizzie's mother, but rumor had it that Nan was the same way.

She could hear Hank and Tom talking on the back porch below Lizzie's room, but she couldn't make out what they were saying. It was best she didn't know, anyway. There were a lot of things it was best not knowing. That's why she never asked Caitlyn about Alex Culpepper.

Anna closed the drawer and picked up the laundry basket. Lizzie was leaning against the railing at the top of the stairs, her red hair escaping from the French braid to form little tendrils around her face. Anna was struck again by how solemn her expression always was. The girl rarely smiled, although when she did, it lit up the whole room.

"Daddy's leaving."

Anna felt a surge of maternal love and reached around to hug her.

"He'll be back," she whispered.

"I know." Lizzie pulled away and stood up straighter, her head high. She was a tough one, but sadly it was because she had to be. "He says you and Joan will keep us safe."

Anna nodded. "That's right. We won't let anything happen to you or Teddy."

Lizzie cocked her head and narrowed her eyes. "But it's really Will and Murph who are protecting all of us, right?"

Leave it to Lizzie to know what was what. "That's right."

"They couldn't protect that woman, though, could they? So how safe are we, really?"

Lizzie was wiser than her eleven years, and Anna always had to watch herself or she'd be too candid with her, forgetting that she was still a child.

"We are very safe here," she said. "There's nothing to worry about."

Lizzie gave her a look that told her she hadn't been quite successful in her reassurance. Maybe because she hadn't convinced herself of it.

"Now go on downstairs and say goodbye to your father."

Lizzie bit her lip, and Anna had the sense she had more questions, but to her relief, the girl turned and made her way down the stairs, her fingers sliding along the banister.

"Can't keep the driver waiting." Hank announced through the screen door.

From the top of the stairs, Anna could see Ted peeking around his waist.

"Come say goodbye, Lizzie." Hank motioned for the girl to come closer, and she bounded forward, swinging the door open and grabbing his hand. He ruffled Ted's hair, taking the boy's hand with his free one, and the three of them disappeared down the steps, the door slapping shut behind them.

Lindsey, Hank's new assistant, had gone on ahead earlier, so it would be Hank and Tom heading back to the city together. Anna took her time going down the stairs, and as she reached the bottom, Joan appeared at her side.

"You okay?"

Anna started at the sound of her wife's voice, then relaxed, finding Joan's hand and squeezing it.

"I'm fine," she said.

And she would be, with Joan by her side. What would she do without her? Anna marveled again at her good luck in meeting her almost three years ago, when her marriage to Hank ended. It had been such a random meeting at the local farmer's market, just weeks before the house was ready for guests. There had been a spark between them, something Anna had thought she'd never feel again, and while their relationship moved quickly, it never felt rushed. Only right.

Anna smiled to herself, recalling when she first saw her, Joan had been checking out the tomatoes, her hair tousled in a loose knot on the top of her head, her features striking with high cheekbones and a clear complexion.

She wore a simple pair of worn jeans and a white T-shirt, and Anna had never seen a woman more beautiful.

Joan had caught her staring and smiled. "I'm Joan," she'd said, as though it was the most natural thing for them to meet.

They'd been together ever since. Joan had quit her job because she was looking for a more relaxed lifestyle, and her finance background helped tremendously with running the small business. Joan always said that timing was everything.

Anna reached around her waist and pulled her close, her lips brushing Joan's.

They watched everyone from behind the screen door. Lizzie and Ted were running around, shouting their goodbyes, their arms flapping in the air. Kate stood stiffly, her arms folded across her chest. She certainly wasn't the mother type.

Lizzie came back and was trying to engage Kate in conversation, and to the woman's credit, she unfolded her arms and seemed to be answering the girl's questions.

Joan cocked her head toward the scene outside. "You going to be okay with Wife Number Six here?"

Hank was kissing his new wife, a kiss that was a tad too intimate for the driveway. Kate pulled away, but the way she looked at him told Anna that maybe Hank had actually found a woman who truly loved him. Time would tell if it was for the right reasons.

Anna shrugged. "It'll be fine." Although she wasn't quite sure. She'd known Kate in her capacity as Hank's assistant, but her new role as wife left some questions as to how their relationship would go. She was having doubts about sharing Nan Tudor's journal with her, but it was too late now.

"Maril's staying, too?"

Maril had shown up out of the blue, most likely sent by her mother. She was hovering behind her father, hoping for a glance her way. Just like

Catherine. Sad, really. Hank could do more for Maril, but like with his wives, once he left, he never looked back.

"Yes, I suppose so."

"Let's pretend they're paying guests, and we can get through this." Joan frowned. "Where's Cromwell?"

Good question.

"I don't trust that man," Joan said, a venom in her tone that Anna had never heard before.

"Did he say or do something?" she asked, concerned.

Joan gave her a tight smile. "Nothing more than usual." But there was something behind her words, something Anna couldn't put her finger on.

She would talk to her about it later, because there were more pressing things right now.

Joan gave her a peck on the cheek. "I'll go put on a fresh pot of coffee. I'm sure everyone will need it."

"I know I will."

As Joan headed back to the kitchen, Anna leaned against the railing and sighed. It was going to be a long couple of days.

Heavy footsteps were coming down the stairs behind her. She twisted around to see Tom, holding his overnight bag. She started to say goodbye, but he held up a hand. He leaned in toward her, his mouth so close to her ear she could feel his breath.

"She was never here." Tom's voice was low. "You never saw her."

12

Alex Culpepper had changed his cell number. Kate clutched her phone and debated what to do. She'd left voicemails and texts for Caitlyn that had gone unanswered. Not exactly a surprise, considering, so going through Culpepper was her best bet. If anyone knew where Caitlyn Howard might be, it would be him—and it was now more important than ever to find her. Before Jane Rocheford told anyone else that Caitlyn had gone missing on her way to see Hank only days before a body was found. Not to mention that Caitlyn had somehow gotten her hands on Nan Tudor's diary—a diary that Hank would undoubtedly not want anyone to see.

Kate had only one option when considering how to reach Culpepper, one she wasn't keen on, but there was no other way. She tapped out the number on her screen and waited.

"Hello?" Jane Rocheford wasn't only Caitlyn's publicist. She also worked for Culpepper. She'd introduced them.

"Jane? It's Kate Parker." She paused, then added, "Kate Tudor."

"Did you find Caitlyn?" A tinge of hope laced her tone.

"No, not yet. I was hoping you could give me Alex Culpepper's private cell number."

Jane was quiet for so long that Kate thought the call had been dropped. And then, "I already asked him if he knew where she was. He said he doesn't."

"I'd like to give it a try."

"I can't give that number out."

"I just want to make sure she's okay."

Jane hesitated, as if she were weighing whether Kate was telling the truth. After a second, she said, "He's on set. He might not even have his phone on."

"Let me try."

"You're worried about her. That body . . ." Jane's voice faltered.

Kate sighed, giving the impression that was the only reason she wanted to reach Caitlyn. "It's best to make sure."

Jane rattled off the number. "Let me know if you hear anything, okay?"

"Sure."

"I don't think it's a good idea," said Will Stafford, the head of Anna's security detail, when Kate explained she needed a ride to the train station.

"I have to go to the city for a couple of hours." Kate wasn't about to give him more than that, and she looked to Anna for support. Surprisingly, the other woman shrugged.

"I agree with Will. There's too much media watching us."

Anna was supposed to be on her side. She knew how important it was to find Caitlyn now, and Kate didn't want to talk to Alex over the phone. She didn't know who'd be listening in, so she'd set up a meeting for early afternoon.

Kate frowned at Anna, staring at her until Anna finally rolled her eyes. "Okay, okay, I know." Anna turned to Will. "She has to go."

Will looked from Anna to Kate and back to Anna. "Then she has to do what I tell her. No questions."

"Fine." Kate didn't have a choice. "But you can't ask any questions, either."

His lip twitched, like he wanted to smile but kept it at bay as he told her to dress in yoga clothes, pull her hair up in a ponytail, and not to wear makeup. "Meet me at the garage when you're ready," he instructed.

Anna followed her upstairs.

"We can trust him, right?" Kate asked as she pulled her workout clothes from her small bag. She'd thrown them in at the last minute, thinking that she might want to work out in Anna's basement gym, not realizing they'd come in handy like this.

"Yes. He won't be a problem. I trust him completely."

"Where did you find him?"

"Joan hired him."

"What's his background?" Kate asked from behind the bathroom door as she wriggled her way into leggings and a sports bra.

"Military. West Point. Afghanistan. Iraq. Five tours."

Kate scrubbed her face clean. When she looked up in the mirror, her eyes were pale, lashes almost invisible, and the freckles danced along her nose and colorless cheeks. She couldn't remember the last time she'd gone out without makeup.

Anna was still speaking. "Honorable discharge. He was wounded in an IED explosion in Kabul, but I don't know much more than that. I haven't seen any signs of a physical wound. He's proven himself here and has built a good team."

Kate worried a little about Anna's choice of words. If there was no physical sign of a wound, that could still mean he had post-traumatic stress disorder or some other mental health issue as a result of his time in a war zone. But there was no other way she was going to get out of this house and into the city without him, so she didn't have a choice but to trust Anna's instincts about the man. Still, she had one other question.

"But even though his team is supposed to be so good, why didn't they see anything over at that marsh in the last few days?" Kate stepped back into the bedroom, looking like any other Greenwich housewife heading for her daily workout.

Anna sighed. "No one saw anything. It makes me think that whoever that poor woman was, someone tried to bury her at sea and she floated into the marsh."

Kate grimaced. "We can only hope," she muttered, adding more loudly, "All set. I'll see you later. Hopefully Alex will tell us where Caitlyn is. Make sure you keep that journal hidden."

She ran into Joan on her way out, and she made the excuse that she'd found a class she wanted to take. Joan looked dubious. Anna might have to answer some questions. It was uncomfortable lying to a spouse but sometimes necessary. At least Maril hadn't seen her; Anna had sent her to the private beach with the children this morning and they were still there.

Kate met Will in the garage where the silver Subaru sat waiting. He gave her a once-over and a quick nod of approval before opening the passenger door for her. He was wearing jeans, a black T-shirt that showed off muscular arms, and a baseball cap over his close-cropped hair. There was a look about military men, and Will Stafford had it, would probably have it for the rest of his life. She climbed into the car and settled into the seat, her small black gym bag in her lap, pulling the seatbelt over her chest.

"You ready for this?" he asked when he got into the driver's seat.

She nodded.

He handed her a ball cap that matched his own. "Put this on. Do you have sunglasses?"

She'd never disguised herself like this before, even when she was accompanying Hank. "Is this really necessary?"

Will's eyebrows rose. "Yes."

His familiarity with disguise made her wonder more about his background. What, exactly, had he done in the military? But as the gate swung open and the car pulled out into the road, she was distracted by the vans and cars parked on the opposite side of the street, cameras aimed at the Subaru.

"Don't look," Will said. "Look at me. Tilt your head down so they can't get a good shot."

"Will they follow us?"

"Most likely." His tone was matter-of-fact.

"I've never noticed this many before."

"There's never been a murder before." The words sat between them for a few minutes before Will spoke again. "I can't drop you at the train station. They'll be all over you. Let me take you where you need to go."

She'd wanted to take the train, be truly invisible when she got to the city. No one would know where she was heading.

He noticed her hesitation. "It's safer, in more ways than one."

She spotted two cars tailgating in her sideview mirror.

Will grinned. "I can lose them."

She barely had time to register the way he weaved in and out of traffic and finally onto the highway because he entertained her with stories about drag races on long stretches of empty road and demolition derbies at his hometown speedbowl. She didn't think things like that existed anymore; they were a throwback to another era, like poodle skirts and the twist.

"Maybe not in your world," he said with a wink. "And I'll tell you something I've never admitted to before." He paused for effect, then said, "I was a sandbagger."

"I have no idea what that is."

"I always entered races I was overqualified for so I would win."

"So you were a cheater."

He gave her a sidelong look, then his eyes went back to the road. "Aren't we all, in some way?"

She didn't like where this conversation was going.

"How do you like working for Anna?" she asked, changing the subject.

"It's a good gig. Pays well."

"They might need some extra security now," Kate said. She didn't care that Anna felt they would be "fine." Now that she had the opportunity, she could talk to Will directly about it.

"Oh, don't worry," he said with a smile. "Already taken care of. I'm staying on the property and have hired a couple more guys."

"Anna gave you a room?"

He chuckled. "Not in the house. Over the garage. I've got the equipment and an office up there."

"Equipment?"

"Computers. Alarms. We monitor everything. Screens showing the entire property from every angle."

Kate thought about that for a moment, what Anna had said about none of his team seeing anything suspicious in the last few days. "So you technically shouldn't miss anything on the property? What about over near the marsh? Do you have cameras aimed there, too?"

Will grinned. "You sound like those cops." He hesitated, the smile disappearing as he sighed. "I know what you're thinking, but we've got nothing from the night before the body was found."

"What do you mean, 'nothing'?" She didn't like the sound of that.

Will shook his head. "Nothing was out of place, no one was where they shouldn't be. The camera angle doesn't capture the marsh. Maybe if they had the cameras on next door . . ." He shrugged.

Goosebumps rose on Kate's skin. "What do you mean, *if* they had the cameras on next door?"

"From what I hear, there was some sort of computer malfunction over there. Been going on a couple of weeks now. No security video at all. Cops asked me if I knew anything about it, but I don't work for Tudor. He's got his own people. I don't know their setup."

No security video? It couldn't be a coincidence, and from Will's expression, Kate could tell he was thinking the same thing.

No witnesses.

September 30

I quit my job today. It was our first real argument. He was angry, said that I couldn't leave him. That I was abandoning us. What us? There is no us as long as he's still married to her. He tells me he wants me, that divorces take time. He doesn't understand that working for her isn't working anymore. I'm not leaving him, I'm leaving her, my job, Tudor Enterprises. He said he could have me transferred, but I'd rather not go to another department and be the subject of gossip.

I've stayed in the job to try to prove that we aren't sleeping together. Because we're not. Not yet. But no one believes it.

Last week, Tom came to me and told me I had to quit.

Hank likes Tom, trusts him, because he's so good for the company. He's been able to help Hank negotiate any deal he wants, and his companies have expanded so much in the last few years. But there's something beneath Tom's surface, something that goes beyond helpful and borders on a kind of evil. Tom likes to be cruel, like a cat with a mouse, toying with Hank's enemies and digging up shit, dangling threats until he gets what he wants. It's not working with Catherine, though. He's been using all the tricks in his book on her, but she's smarter than he is. She's tougher than Hank or Tom knows. She's got her own people who are just as ruthless. Rumors have it that she's got a Cromwell of her own, someone off-site, someone who is loyal only to her, not to Hank. No one seems to know who it is—I've tried everything to find out. There's speculation that it's a lover, *that's why it's a secret who it is. We don't even know if it's a man or a woman. Eustace Chapuys, a weird little guy who runs her communications office, is always poking around trying to find out, but she hasn't even told him, apparently. Hank doesn't believe me, though. I've tried to tell him. He doesn't like it when I speak up, but I can't stay quiet on this. I worked for the woman. I saw who she is, how she operates. He only saw the meek Catherine who would give him everything he wanted. Who would say anything he wanted her to say. He doesn't understand her tenacity, her insistence that she will be his wife forever.*

Tom said we have to make it harder for her to get any more proof that Hank and I are having an affair. We've tried to be careful. We never meet in public, or go out to dinner, or do anything that a man and a woman in love do. Instead, he comes to my apartment and we drink wine and talk books. But Tom told me that as long as I work for Catherine, as long as I'm there, she's watching me. He said he knows she's got people following me, and he's not able to protect me anymore. Protect me and Hank.

I submitted my resignation, effective immediately. Within 24 hours, I found myself settled in a cottage on an estate in the Berkshires, arranged by Tom. The woman who owns the main house on the property is leery of me, but she's well paid for her discretion. I'm uncertain how long I'll have to be here. Hank doesn't know where I am—he's pretty angry with Tom for keeping this a secret, but Tom tells him that it's necessary for the divorce. He does call me and we talk. Or argue. He pleads with me to tell him where I am so he can come to me. It's breaking my heart.

Tom better settle this divorce soon.

13

The taxi came to a stop in front of the brownstone on the Upper East Side in Manhattan. Will had dropped Kate off in Times Square in front of the Hard Rock Café, and when the Subaru was safely out of sight, Kate went over to Madison Avenue to hail a cab. If Will suspected she was ditching him like that, he didn't let on, just said that he'd meet her at that same spot in two hours. She couldn't let him know what her true destination was—and risk having him see Alex arrive.

Alex Culpepper said he'd meet her; he promised he'd keep the paparazzi away. Kate wasn't sure how he'd do that, but he said she should leave it to him. She was being forced to trust too many people lately. Caitlyn should have stayed put at that rehab center. She'd said she would. Kate should have known she was lying. The girl was all about lies.

Kate fished her keys out of her gym bag and opened the heavy door. She paused at the line of mailboxes and retrieved a pile of junk mail that she stuck under her arm as she made her way down a short hallway, where she let herself through yet another locked door. There was no elevator in the walkup, and she climbed the stairs to the third floor. When she reached the next door, she took a deep breath.

Kate put her key in the lock and pushed the door open, stepping into her world. It wasn't a big apartment, but it was full of her things, things she wasn't yet ready to bring to the penthouse. They belonged here; time would tell if they could make the transition.

Hank wanted her to let the apartment go, but she kept stalling him, saying she hadn't gotten around to dealing with it. The penthouse she shared with Hank was on the Upper West Side, directly across the park. If she went up to the roof, she might actually be able to see the building.

She dropped her bag on the floor as she stepped into the living room. The oversized brown sofa was plush and soft, bright red and blue pillows tucked under the curves of its arms, a pink cashmere throw folded over the back. Rings from wet glasses and mugs had created a design across the teak coffee table that looked like it had been made that way rather than residue because someone hadn't used a coaster. Shelves lining the wall behind the sofa were overflowing with books and artifacts from her travels: small glass jars filled with sand from the Greek islands, carved wooden statues from the Dominican Republic, needlepoint pandas from China, a jade Buddha bought at Stanley Market in Hong Kong.

An original oil painting she'd found at a stall along the Seine in Paris hung on the wall across from the shelves, its long sweeping brushstrokes a blast of color to match the pillows on the couch.

Her eyes landed on the photograph of her parents, smiling at each other as they posed on the Great Wall. Kate remembered taking that picture, a family vacation when she was twelve. They'd given her a camera for her birthday, and she took dozens of photos as they traveled throughout China: Beijing, Shanghai, Xian. Her childhood had been happy, full of travel and laughter. Her parents were both teachers, and they believed travel was education.

She wished they were still alive. Her mother died first, breast cancer. Her father followed three years later from prostate cancer. Kate missed their wisdom, their conversation. She wondered what they'd think of Hank, about her marrying him. They'd met her first husband, and while they didn't say anything, she knew they didn't approve. She had been too young. Her second had been an impulse; it hadn't been long after her father had died, and she'd been lonely. It was the wrong reason to marry someone she barely knew, and it was over in less than a year.

Kate put the kettle on the stove and fished out a tea bag. She wished she had more time. Hank didn't know about the stolen hours she'd spent here, surrounded by her things, away from her job, from her responsibilities. Was it wrong to still want that? Time alone to be herself, not an assistant—or a wife. Kate admonished herself. It was too soon in her marriage to think like that. But she'd always been Kate Parker. It was going to take a little time getting used to being Kate Tudor.

A buzzer startled her as she poured her tea, her hand jerking and spilling hot water onto the countertop. Kate frowned, glanced at her watch. How did he get here so quickly? She mopped up the spill with a napkin before going over to the small intercom by the door. She pushed a button. "Yes?"

"It's Alex."

She held the other button long enough for him to push through the front door downstairs. When the second buzzer sounded, she held the button again and opened her door, waiting. She heard his footsteps on the stairs as he approached, finally appearing in her doorway.

Kate was taking a risk having Alex meet at her apartment, but she couldn't think of anywhere else where they could have the privacy they needed.

He gave a quick nod as he brushed past her, his bleached-blond hair long in front and covering half his face. When he looked up, she again was struck by how good looking he was. She could understand why Caitlyn would be taken in by him. His blue eyes flashed as he grinned, his shoulders slightly hunched, as though he were embarrassed by his height, which Kate put at a couple of inches over six feet. He wore a tattered plain black T-shirt and a pair of denim cutoffs with Tevas on his feet.

Her conversation with Will suddenly popped back into her head. He said everyone cheats. Caitlyn had certainly cheated, and Kate had felt superior because she hadn't slept with Hank before his divorce. But they'd been cheating from that moment in the office when her eyes had locked with Hank's and she knew they were going to be together at some point. It was as palpable as anything she'd ever felt.

Alex leaned against her kitchen island, his eyes full of curiosity as to why he'd been summoned.

"Did you get past them?" Kate asked, knowing he would understand she meant the paparazzi.

"Took the subway. No one ever thinks I'm going to take the subway."

That's how he got here so quickly.

"It's easier in New York than LA." He ran a hand through his hair, pushing it back so she could see the curiosity in his expression. "So what do you want? Why did you need to see me?"

Might as well get right to it. "Where is Caitlyn?"

He frowned. "Why are you looking for Caitlyn?" He wasn't answering her question.

"Have you heard from her?" Kate asked.

"I haven't heard from anyone. I've been on set. I'm surprised you managed to get through to me."

She didn't tell him that it was because of Jane Rocheford, but if he thought about it a little, he might be able to figure that out. He wasn't exactly known for his intellect, however.

"When was the last time you saw her?"

He shifted from one foot to the other, his shoulders slouched even more as he stared at the floor. Kate was reminded how young he was. She supposed she shouldn't be surprised that Caitlyn had been so smitten with him. She was as young as he was. Younger. And Hank was forty years older.

"What's the third degree all about?" he asked, finally meeting her eyes.

"Have you seen her in the last few days?"

"Maybe. I don't see that it's really your business."

"Where did you see her? Just tell me, Alex. It's important."

"Okay, okay. I went up there. To that rehab place. They're divorced now anyway; I didn't think it would be a problem." She heard anger in his tone, even though he was trying to tamp it down.

Kate had agonized over her negotiations with him, the deals she made to get him the Bond role so he'd leave Hank's wife alone. Now *she* was married to Hank, so what did it matter anymore? It was time to stop dancing around what was going on.

"Caitlyn's missing. She left the rehab center, went to see Anna Klein, and then disappeared. She was hysterical and drunk. From the way it sounds, you might be one of the last people who saw her. If you have any idea where she's gone, you have to tell me."

For a moment, she saw concern and confusion in his face. "Missing?"

"Where is she?"

Alex shrugged. "I thought she was still at rehab."

Kate shook her head. "She's not. Jane says no one has seen her. She called me, upset that she couldn't find her."

Alex frowned. "Is this why the police are trying to reach me?"

The police? Had Jane told them Caitlyn was missing? "I don't know," she said truthfully. "You didn't talk to them?"

"No. I told you, I've been busy on set."

"She didn't tell you she was going to leave rehab?"

He bit the corner of his lip. Kate could tell he was debating what he should say. Finally: "When I saw her, she said she was going to go see *him*."

Kate knew who he was talking about. "Jane said she was going to go see Hank, too. Do you know why?"

"She was going to tell him about the book."

Her heart began to beat faster. "What book?" she asked, although she had no doubt he was talking about Nan Tudor's journal.

"She'd left a book at my place and wanted me to bring it to her. She said she might be able to use it against him. He wasn't giving her enough money. She said she might be able to help me out, too."

"We have to find her."

"What's going on, Kate?" He'd heard the urgency in her voice.

She took a deep breath. "That book could get her into trouble; it's better if she talks to me before she talks to Hank." Hank certainly wouldn't like the idea of his ex-wife blackmailing him.

"I'm not sure that book is the only thing that could get her into trouble," Alex said.

Kate frowned. "What do you mean?"

Alex gave her a pitying look. "There's something you should know, Kate." He hesitated a moment. "Caitlyn's pregnant."

14

Alex's voice was soft, so surely Kate had misheard. "She's what?"

"It isn't mine."

Kate gave a short snort. "Don't lie to me."

"I'm not lying. She told me about it when I brought her the book. We had a fight. I figured that's why I haven't heard from her. It got pretty ugly."

"What did you fight about?"

"She wouldn't tell me who the father was, but she said it wasn't me."

"Who else's would it be?"

"We hadn't been together, you know, like that, in a little while. I've been tied up with this movie for the last few months. I didn't want to screw it up, so I told her we had to put things on hold until I was done. I needed to focus. She was pissed about that. She said now that she and Hank were split up, we could do anything we wanted, and it was fucked up that I was too busy."

Kate was trying to wrap her head around this.

"I told her I'd marry her," Alex was saying. "But she said she didn't want to get married again. She was going to raise the baby on her own."

That didn't go along with Caitlyn's narrative. She wasn't exactly mother material.

"She said she was going to go away. That's what the money was for. The money she was going to get out of *him* in exchange for that book."

Kate finally found her voice. "Why did she tell you?"

Confusion crossed his face. "What do you mean?"

"If you aren't the father, why did Caitlyn tell you she's pregnant? She's going to go away anyway. You would never have known, right?"

"I never know why she does anything," he said bitterly, hesitating a second before adding, "It could be *his*. That might be why she wouldn't tell me."

Kate stepped back, away from him, as though his words were contagious. She knew who he meant. "That's impossible," she said. "Hank hasn't seen Caitlyn in months. He won't see her." But it hadn't been for lack of her trying. Alex's story about how Caitlyn was unhappy about Hank's refusal to give her more money was true. Hank had told Kate himself about Caitlyn's persistence. Caitlyn had signed the prenup, though, so she'd signed any rights away. She should've known Hank wouldn't give in. Still, she'd left voicemail after voicemail, messages at the office, at Hank's apartment building with the concierge, the doorman. She tried to get into the offices, only to be stopped by security.

"Are you so sure?" Alex asked.

Kate considered the question. Could Hank be the father of Caitlyn's baby? No. They hadn't been together in a long time, and despite Alex's insinuation, Hank had not seen Caitlyn. Kate had been on the front lines of the collapse of Hank and Caitlyn's marriage. Hank had divorced himself from Caitlyn long before the courts made it so. But despite herself, doubts began to creep into her head. She'd been there at the beginning, too, when Hank started his affair with Caitlyn, been head over heels infatuated with her. If Caitlyn had come to him, given him any idea that she wanted him back, wanted him in her bed, he might have given in. It wasn't as though he and Kate had had sex before their wedding.

Maybe she should've just had an affair with him. She had suggested that, telling him that they should get to know each other in that way first. But he insisted that it had to be marriage.

"I want to make an honest woman of you, Kate," he'd said when he slipped the diamond on her finger. "I want you to be my wife. Share my life, share everything. I don't want to go halfway. You deserve so much more."

The way he'd looked at her, his desire and *need* for her dizzyingly attractive. She had wanted it as much as he did when he put it that way. She hadn't needed much convincing.

Remembering, she pushed the doubts away. He'd been done with Caitlyn. He'd wanted *her*. "Hank can't possibly be the father of her baby," she told Alex.

He rolled his eyes at her. "How well do you really know your husband, Kate?" The way he asked made her wonder if he knew more than he was letting on. "Caitlyn's naïve," he added. "I told her he'd destroy her. He was sucking the life out of her. He threatened her, said he'd fix it so she wouldn't be able to work anymore. But when he called her, she went. She can never say no to him. She's not *allowed* to. He owns her, and she has to do what he wants. He holds all the cards."

Before Kate realized what was happening, Alex stepped closer, trapping her against the kitchen island, pinning her arms at her sides.

"This was *after* you thought you'd handled the situation with me and her," he hissed. "*After* you thought Caitlyn was out of the picture and he started romancing you. Priming you to be the next one. You were never in control. You know that, right? He's going to do to you what he's done to her. And then he'll move on like you never even existed."

Kate tried to twist away, but he was too strong. Her heart was pounding, and she struggled to take a breath.

"How does it feel, Kate?" he asked, his breath hot against her cheek. "How do you think *she* feels?"

She thought about the gun in the drawer of her bedside nightstand, but he had her trapped.

Yet as suddenly as he'd moved in, Alex let her go and took a few steps backward, his hands up in surrender, the anger dissipating. Kate rubbed her arms where he'd held them, not taking her eyes off him.

Finally, he dropped his hands and gave her a sad smile.

"They both betrayed us, Kate. There are consequences for that."

15

CATHERINE

Catherine poured herself a cup of tea as she stood at the island in the middle of her kitchen. The shiny, dark gray granite showed every spot, every smudge. She focused on a fingerprint next to her mug. Was it hers? Was it Lourdes's? Was it Maril's? She remembered watching one of those crime shows on TV about how fingerprints were as individual as a person's DNA.

She missed Maril. Her daughter had gone to Anna's to keep tabs on what was going on with Hank—and to keep tabs on the children. The police and the media were crawling all over that property; the children needed a distraction. She didn't hold anything against those little ones, it wasn't the girl's fault who her mother was. And the boy—he would never know a real mother's touch.

Catherine carried her cup upstairs to her bedroom. It was midday, but she had the curtains drawn so the room was dark. She put the cup on her nightstand and crawled under the thick comforter, protecting her against the air conditioning. Her laptop rested on the pillow next to her, and she slid it over onto her lap, opening it to reveal photographs of Kate Parker. There weren't as many of this one as there had been of Caitlyn Howard;

Kate hadn't been quite so publicly visible. Most of the pictures showed her with Hank or, rather, following Hank as part of his entourage.

This wasn't healthy, searching for images of her husband's newest wife. But it was better than giving in to her addiction down the hall. She had to maintain some self-control where that was concerned; otherwise, she might sabotage everything she'd planned so carefully.

The landline phone rang, startling her. She tensed slightly when she saw the number on the screen.

"Yes?" she asked when she answered.

"There might be a problem."

This wasn't what she'd expected to hear. "What?"

"It's gone."

Catherine's grip tightened on the handset. "Are you sure?"

"They searched her room at the rehab center, but they didn't find it."

Catherine should have known something would go wrong if she didn't handle it herself. But she couldn't fathom the idea of stepping outside. It had been too long. It would be like Dorothy in Munchkinland after spending her whole life in Kansas. The colors would be too bright.

It had seemed to creep up over time, this desire to stay at home, the panic that struck her when she merely thought about leaving the house. It was as though the moment she stepped over the threshold she would die. Catherine knew what agoraphobia was. She'd self-diagnosed with help from the internet. Maril didn't like it, tried to lure her out with promises of spa days, leisurely lunches, and cocktails, and even resorted to tough love, threatening psychiatrists and antidepressants. She didn't tell Maril she already had a stash of antianxiety medications, a doctor who came to the house regularly. Anyone would do anything for a price.

"I thought you took care of this." Catherine tried not to raise her voice, but she wasn't successful.

"I'll find it."

That was more like it. "Are you sure?"

"Leave it to me. Have I ever let you down?"

Catherine replaced the handset in its cradle and settled back on her pillows, sinking into the folds.

She recalled how Caitlyn Howard had shown up here without any notice, dressed like a teenager, in a pair of torn jeans, a loose white T-shirt, her hair blazing red, piercings lining her earlobes.

"I need to talk to you," she'd said.

Lourdes had gone for the day, and Catherine had opened the door against her better judgment. But she'd been curious why the girl was here; none of the other wives had ever visited her, and this one, in particular, was so unexpected. Maril had told Catherine about her new "stepmother," who was fifteen years younger than she was and an actress. Catherine had found a movie that the girl had been in, not a starring role but a surprisingly good supporting one as the best friend. She'd been even younger then, maybe only thirteen or fourteen, and being Hank Tudor's wife had certainly been the farthest thing from her mind.

Catherine had studied her for a moment. While the camera was very kind to her, the girl was possibly even more beautiful than she appeared on-screen. She had a natural grace about her, and Catherine could understand why Hank had been taken in by her. No man would have been able to resist her if she'd set her sights on him. For the first time, Catherine found herself forgiving Hank for this indiscretion. He was a man, after all, and couldn't help himself. And surprisingly, she also found herself feeling sorry for him. This girl—woman—in front of her had broken his heart.

Catherine led her through the great room and back to the kitchen. She may have let the girl in her house, but she wasn't going to let her think that she was important enough for any other room. Caitlyn didn't seem to care—or notice. Catherine wondered if it was her upbringing—or perhaps she hadn't expected more, considering. What did Hank's wives say about her? Did they get together over a glass of wine and gossip and laugh about the woman who was still waiting for him to come back?

Caitlyn slid onto one of the chairs at the island, making herself comfortable. Catherine admired that, her moxie. And even though she didn't approve, she didn't admonish her, just stood in front of her, hands on her hips, and asked, "What do you want?"

"I need information," she said.

"Information about what?"

"Hank."

"He's not your husband anymore."

"The divorce isn't final."

"But you've been carrying on with that"—she didn't quite know how to put it—"*actor*."

Caitlyn rolled her eyes at her. "Hank carried on with Nan when he was with you. He carried on with Jeanne when he was with Nan. It's only a matter of time before he ends up marrying his assistant, Kate Parker. I'm not blind, I can see what's going on between them. Men like him have patterns."

Her words stung, but they weren't false.

"What do you want from me?"

"He's going to take everything, my life, my career, and leave me with nothing. He can't get away with that. He can't get away with what he did to you, and while he gave Anna that house, he treats her like a fucking babysitter for those kids he doesn't have time for." Her tone grew sharper with each sentence, her forehead furrowing into a frown.

Catherine hadn't had a lot of sympathy for her, but there was something oddly endearing about her anger, an anger she was not unfamiliar with. She loved Hank, but she hated him, too, for what he'd done. She would take him back in a minute, but making him suffer was never far from her mind.

Still, she resisted. "You will be better off forgetting about him. I don't believe I can help you."

"You mean you *won't* help." Caitlyn's tone was accusatory, but Catherine didn't hold that against her.

"I don't know what you think I can do for you."

"Don't you want to get even with him? Don't you want to make him as miserable as he's made you? Don't you want him to come crawling back to you, his tail between his legs, realizing that no one else could ever want him as much as you do?"

Everything she said was true. Catherine had thought all of those things these past years; she'd thought them—and done things that she'd believed would bring him back to her. But so far, she was still living alone in this big house. Waiting.

She admitted curiosity about what Caitlyn Howard might be suggesting. "What do you want?"

"Nan Tudor."

Catherine's heart skipped a beat, hoping that her expression didn't change. "What about her?"

"She disappeared."

Catherine had to tread lightly. Caitlyn didn't know anything. She could never know anything. "That's what they say."

Caitlyn sat up straighter. "You don't think so?"

Catherine gave a short chuckle. "She was there one day and then she wasn't. Yes. I suppose you can say that she disappeared."

"Do you think that Hank had anything to do with it?" Caitlyn leaned toward her, studying Catherine's face.

Catherine tried not to react too strongly. "Of course he had something to do with it. He was seeing Jeanne. Nan knew about it, and she knew she was out. That he would divorce her. So she left."

"But why would she leave Lizzie behind?"

That was when Catherine decided to give her the diary. It was a spontaneous decision, but a gamble worth taking. She held up her hand. "I've got something that might interest you," she said. "I'll be right back." She made her way upstairs and unlocked the door. She passed the computer screens without a glance and went into the closet. The small built-in safe had a keypad lock. She punched in the code, and the door popped open. Reaching inside, she grabbed the book, caressing its cover before shutting the safe's door and heading back down to the kitchen.

Caitlyn was still sitting at the island, her fingers tracing an imaginary circle on its surface.

Catherine handed the book to her.

"What's this?" she asked.

"Read it. You might find what you're looking for." Hank didn't know it existed, that secrets were laid out in black and white. She'd wondered what she should do with it, how she could use it.

"Where did you get this?" Caitlyn, her eyes wide, had asked after flipping through the pages.

Catherine waved her off. "Just take it."

She might have suggested that Caitlyn use this against Hank. Blackmail him with it. Or maybe she didn't. Maybe it was all the girl's idea.

Either way, no one would be able to tie it to her.

May 15

He's filed for a divorce. Officially. It's about time. One thing I've learned being away is that absence really does make the heart grow fonder. He's been sending me love letters, through Tom, and he's gotten more and more lovesick as the months have gone on. He's promising me everything: marriage, a family, a share in his business. He says he doesn't want a prenup, that it would "sully" our deep love for each other. Tom disagrees, but Hank is being adamant. It's all a bit heady for me to take in. I have never felt so completely loved. He is willing to sacrifice everything for me. Me.

I'll only admit it here, but it's incredibly empowering. He'll do anything I ask him to, but I'm careful not to push it. I have to balance this new leverage I've got. I want him as much as he wants me, but I also want the life he's offering. I want the power that being Mrs. Hank Tudor offers. I want what Catherine has—or, rather, had.

Maybe I should feel bad about her. He loved her once. I know that. And she's been instrumental in building the business. She was kind to me when I started working for her, and treated me with a lot of respect. It was only later, when she suspected about me and Hank, that she changed her attitude toward me. Still, she only became distant and reassigned me to duties that I wasn't sorry to give up when I quit. She was never cruel. I wondered sometimes why she didn't fire me, but maybe she was in a little bit of denial. Or maybe she wanted to keep me close, keep an eye on things. Who knows.

But she's not going to win this. He's moved out of their house, bought a new penthouse in the city. He wants ME.

This is why I have to go back. It's time to stake my claim and begin my new life.

16

ANNA

Anna kept her eye on the clock. Kate should be back by now. Joan seemed oblivious to her worry as they went about their day, cleaning the empty rooms, doing laundry. Maril was helpful by keeping the children busy. After the beach, they'd gone out for ice cream, the quiet settling over the house like a warm blanket. When their work was finally done, and with no guests to be concerned about, Joan headed to the pool to do some laps and Anna took her tea out onto the porch and settled into a wicker chair.

She glanced over at the marsh next door, and she could see the yellow crime scene tape flapping in the breeze. How could something so brutal happen so close to her home? Her inn had become a refuge—for her guests, but also for her and Joan. And the children. They felt safe here. Ted had never known anywhere else. Did Lizzie remember the brief time with Jeanne before Anna came into her life? She'd been so little when Nan left, only three, but every once in a while, she'd claim to remember her— "She smelled like flowers, Anna, really. Like the lawn right after it's cut. She was so beautiful. She had long hair, like me, but it was brown, not red." It was possible the memories were real.

Anna had skimmed the journal before she tucked it away, enough to see how much Nan had loved her daughter. By all rights, it belonged to Lizzie, but Anna's instincts told her to keep it hidden for now. Lizzie was getting older, but Anna didn't think she was old enough yet for the revelations within its pages.

She didn't like having the diary, worried that Lizzie would discover it, but Kate said it was easier to keep it here until they could figure out what to do with it. Figure out how it made its way from Nan, who'd been missing for eight years, to Caitlyn. Had Hank known about it? That Nan had chronicled their courtship, their marriage? There was so little that he *didn't* know. None of them had secrets they'd been able to keep from him—or Cromwell.

Anna took another sip of her tea. It had grown cold, but she didn't mind. She wondered about Kate, the sixth wife, if she'd survive. Kate seemed as though she could handle him, but sometimes she was a little too cocky, a little too independent. Hank liked a woman whom he could believe was subservient, even if she wasn't.

The sound of tires on the cobblestones made her sit up straighter. A car door slammed, and she stood and walked around to the front of the porch. Trooper Pawlik—that older officer who'd spoken privately with Hank—was already coming up the steps. Will Stafford's second man, Murphy, was on his heels.

Anna nodded at him. "It's fine, Murph," she said, although it wasn't. Not really. Hank wouldn't like it if she talked to the trooper without either him or Tom present.

Pawlik acted as though the exchange hadn't taken place. "If you don't mind, Ms. Klein, I've got some follow-up questions." He didn't wait for a response, but met her at the door. She wasn't quite sure what to say; it was clear he was going to ask his questions anyway, so she led him into the house.

"May I offer you some coffee?" Anna asked, bringing him into the kitchen. It seemed a little less formal here, rather than in the great room.

"If it's made," Pawlik said.

Anna took a mug out of the cabinet. "How do you take it?"

"Black."

She poured a cup as Pawlik hung back, his eyes taking in everything about the room: the white wood cabinets, gray granite countertops, stainless steel state-of-the-art appliances. She'd never seen a man so interested in kitchen architecture.

"What can I do for you?" she asked, setting the mug in front of him on the island, where he'd perched on a stool. He'd taken off his hat, and she could see he was balding. He had a ruggedness about him that she liked, reminded her of the boys back home.

"Thank you." He took a sip of the coffee. "I'd like to talk to Mrs. Tudor as well."

"She's not here. She went to a workout class. I'm not sure when she'll be back."

He gave her a curious look as though he knew she was lying, as though he knew Kate had gone into the city rather than around the corner. But he didn't call her on it, merely said, "I was wondering if you've seen anyone else around the house next door."

She shook her head. "Not since yesterday. It's been quiet since your people left."

"No one showed up?"

She wasn't sure what he was getting at. "No. I mean, the media's been lurking, a little more than usual, of course."

"What about Mary Brandon? Have you seen her again?"

"Haven't you talked to her by now?"

Pawlik gave a low chuckle. "It seems that anyone associated with your ex-husband doesn't want to talk to the police. I've only spoken to her voicemail so far." He hesitated, but when she didn't say anything, he asked, "Did you talk to her when she was here?"

"No."

"But she *was* here?"

"Not *here*. But her car was over at the house."

Pawlik frowned. "You saw her car? Did you see *her*?"

"No."

"I was under the impression you did."

"I didn't mean to give you that impression, because I only saw her car."

Pawlik pulled a little notebook from his back pants pocket and flipped through it, then looked up at her. "You said you saw her."

"No."

He stared at her, as though he couldn't believe he'd gotten it wrong. "How do you know it was her car? Could it have been someone else's?"

"It was a Rolls. I just assumed," she said, realizing now that Mary may not have been the person over at the house.

"How long was the car there?"

"I don't know, maybe about an hour or so. I didn't see it leave. It was gone the next time I looked."

"When, exactly, was this?"

"Three days ago."

"Was that before or after Caitlyn Howard was here?"

The question took her aback.

"Ms. Klein?"

"Yes, I'm sorry. Why do you want to know about Caitlyn?" Tom's words still resonated: *She was never here.*

Pawlik studied her face, and she had the distinct feeling he knew exactly what she was thinking.

"I received a phone call from a Jane Rocheford. She said Miss Howard is missing and she's concerned about her. Ms. Rocheford seems to think that your ex-husband is disposing of his wives."

Anna chuckled. "That's ridiculous."

"You're aware this is not the first time a woman's body has been found on your ex-husband's property."

"What does that have to do with this?"

Ignoring her question, he said, "I have a report that Miss Howard was here recently. I have to follow up. I hope you understand." He said it kindly, but the steely stare told her that he wasn't going away without getting some answers out of her.

It wasn't a surprise that word got back to him about Caitlyn's visit. Pawlik had spoken to all of her guests who'd been at the inn the last several days before the body was found—and he'd spoken to Will Stafford and Murphy. It wasn't as though Caitlyn had been discreet, especially with the way she was carrying on.

"Caitlyn was here four days ago," Anna admitted. She hoped she was doing the right thing. She'd be careful about what she said.

"The day before you saw the car over at your ex-husband's house?"

"Yes, I suppose so."

"Why was she here?"

That was a good question. "I'm not sure."

"You hadn't invited her?"

"No."

"How well do you know her?"

"Not very well."

"But she came here. If you don't know her well, why would she come see you?"

"She didn't say why she was here. She had been drinking." It wasn't exactly news that Caitlyn Howard had a substance-abuse problem, considering how her stints at rehab were documented in the press.

"Do you think she was reacting to her husband marrying another woman?"

It was a question Anna hadn't expected. Caitlyn should never have married Hank in the first place. While she'd seemed so innocent at first—wide-eyed as Hank showered her with his attention, gifts—she wasn't all that innocent. By marrying Kate, though, Hank had truly set her free to be with Alex.

"If you weren't very close, why would she feel she could show up drunk on your doorstep?" Pawlik asked when she didn't answer.

"I really don't know." Anna wondered what scab he was picking at, because he clearly had an agenda.

"What do you know about her relationship with Alex Culpepper?"

She forced a smile. "What everyone knows. It's all over the tabloids."

"She never confided in you about him?"

"No."

"He wasn't with her that night?"

Anna frowned. "No." What was he getting at?

Pawlik began scribbling in the small pad with a stubby pencil he produced from his breast pocket. "How long did she stay?"

Anna shrugged, trying to force herself to relax mentally, even though she was wound tighter than a rubber band. "Not even half an hour. She was upset."

"Did she say what she was upset about?"

"No."

"You didn't find that unusual?"

"Not particularly."

He studied her face, trying to sense whether she was telling him the truth. She tried not to shift in her seat.

"She showed up alone?" He was smooth, moving from one thing to the other seamlessly.

"Yes."

"When she left, was she alone?"

"Yes."

"She had a car?"

"Yes."

"But you said she was drunk. If she were driving herself, why didn't you stop her?"

Why didn't she? Anna thought about it for a few seconds. "She left the house while I was making coffee. I hoped to sober her up. I didn't know she'd gone."

"You're sure there was no one else with her?"

"I don't know. I didn't see anyone." He was rattling her too much. She couldn't think straight. She struggled to regain her composure. Will didn't say anything about someone being with Caitlyn. "Will Stafford, who heads up my security team, saw her come in, but he didn't see her leave. One of the other security guards did. I can arrange to have you talk to him."

Pawlik nodded, making a note. "Yes, I'll need to do that."

"Certainly."

"She didn't say where she was going when she left?"

Anna forced herself to keep her tone measured. "No."

"What kind of car does Alex Culpepper drive?"

"I—uh, I don't know."

"You said you saw a Rolls-Royce next door the next day, and you assumed it was Mary Brandon. Do you know anyone else who drives a Rolls?"

Anna laughed. "You're kidding, right? We're in Greenwich. If it's not a Rolls, it's a Tesla."

Pawlik nodded. "Fair enough." He shoved the pencil and notepad into his breast pocket. "Is your wife here? Perhaps she saw something that you didn't."

"She won't be able to help with your questions about Caitlyn."

"Why not?"

"She wasn't here that night."

He cocked an eyebrow. "Where was she?"

"She went to the movies. One of us has to be here when we have guests, and she hadn't had a night out in a while. I urged her to go." Too much information, but she wanted to head off his questions.

"What time did she get home?"

"Midnight." Joan's voice came from behind her, and Anna turned to see her walking toward them. Her hair was still wet from her swim. "I'm afraid I don't have any proof of the time I came home. Is that a problem? I might be able to find the ticket stub. Would you want that?"

Anna resisted the urge to smile. Joan had been a tough businesswoman, and she knew how to stand up for herself.

Pawlik stood. "No, that's fine."

"And I didn't notice any car next door," Joan volunteered. "Anna mentioned it to me, asked if I'd seen Mrs. Brandon, but by then, the car was gone."

Pawlik was nodding. "Thank you. If you remember anything at all, though, please let us know." This was directed at both Anna and Joan.

"Certainly," Anna said.

"I appreciate your time. I'd like to speak to Will Stafford."

"He's not here right now. He's gone out on an errand." Anna wondered again how long it would be before Will brought Kate back from the city.

Pawlik frowned, as though he suspected she was hiding something, but then nodded. "What about the security guard who saw Miss Howard leave?"

Anna took her phone off the table and punched in a number. "Can you come up to the house and talk to Trooper Pawlik?" After a second, she put the phone down. "He's the same guard who let you through the gate. His name is Murphy. He'll meet you out front."

Pawlik tipped his hat and made his way back out through the great room, disappearing from sight. Anna didn't bother to follow him. He knew his way around. She stood, her hand on the countertop, trying to make sense of the conversation.

"You know what he was doing, don't you?" Joan asked, interrupting her thoughts. "That body. They think it's Caitlyn Howard. And that whoever showed up here the next day in that Rolls dumped her body in the marsh."

17

The ride home with Will was quiet. He was distracted. Something had happened between the time he dropped her off and picked her up, but Kate didn't know him well and didn't feel she could ask him what was wrong. Seeing him reminded her of what he had said earlier about the security cameras not working at Hank's house. Hank paid his team well, and it was hard to believe the malfunction was a coincidence.

Her phone pinged with a text from Anna, asking if she was okay. It seemed like an odd question, as though she shouldn't be. As though Anna was privy to what Alex had said and done.

Everything's good, she texted back. *Will fill you in when I get back.*

The thumbs-up emoji popped up on the screen. Kate stuck the phone back in her gym bag. Did she really want to fill Anna in? Would she actually admit that her husband might have slept with Caitlyn and the girl was having his baby? Maybe she should have stayed in her apartment and worked this all out in her head before going back to the inn.

Through the window, she watched the landscape slip past as she slumped down in her seat, her eyes closing.

"Wake up." Will's voice came through the sleepy fog in her head.

They were almost to the inn. Kate pulled the ball cap down over her eyes as the paparazzi came into view. When the car pulled into the garage, she and Will got out at the same time, the sound of the slamming doors echoing against the walls.

"Thank you," she said, but Will had already disappeared through a door that probably led to his security hub.

Anna was making a salad for supper when Kate came into the kitchen. "How did it go?" Anna asked.

Kate looked around, but she didn't see Joan. "It was, well, interesting." She still couldn't decide if she should tell Anna. Could she trust her?

"That police trooper was by," Anna was saying. "He was asking a lot of questions about Caitlyn's visit here. He asked if Alex Culpepper was with her that night."

"Alex told me he hasn't seen her since he dropped the diary off at the rehab center," Kate said.

"You didn't get the sense he might be lying?"

Kate frowned. She hadn't even considered it. Should she have?

"I was worried about you with him," Anna said.

Kate brushed off the concern. "I was fine. He was fine," she said, more brusquely than she intended.

But Anna wasn't paying attention. She was looking out the kitchen window, shaking her head. "Those kids," she muttered. "Where's Maril?"

Before Kate could ask what was going on, Anna turned to her. "Lizzie and Ted are heading to the beach. I don't know where Maril is, and I have to finish getting dinner ready. Can you go out there with them?"

It may have been worded like a request, but Kate heard it as more of an order. "Sure," she said, dropping her gym bag on the floor next to the door as she went outside.

She caught up with Lizzie and Ted as they crouched on the beach, using their plastic pails and shovels to start construction on a sandcastle. Kate kept her distance, watching them silently communicate with each other. She'd been fairly happy as an only child, but sometimes she wished she had that sibling support and connection, especially when her parents fell ill. It had been hard to handle alone.

She took off her sneakers and socks and dug her toes into the rough sand. Should she go over and help with the sandcastle? Watching Lizzie and Ted, she didn't feel any kind of maternal rush. Maybe Anna had hoped, though, and that was the reason she'd sent Kate out here. It wasn't fair to ask Anna to continue to be responsible for them now that Hank had a new wife.

Did Hank expect her to get pregnant? She'd never even babysat when she was younger; her biological clock had not begun to tick. They hadn't had that discussion; she assumed that because he had three children already, he didn't want any more.

If Caitlyn's baby really was Hank's, what would his reaction be? Would he embrace being a father again? How would that affect his relationship with Kate? She didn't think he'd leave her to go back to Caitlyn, but the baby could change everything—and in ways Kate couldn't even fathom.

"Lizzie!"

Ted's screech pulled Kate out of her thoughts. Lizzie was standing over Ted with a bucket of water, threatening to douse him.

"Lizzie!" Kate heard her own voice, much like her mother's, and the girl froze as she stared back at her, the bucket teetering. But as Kate began to head toward them, she heard a voice behind her.

"You the new one?"

Kate pivoted around to see an older woman walking toward her. She wore an oversized, button-down white shirt over a pair of baggy linen cropped pants. The wide brim of a straw hat obscured her face, but she tilted her head a little so Kate could see the large dark sunglasses, the bright red lipstick.

"You the new one?" she asked again.

What was this woman doing here? She'd thought that the only access to this beach was through Anna's property.

"You're not stupid like the last one, are you?" The woman's tone was low, serious, as she came around and stood next to her. "He doesn't like stupid women."

"I'm sorry, but I don't know what you're talking about," Kate said, although she was almost certain that she did. This woman knew Hank, knew about his wives. Not that this wasn't a small community and everyone probably knew everyone, but it was disconcerting all the same.

The woman gave a short snort. "You're the new one. I saw your picture in the paper." The woman stepped closer, tipping her head back and peering at her through the glasses that reminded Kate of an insect's eyes. "You're not as young, but you're pretty enough. Not like the second one, though. There was something about her. Too bad about her."

What did she know about Nan? The question was at the tip of Kate's tongue. She wanted to ask, but she didn't know this woman and couldn't trust her. She forced a stiff smile and said, "Nice talking to you." She began to turn when she felt the woman's fingers around her wrist.

"Be careful." The woman's grip tightened.

"Be careful of what?" she couldn't help but ask.

Even though she couldn't see her eyes, Kate could sense the woman's gaze on her face. Flustered, she wanted to look away but forced herself not to. After a few seconds, the woman spoke. "She thought she had it all under control, but she was wrong. He got angry when he realized what she was up to. She disappeared not long after."

Questions began to swirl around in Kate's head: Who was she talking about? Caitlyn? Caitlyn, who told Culpepper she was going to blackmail Hank over the diary? That would have made Hank angry. It would've made him furious. But how could this woman have known about that? It was impossible. Wasn't it? Caitlyn had gotten her hands on that diary somehow. Someone other than Caitlyn and Alex knew about it.

Before Kate could sort out her thoughts, the woman let go and folded her arms across her chest. "He covered it up. Money will do that, and there's plenty of that to go around." Her cheeks reddened slightly, and she bit the corner of her lip. "That'll be the case this time, too, mark my words."

Kate froze. Was she making a reference to Martha's Vineyard?

"You don't know, do you?" the woman asked.

"Know what?" Did she really want to know anything? It was always better not knowing.

The woman looked over toward the children at the water's edge. Ted was back to building the sandcastle as Lizzie unabashedly stared at them. "I can see their mothers in them." She turned back to Kate. "Are you going to have children?"

The question made Kate bristle. This woman was a stranger, and she had no right to ask such a personal question. She shouldn't have engaged with her. It was like the homeless people on the streets in the city. Don't make eye contact, walk swiftly past. She stood up a little straighter.

"I thought this was a private beach," she said coldly.

The woman slipped off her sunglasses, and her green eyes held Kate's. "Watch out for yourself." She spun around and started to walk away, leaving a trail of footprints in the sand. Kate stared after her. But suddenly, the woman turned and said, "If you want answers, you should ask Catherine." She hesitated a moment, then added, "If you talk to her, tell her Margaret Pole sent you."

Kate watched the woman square her shoulders and march across the beach, stopping every now and then to pick up a stone and put it in her pocket. Crazy woman. She couldn't help but wonder, though, about what the woman had said. Talk to Catherine? Hank's first wife? Why would she do that? What, exactly, did Catherine know?

And who *was* Margaret Pole?

18

ANNA

Anna hadn't lied to Kate. Not exactly. When Kate asked Anna if she knew Margaret Pole, she merely said, "I've seen her around." Before Kate could press for more, Anna added, "Let me tell Will, and he can make sure she doesn't bother you again."

Kate frowned. "It's not so much that she *bothered* me, but she insinuated that she knew something, though, about Hank, maybe Caitlyn. Maybe Nan."

Anna gave a short chuckle. "Everyone around here knows about Hank and his wives, Kate. The gossip is something I had to get used to, because it's not going away."

"She told me to talk to Catherine."

"About what?"

Kate shrugged. "I have no idea."

Anna wasn't sure how long she could put Kate off, but if she admitted to knowing Maggie, she'd be expected to explain how, and she couldn't tell her. She hadn't even told Joan about her. It wasn't as though she saw Maggie all the time; just the opposite. She'd only seen her a handful of times since they'd met, and it was always at a distance. That's what they'd agreed upon.

She shouldn't have been surprised that Maggie approached Kate, especially while she was with the children on the beach. Maggie would naturally be curious about Kate, about her marriage and possible new role as mother to Hank's children.

Anna had met Maggie right before she'd opened her inn. The renovations were finished; the first guests were due to arrive the next day.

Anna remembered the anxiety that had settled under her skin. Hank was encouraging, even though she knew she was in over her head. She didn't have a head for finances—that was where Joan came in, not long after—but Hank told her finances could be managed. It was her job to create an environment that was warm and welcoming, a place that people would want to return to.

"What about a basket of slippers?"

The voice had startled her as she opened the front door, not expecting to see anyone there. The woman was hovering on the front porch, her hands on her hips, surveying the entryway.

"What do you mean?" Anna asked.

"A basket of slippers. For the guests when they arrive. It will feel like home. That's what you want, isn't it?"

Anna eyed the woman carefully. She wore a pair of loose linen slacks and a white button-down cotton cardigan. Her hair was a mass of white curls pinned on the top of her head with chopsticks. Her eyes were a bright green, so green Anna wondered if she wore colored contact lenses, and her smile was kind.

"The inn's not open yet," she tried. Where was security? No one should be able to get past them and to the door. She peered around the woman, but she couldn't see anyone else.

"I know you're not open. But you really should have a basket of slippers."

The woman's comment distracted her. It was a good idea. This was why she'd been so uncertain about this. She didn't have that instinct, yet this stranger did.

"You can get a nice basket in the center of town. And there's that place that sells slippers."

Anna knew of the store. She nodded slowly. "Do you live nearby?"

The woman shrugged. "Close enough." She slid past Anna into the house, touching surfaces, eyeing the paintings on the wall, the books on the shelves.

Anna followed her, uncertain what the woman was looking for. "Can I help you?" she asked.

The woman whirled around and faced her. "You're his ex-wife." It'd been said matter-of-factly.

Anna had wondered when it would happen. When someone like this woman would intrude into her world, asking about Hank, the curiosity unavoidable.

"Yes," she said. "Do you want to book a night at the inn? We open tomorrow." She wasn't going to humor this woman. "Who exactly are you?"

The woman grinned and held out her hand. "I'm Margaret—Maggie—Pole."

Anna hesitated, then took her hand. It was warm and thin, but strong. "Anna Klein."

But the woman had already pulled her hand away, nodding. "Yes, I know, dear."

Of course she did.

"Are the children here?"

This was getting out of line. "I have to ask you to leave," Anna said firmly, but the woman, Margaret Pole—Maggie—was moving into the kitchen. Anna followed, her eyes settling on the phone that sat on the island in front of Maggie. She had no way of calling for help if she needed it. Would she need it? Maggie was smaller than she was; she wasn't carrying a bag that could conceal a weapon. The knife block was in the corner next to the fridge; maybe Maggie wouldn't see it.

The woman suddenly twirled around and faced Anna. "You don't have to worry about *me*, dear. I'm the least of your worries." She cocked her head and studied the younger woman's face. "You signed the nondisclosure agreement, didn't you?"

She hadn't had a choice.

"It was a rhetorical question," Maggie said, assessing the kitchen, moving toward the back door that led to the patio.

Anna felt helpless. This woman knew who she was, but Anna didn't have a clue who *she* was.

As though reading her mind, Maggie paused at the door and turned to face Anna. "I have a vested interest in you, my dear. Hank still seems to like you. Of course, that could change at a moment's notice. It all depends on what he hears about you, if he hears something that he doesn't like, if he hears that you are going against his wishes." It was a veiled threat; there was no denying it. After a moment, Maggie said, "All I ask is that I can see her. She doesn't have to know anything, but I need to know she's safe and happy."

Anna frowned. She didn't understand. "Who's safe and happy?"

"Why, Lizzie, of course," Maggie said, opening the door and stepping outside. "As long as I know she's well cared for, you have nothing to worry about. You can open your inn and accept Hank's generosity. You'll probably have a lot of success." She smiled at Anna's confused expression. "Hank is going to marry that girl. That teenager. He has no intention of turning her into a mother, nor does he want to. You, on the other hand, are the responsible one. Those children will stay with you. And I will be close by."

"What is your interest in Lizzie?" Anna asked after a moment. Maggie Pole might look like an innocent older woman, but there was a hardness behind her eyes. She knew something. "Are you in touch with Nan?"

"I made a promise," Maggie said. "You are going to help me keep it."

"Do you know where Nan is?" Anna pressed.

Maggie pursed her lips, studying Anna's face as though trying to decide what to say. Finally, she spoke.

"Nan is dead."

January 10

My office windows overlook Battery Park and the harbor. He came through, as promised. Catherine is gone; this was her office. That mousy little thing, Jeanne, is sitting at my old desk outside. She was here when I started. It doesn't matter whether she reports anything back to Catherine now and she does a decent job. I like pretty things, though, and Jeanne is hardly pretty. She doesn't do anything to make herself up. Every woman can make herself attractive if she tries. Makeup would go a long way with this one. A little color in her cheeks, a little mascara, some lipstick, she might not be a knockout, but she'd brighten the place up. Some heels rather than the flats, a pencil skirt and a silk blouse rather than the flouncy dresses that look like a throwback to the '80s. I'm not sure I can legally ask her to get a makeover, so I'm keeping my mouth shut. Anyway, I can't afford to hire someone who's better looking, or Hank might be tempted to move on. I still won't let him fuck me the way he wants—the way I want him to. We are still only all fingers and hands and tongues, and we can make each other come with explosive orgasms, but I have to hold back something until I know for sure that I can get the other things I want first; if I let him inside, he'll see me as any other woman. This way I can be in control.

Reading this, it makes me sound heartless. But I'm not. I'm scared. I'm scared that the moment I give in, he'll lose interest in me. I'm not usually so insecure about myself, but I see the way he is. How powerful, how in control, how desirable. Other women want to fuck him, and he cheated on Catherine—not only with me. He discarded those women. I won't be discarded. I won't allow that. This way, he wants me all the time. The hope each time that I'll give in makes his desire even stronger.

It's getting more difficult to say no, though, the longer it goes on. He's not hiding his relationship with me. I'm going to all the meetings, all the dinners. Openly. He's telling everyone I'm his fiancée, that we're going to be married. But I can't shake an ominous feeling. He's still married. To her.

She won't sign the papers, even though he keeps telling me that Cromwell's working on it. She says she loves him, even though she knows about me. What kind of woman puts up with all this for so long?

19

Lizzie and Ted ran around on the lawn after dinner, their screeches gleeful as they hit badminton birdies with Wiffle ball bats. Lizzie's red hair flew in the breeze, long and flowing, redder than her father's. She had Nan's eyes, smoky-gray eyes that bored into your soul as she looked at you. Lizzie was smart, too; she had Hank's number, and Anna had said that in the past months she'd been asking a lot of questions about her mother. Hank apparently always managed to ward off the questions by rushing to work, but Kate wondered how long he'd be able to evade the topic. Lizzie was notoriously relentless.

Kate settled into a wicker chair on the patio, pulling her legs up underneath her as she put her glass of wine on the small glass-topped table next to her. She had helped Anna and Joan clean up the dishes, and they were now seated in a matching pair of Adirondack chairs on the lawn, hands entwined, keeping an eye on the children. Maril was swimming laps in the pool.

It all seemed so normal, considering what had happened just days ago. A woman brutally murdered.

Kate had brought her tablet out with her, and when she pulled up the search engine, she typed Margaret Pole's name into it. She was glad to have something to do other than stew over whether Hank had slept with Caitlyn. No matter how she tried to tell herself that Hank had still been married to

Caitlyn when their romance had begun, that she had no right to assume a married man would actually follow through on spoken promises, she'd still expected that he was being faithful to *her*. Kate shrugged the thoughts away and scrolled through the internet results on her search.

She didn't see anything related to the woman she'd met on the beach, so she added "Greenwich" and searched the white pages. There it was. She tapped the screen and discovered a Margaret Pole's address and phone number—xxx'd out; she could pay and get the number. According to this, Margaret Pole was seventy-eight years old and had no political affiliation.

None of this was particularly helpful. She went back to the previous search and scrolled absently through the results. Nothing. She clicked on News, but she was beginning to think this was an exercise in futility. How could Margaret Pole know anything at all about Nan or Catherine Tudor except local gossip?

Kate absently typed "Tudor" in the search engine next to Margaret's name. She sat up straighter when she saw the image that popped up on the screen. A picture from the society pages of Hank's sister, Mary Tudor Brandon, and longtime family friend Margaret Pole at a gallery opening in New York City twenty years ago. Margaret was barely recognizable as the woman Kate met on the beach. This woman wore a red chiffon evening gown, her blonde highlighted hair styled in a short bob that accentuated her delicate aquiline nose and long white neck. She was posed with her hand on Mary Brandon's arm, looking at her with a bemused smile as though Mary had told her a funny story. Mary was particularly elegant in a silver dress that clung to her slender body. She looked exactly the same today as she did then. Her hair had the reddish-blonde hue that Hank used to have before he went gray. She must dye it, as she was almost sixty, but she still retained her youthful beauty and had few lines on her face. It might be the result of a very good facelift; it was natural enough that she merely looked extremely well rested. Kate wondered about her marriage to Charlie, Hank's best friend and serial philanderer. How had Mary put up with it all these years?

Kate didn't know Hank's sister all that well. They'd had very little interaction, and only when she was Hank's assistant. Mary sent an obligatory note after the wedding, but nothing more. Kate tried to brush it off. After six marriages, she couldn't blame her. She hoped that they could get to know each other, though, and perhaps Kate could win her over.

On impulse, Kate picked up her phone and scrolled through her contacts until she found Mary Brandon's information. Without thinking about it, she hit the CALL icon. And to her surprise, she heard, "Hello, Kate."

"I didn't think you'd pick up," Kate said, not in an accusatory way but matter-of-fact. She'd figured she'd have to leave a message.

"I apologize that I haven't been in touch since you and Hank..." Mary's voice trailed off.

Mary hadn't wanted Hank to marry his assistant. If Kate had been her, she probably wouldn't have wanted that, either. It caused too much scandal, and Hank Tudor was already at the epicenter of enough gossip.

"I know you don't approve," Kate said.

"It's not that—"

"Yes, it is," Kate interrupted. "Don't insult me by trying to tell me otherwise."

"Well, at least you're not like Caitlyn." Mary's tone dripped with contempt, and Kate suddenly felt a lot more compassion for her predecessor.

She wanted to turn this conversation to the reason she called. "You know about the body in Greenwich." It was a statement, not a question.

"Of course."

"Have you spoken to the police yet?" Kate asked.

"Why do you care?"

"Because the longer it goes on—"

"No one's identified the body. I understand it's difficult because of the water and bloating. But you should know that the longer it takes, the better for everyone."

"Better how?"

"From a PR standpoint, of course. I'm surprised you even have to ask."

Ignoring the snide comment, Kate pressed on. "The police have been wondering about you. Where you've been."

Silence. Finally, "Maybe it's good for them to wonder. For the time being." She hesitated. "Don't get involved in this, Kate. It's not healthy. Just be with my brother. Make him as happy as he can be until he divorces you."

She sounded so sure that there would be a divorce. Kate bit back what she really wanted to say: *I'm not naïve.* But maybe she was. She'd noticed Hank noticing Lindsey already. And then there was Caitlyn and her pregnancy . . . What had she gotten into?

Mary cleared her throat. "I have to get going. We never talked. Understand?"

"Wait. Who is Margaret Pole?"

"How do you know about Margaret?" Mary's tone was sharp, defensive.

"I met her. Random meeting," Kate explained.

"What did she say to you?"

"She seemed interested in meeting me. She seemed to know about Hank's, um, previous marriages. I mean, that she actually knew his other wives, not that she'd only read about them." She didn't want to admit she'd done a search on the internet.

Another silence, then, "She's an old acquaintance. I've heard she's got a touch of dementia."

Kate could tell she'd chosen her words carefully, not willing to give her more than that.

"She told me to watch out for myself."

Mary laughed. "Of course she did. Everyone knows that my brother chews up his wives and spits them out. It's no one's fault but your own that you decided to ignore that small impediment in his personality."

And then she hung up, leaving Kate feeling foolish. Was that all that Margaret Pole had meant? When she told her to talk to Catherine, it was probably a roundabout way of reminding her what could happen to Hank's wives. Even her allusion to Hank covering something up didn't have to be as sinister as Kate thought. Hank covered things up all the time. She was no stranger to covering things up, either, like with Caitlyn and damage control with Culpepper.

At least Mary Brandon was alive and well. The last three years had taught her how to keep secrets, so she tucked that one away.

"Hello, Kate."

Hank's voice startled her. She looked up to see him walking toward her, his expression curious, as though he were seeing her for the very first time.

"You didn't tell me you'd be back tonight," she said, folding her arms across her chest. She wasn't ready for him to be here. She hadn't yet thought through what she was going to say when she confronted him about Caitlyn's pregnancy.

She could see the tightness around his mouth. It must not have gone well with the shareholders. He came closer, reaching over and touching her cheek. He smelled of whiskey. "I came back early from the city. I met with the police." His gaze fell on the marsh, where the body was found.

"It was Caitlyn," he said then. "I identified her body."

20

Kate jumped up and wrapped her arms around him. He held her tight for a moment, then pulled away. She peered up at his face but couldn't read him. It was as though he'd slipped on a neutral mask.

"You're sure?" she asked.

He nodded. "It was the tattoo."

"Tattoo?"

"A rose. On the inside of her thigh."

Kate caught her breath. Caitlyn had been Hank's "rose without a thorn." He'd made that declaration to the press when he announced their engagement. Kate had coined the term for him. It was her job.

"Who could have—"

He put his hand up, stopping her from continuing. "It was a horrific act of violence. Despite my, um, feelings for her, she did not deserve such an end. I have already spoken with her parents and expressed our condolences." He reached over and stroked her arm. "I'm glad you've been here for Anna and the children, but I do wish you hadn't taken your little trip into the city today." His tone was stern, as though she were a disobedient child.

He knew. Despite Anna's assurances that Will Stafford was to be trusted, clearly he couldn't be.

"Why was Culpepper at your apartment?"

Kate was struck by the change of subject, as though Caitlyn's murder was a mere footnote to her meeting with Culpepper. He was looking at her expectantly. She thought about his question. How had he found out? While Alex might have managed to evade the paparazzi, Will must have followed her from Times Square without her noticing him. Was this why he'd been so distracted on the way home?

"I know Culpepper was there, so don't even try to say he wasn't. I want to know why," Hank prodded.

"I asked him where Caitlyn was." She might as well tell the truth. "Jane Rocheford said she was missing. He was the one most likely to know where she might be." The words caught in her throat as she realized Jane had been right to be concerned.

"Why did you meet at your apartment?" Hank's eyes narrowed as he studied her face.

She needed to turn this conversation around. "I thought it would be the best place to stay out of the eye of the media."

"There are eyes everywhere, Kate." His tone was ominous, and she made a mental note to keep that in mind. Her life was no longer hers. She was going to be watched, not only by the media but by her husband. She'd made that choice willingly; she was now beginning to realize what it meant.

"You could have asked him over the phone," he admonished. "You know the police want to talk to him?"

Alex had said that. That the police were trying to reach him. She remembered Anna saying Pawlik had asked if Alex was with Caitlyn the night she was here. Could Alex have been involved in Caitlyn's murder?

She shivered involuntarily. She'd met him alone in her apartment, and he had frightened her. She should be more careful. Even if Alex wasn't involved in Caitlyn's death, *someone* was, and he was still out there somewhere.

"I understand you're not used to this. The fact that you cannot come and go as you wish anymore. We have security for a reason. I know that will be difficult for a while, but you'll settle into it." He hesitated, then added,

"I don't want something to happen to you like what happened to Caitlyn. You're too precious to me."

Hank was so concerned about security, *her* security, but was he doing anything about the fact that the cameras at his house hadn't recorded anything? Cameras that might have helped the police find the person who murdered Caitlyn? But before she could ask about that, he continued.

"I'm sorry our marriage has to start out this way, but I promise it will be over soon and I can devote more time to you then."

"Devote more time" to her? Kate knew the way Hank worked. Tudor Enterprises always came first.

"We never got a proper honeymoon," he reminded her. "Maybe we should leave for Tuscany as soon as all this"—he waved his hand in the air—"is over."

"I've got everything I want right here."

He gave her a smile and reached for her, grazing her lips with his. "It's too crowded here." He stepped away. "Right now, though, I'm going to go upstairs and take a shower." He picked up his brown leather carryall from where he'd dropped it on the patio tiles and disappeared into the house.

He was right. The house *was* too crowded. Kate hadn't expected the sheer mental exhaustion of having children around. And then there was Maril. Sometimes Maril wanted to be best friends, but then there were the times when it was more than obvious that Maril wanted to drive a wedge between her and Hank. She shouldn't be surprised; Maril was so loyal to her mother that any idea of befriending her father's newest wife would be complicated.

The cool evening air caused goosebumps to rise on her skin—or more likely it was the thought of Caitlyn's body in the marsh. She felt a sudden rush of sadness. The young woman had been unpredictable and even unstable at times, but she had also embraced life to its fullest. Her laughter could light up a room, and Kate was hard-pressed to think of anyone—man or woman—who hadn't been captivated by her. For all the trouble Caitlyn had caused, she didn't deserve to die.

And what about her pregnancy? The police would know about that; there would be an autopsy. Did they tell Hank when he was there today? Did he know?

Kate glanced toward Anna and Joan, their hands still clasped together. There was no sign they'd noticed Hank's return, and she certainly didn't want to interrupt their moment of tranquility. They'd learn about Caitlyn soon enough.

Kate picked up her phone, tucked the tablet under her arm, and headed upstairs after her husband.

He was still in the shower. Kate peered into the mirror at her reflection. The stress of the past days showed in the bags under her eyes. The window was open, and the lace curtain fluttered with the breeze. Long Island Sound spread out beyond the house, a couple of sailboats moving across the water. The children's voices rose off the lawn, their chatter disappearing over the horizon.

It was almost as though nothing had changed, that Caitlyn wasn't dead, that someone hadn't murdered her.

Kate rounded the bed and tripped over something. Hank's brown leather carryall. She leaned over and grabbed it, putting it on the bed. She unzipped it and saw Hank's toiletry bag, a couple of pairs of boxers and socks, and two golf shirts.

She fingered the fabric of his shirt, taking out the clothes he'd already worn and dropping them in the wicker laundry basket next to the dresser. It was busywork, she knew, as she tried to sort everything out in her head. How was she going to ask him about Caitlyn's pregnancy?

Something was at the bottom of the case. She tried to close her fingers around it, but it was stuck in the seam. She lifted the bag and dug her fingernail into the crease. It came loose, and when she opened her hand, the light hit it and it glinted brightly.

It was a diamond ring.

Caitlyn's ring.

21

Kate studied the marquise diamond in a French-cut basket setting. It was elaborate and overstated. Kate's round diamond in a simple gold setting was all she'd wanted. But Caitlyn was all about making statements, and this ring had been front and center in a magazine article about the young actress's engagement to Hank. Kate herself had guided the press coverage along with Jane Rocheford, and she oversaw the photo shoot. There was no doubt in her mind what she was holding.

How did it end up in Hank's carryall?

The question tugged at her as she thought about how her husband had come home unexpectedly, acting so normally, as though he hadn't just identified the headless body of his ex-wife—his pregnant ex-wife—found on his property.

If she said nothing, then it was as though it never happened, she'd never found the ring and she could pretend that nothing was wrong. That was probably the smart move. She could put it back in the carryall and no one would be the wiser. Except for her.

Kate went out onto the balcony. The sun was low over the horizon, bright pink and orange streaks coloring the sky. She sunk down into one of the chairs, the ring still in her palm, biting into her skin.

"Kate?"

She hadn't heard the shower turn off, but she wasn't startled. It was as though she'd been expecting him. That he'd known what she'd found and that she needed to ask him about it.

Hank caressed her shoulder and leaned down to kiss her neck. He was wearing a plush white terry cloth bathrobe. His hair was wet, slicked back behind his ears.

Kate wriggled away. He gave her a curious look, frowning, and then sat across from her, the small table between them. Kate held her hand over the surface, opened it, and the ring dropped with a small *clink*.

She raised her eyes to meet his, which glanced so quickly at the ring that she almost missed it.

"Where did you find it?" he asked, as though the ring was merely something he'd misplaced.

"I was unpacking your bag. It was stuck in the seam." She stared him down, daring him to tell her about it, how he had gotten it.

"What do you want me to say?"

"How did it get there?"

"I must have left it there." His response was casual, as though she'd asked how the weather was.

"What I'm asking is, why is it in your possession?" She was aware her tone was formal. She should have pretended to merely be curious, not confrontational. But it was too late now.

He smiled, a long, lazy smile that didn't quite reach his eyes. "She gave it back to me."

"When?"

"When I told her I wanted a divorce. You wouldn't think that I'd let her keep it, would you?" A menacing tone crept into his voice, a warning that she shouldn't question too much. She'd heard it before, but she'd never been on the receiving end.

Caitlyn wouldn't have given him back that ring. This was the same girl who was going to blackmail him with his second wife's diary for leverage so he would give her more money. Why would she give up this incredibly expensive diamond ring? Caitlyn could have sold it for thousands of dollars. Tens of thousands.

His mouth twitched. She nodded, worried that she'd say the wrong thing, so she said nothing.

"Do you think that I did it? That I killed Caitlyn and then took her ring?" he asked.

"No." It was barely a whisper. She cleared her throat. "No, of course not," she said more loudly. "That's not what—"

"We can't begin a marriage with you suspecting me of anything," Hank said, his voice steady, calm. As though he hadn't accused her of just that: suspecting him of being involved with Caitlyn's murder.

She reached over, put her hand on his knee, and attempted a reassuring smile. "No, I don't think anything like that, of course," she said. "It was a surprise, finding her ring. It doesn't seem in her character to have given it back willingly."

"No. It's not."

Kate waited for him to continue, but he didn't.

"We shouldn't have secrets," she tried.

Hank stared at her, his eyes dark, the anger brewing behind them. "There are no secrets, Kate. You know better than to push. If you do, then I'm not responsible for what might happen."

The threat lay between them. She considered carefully what she would say next. "I'm sorry." She touched his hand. "I'm not, well, I'm still getting used to this. Being your wife, I mean."

She'd played this wrong at the start, but that was the right thing to say. He closed his hand over hers and lifted it to his lips. "I know you're having a tough transition," he said. "But I hope you know how much I love you and how much I want this marriage to work."

"I do," she said. Kate gently pulled her hand out from Hank's. She touched the ring that lay on the table between them, then raised her eyes to his. "What will you do with it?" she asked.

He picked it up and twirled it a little, then took her hand, slipping the ring on her finger. It was dazzling, belying the ominous chill that rushed through her.

She swallowed hard and pulled it off, letting it drop. "No," she said, her voice low, husky. "It's hers." Did he think they were interchangeable? That one would replace the other and not be aware of what had come before? What was he looking for in all these wives?

Kate wanted to feel special, and having that ring on her finger made her feel as temporary and replaceable as the others.

Hank was sitting back, an amused look on his face. "I shouldn't have done that," he said, but his expression told her he didn't mean it.

"What about the baby?" she asked. She couldn't stop herself. She wanted to lash out at him for making her feel so small.

"What baby?" His expression didn't change, but she heard something different in his tone.

"Caitlyn's baby." When he didn't answer, she added, "She was pregnant, Hank."

His hands curled into fists and his jaw tensed as he got up slowly. Kate struggled not to look away from his glare.

"You're playing with fire, Kate. If you know what's good for you, you'll leave this alone."

22

K ate bit down her own anger. "I just want to know if you knew she was pregnant," she said.

He stared at her, and she couldn't read his expression. Finally, he said, "No, no, I didn't know. At least not until the police told me. How did you find out?"

"Alex told me. He said she told him it wasn't his." She was treading on thin ice, but she had to know. Had to know if there was any possibility that her husband was the father of Caitlyn's baby.

"I'm not sure why this concerns you," he said, his expression daring her to ask.

Before she could decide exactly how to proceed, his phone buzzed. He went into the bedroom, grabbed it off the dresser, and put it to his ear. "Yes?" he barked as he closed the French door behind him, leaving her alone on the balcony.

Hank wasn't going to tell her anything. Not even if she came right out and demanded to know. She could hear him murmuring to whoever had called; then it was quiet. She got up and pushed the door open. He didn't even look at her as he grabbed his carryall off the floor and put it on the bed, pulling clothes out of the basket where she'd put them and stuffing them inside.

He was leaving.

He was angry with her. Angrier than she'd ever seen him. And it looked as though he was following a familiar pattern: he'd leave the house tonight, barely saying goodbye—and she might never see him again. That's what he'd done with Caitlyn at the end. What he'd done with Catherine. He just left. Cromwell would pick up the pieces, formalize everything, and Hank didn't even have to participate.

Was she becoming as inconvenient as the others?

This was the beginning for them. She shouldn't have confronted him with the ring. With Caitlyn's pregnancy. She knew better than that. And yet she wanted answers.

If she were truly honest with herself, she wanted to make sure that he hadn't had anything to do with Caitlyn's death. Or with her pregnancy. For some reason the latter was bothering her more than the possibility of the former, since he'd been with *her* the past two weeks and couldn't possibly have killed Caitlyn. But had he chosen *Caitlyn* to sleep with, when he was telling Kate she was the woman he wanted to marry?

She was jealous of a dead woman. A murdered woman. What was wrong with her?

"Where are you going?" she asked, forcing her tone to stay neutral.

He gave her a tight smile. "I'll be back in two days. Emergency board meeting in Frankfurt. Lindsey's meeting me at the airport."

Lindsey. That's right. Kate hadn't seen her since that day at Anna's, the day they found the body. But it wasn't a surprise that Hank had spoken to her, that he'd arranged for her to go with him. Lindsey was his assistant. Kate had to stay behind.

"You have to leave right now?"

"Yes." His tone was curt. He wasn't going to say any more. He'd made it clear what her place was. "You should go downstairs."

"Is Tom going with you?"

Hank cocked his eyebrow at her. "Why do you need to know?"

"No reason." She hesitated a moment. "I'm thinking about heading back to the city. I have to pack up, call the movers."

He gave her a genuine smile mixed with relief. "That's an excellent idea. Make sure you have them move what you want to keep to the penthouse. Everything else can be sold."

Granted, she had some furniture that was falling apart and needed to be replaced anyway. But most of what was in that apartment meant something to her, and she resented the implication that she would so easily discard her old life for her new one. Some things needed to make the transition with her. It wasn't time to get into that now, though. She forced a smile. It was easier to maintain harmony at the moment.

Hank was looking at her expectantly, and for a second, she wondered if he could read her mind, but that was silly.

She nodded. "First thing tomorrow. I'll set it all up."

Hank stopped packing and moved around the bed, his arms around her. "We're going to be so happy," he whispered in her ear, "as long as we put all this unpleasantness behind us. I'll meet you in the city and we can plan that honeymoon I've promised you."

She wanted to believe him, believe *in* him. But to call Caitlyn's murder *unpleasant*, she wasn't quite sure how to respond to that except by extricating herself from his embrace. He didn't seem to notice. Kate wrapped her arms around her torso, hugging herself tight as he finished packing. "You're always leaving," she said before she could stop herself.

Hank met her gaze. "But I'll always come back."

Would he? She couldn't be sure.

He paused at the door, his carryall in his hand. "We can't let Caitlyn ruin what we have. She's gone, tragically. But maybe it's for the best." And then he was gone.

She worried the finger where Hank had put Caitlyn's ring. It was as though she could still feel it there. Kate tried to shrug it off. She couldn't let it get to her. Five wives had come before her, and they'd all had rings of their own. It was the way it worked.

It was only later that she found it on the dresser. Caitlyn's ring, sparkling in the stream of moonlight that came in through the window—he'd left it right where she couldn't miss it.

January 12

It happened. IT. And I'm pregnant. He's elated. He says we'll get married now. He's pushing Cromwell to settle everything with the divorce. He doesn't want me to have the baby if we're not married. It better be soon. We only have eight months. But he's confident it'll work out.

I broke down when we went away on business together. We'd had so much pent-up sexual frustration that it was bound to happen. And of course it was a trip to Paris, my city, the most romantic city in the world. I should have known I wouldn't be able to resist him there.

We spent the first full day in meetings. I was jet-lagged and a bit out of sorts, but pushed through. I'm heading up a new initiative I'm really excited about, and even jet lag couldn't dim my enthusiasm. One of the things I saw when I started working at Tudor Enterprises was the lack of women in management. Sure, Catherine was at the top of the organization, but she was only one of two. Now I'm the one of two. Hank was dubious about my plans to recruit and retain more women; he really can be old school at times. I outlined a plan that would ensure advancement throughout his companies for women at all levels. I've hit some resistance from women, surprisingly. Tudor Enterprises has a reputation of being an old boys' club (see Hank's old-school attitude), and a lot of women start out at the company but then move on to others. It's not a good look, and it's not the way any company should be run in the twenty-first century. I'm also pushing for diversity, combining the two into an inclusivity effort. Hank said I should begin with committees, but I find that committees don't actually do anything except have endless meetings and write a lot of memos. I want to get this done, so I'm starting with human resources and the recruiters.

There was a lot of support during the presentations I organized, and by the end of the day, I was rejuvenated. We had champagne with dinner, and afterward he came back to my room (yes, we had booked separate rooms). He suggested I take a hot bubble bath, gave me a bath towel, and sent me into the bathroom while he made a drink at the bar in the room.

It wasn't until I was submerged in the soapy water, touching myself, that I knew I wanted him more at that moment than any other. I climbed out of the tub, stepped back into the room, not wearing anything, the water dripping from my hair down my body. He didn't need an invitation. He lifted me onto the bed and didn't even bother taking off his clothes, just unzipped his fly and that was that. We were finally completely consummated.

We spent the next twelve hours in bed, doing things to each other that I'm embarrassed to write even here.

I hadn't been prepared, and I know it was that night. Because it had to be. It was too perfect.

I don't know how I feel about being pregnant. That hadn't been the plan, but I was so crazy for him that I didn't think about it. And he never talked to me about it, about whether we'd take precautions. It's not like we haven't had a lot of time to talk. Maybe he wanted me to get pregnant. Maybe this was his plan, even if it wasn't mine. He certainly is happy enough about it. He says that he's getting a second chance, both with me and our child.

My stomach is still flat, but there's a baby growing inside me. Our baby. It all has to work out now. It has to.

23

ANNA

Anna made her way through the hall, her fingers lightly brushing the wall, shadows creeping through the windows. She went down the stairs, the wood cool beneath her bare feet, into the great room. It wasn't a surprise that she couldn't sleep. There were weeks when she had no trouble, but stress brought it on. Lying awake for hours, staring at the ceiling, all of her anxieties—and guilt—bubbling to the surface so she couldn't relax enough to drop off and give herself a break.

Hank had told her about Caitlyn. About how she was the body in the marsh and how he'd identified her. Was it a shock? Not really. She'd almost been expecting it ever since they'd found out Caitlyn was missing. Hank had put his arm around Anna and said all the right things—*It wasn't your fault. Nothing could have kept Caitlyn here if she didn't want to stay. She didn't tell you anything, so how could you have predicted what would happen*—and then he picked up his bag, walked out the door, and climbed into the waiting limo. While the news about Caitlyn hadn't completely surprised her, she *was* surprised that he didn't take Kate with him.

Joan liked to tease Anna about her nocturnal walks, but she understood that Anna's intermittent insomnia was real and this was the only way she could battle it. She hated the sleeping pills, which left her sluggish the next day.

Tonight, though, Joan had begged her to take the sleeping pill.

"That girl was murdered out there," she'd said. "I don't want you to go out there alone."

Anna murmured promises that she knew she wouldn't keep, and once she heard Joan softly snoring beside her, she'd slipped out of bed. She carefully shut the front door behind her as she stepped out onto the porch, making sure her key was in her pocket. She wasn't immune to the fear that had crawled into her life, but she also needed to sleep, and this was the only way. She craved it like Caitlyn craved her booze or her drugs.

Only half an hour, she told herself. That should be enough.

"Ms. Klein?" His voice was almost a whisper.

Will Stafford came out of nowhere, but he hadn't startled her. She'd been expecting him. She made out his shadow, then his face.

"I'll be right behind you," he assured her.

She'd come to an arrangement with him; she would pay the overtime necessary so she could feel safe. The area was relatively isolated, and a woman walking alone was vulnerable. Especially an ex–Mrs. Tudor. She wasn't stupid.

"Thank you for today. For taking Kate," she said, compelled to express her gratitude.

"All in a day's work, Ms. Klein."

She wouldn't have asked him to take care of Kate if she didn't trust him implicitly. He wasn't much older than she was, but she could sometimes see the agonies of war in his eyes when he thought no one was looking. Joan had hired him not long after they met, saying that she needed someone who would be loyal to *her*—not to Hank. Joan also had the ulterior motive of wanting to keep Anna safe during her nighttime wanderings without her ex-husband finding out.

Anna had worried that with Will lurking in the background, she wouldn't be able to find that sweet spot of peace inside her that allowed her to relax. But it didn't take long for her to discover that he could blend into the darkness, become the ghost he was being paid to be, allowing her to disappear within herself, emptying her mind, focusing only on each step. She held the small flashlight, the beam bobbing on the road as her arms swung to the rhythm in her head, a made-up tune that she sometimes found herself humming while in the middle of a mindless task.

Tonight, though, the specter of that body, *Caitlyn's* body, hung over her, and she began to doubt that even her walk would let her sleep. Perhaps she *should* go back and take a sleeping pill. She wasn't far; she could see the front porch light.

She could also see a light on in Hank's house.

Maybe Mary had finally returned. Anna took a few steps toward the house, her eyes trained on the light in what she knew was the great room.

Another couple of steps—the light went out.

Anna stopped, waiting for whoever had been inside to trip the motion sensors and cause the lights to come on outside, but the house lay bathed in darkness. It was possible that the light had been on a timer and no one was actually there. But then why wouldn't she have noticed it before? Anna shook the thought away. She didn't spend a lot of time paying attention to the house next door. She was too busy to notice lights on or off, she told herself. And if someone was there who shouldn't be, there were always the silent alarms.

As Anna ran through all the security on the property, she began to wonder about Caitlyn again. But this time her thoughts were more toward the practical. How on earth had that happened there? It should have been impossible without detection, considering the lighting, the security.

Anna hadn't gone out the night Caitlyn was here; the sleeping pill had done its job. The implication of that suddenly struck her. What if she *had* gone out? Would *she* have been the body in the marsh?

Her body began to shake, and she wrapped her arms tightly around her torso to stop it. This was definitely a mistake. She turned around to go home, quickening her pace.

"Anna?"

His shadow moved across the road, and she turned, expecting Will. But it was Tom Cromwell. Her chest constricted, like a vise tightening with each breath.

"I wouldn't think that you'd venture out after what happened," he said.

He didn't even ask why she was here. He knew. Like he knew everything. If it weren't for Tom, she never would have met Hank. Tom had shown up on her doorstep and offered her more money than she'd ever imagined. But it was her father's business, so she refused. He proceeded to wine and dine her, and it was only when he realized she still wouldn't sell that Hank showed up to close the deal.

"Was it you over there? At the house?" Anna asked. "I saw a light."

"Hank asked me to check on something," Tom volunteered without really answering her question. "I saw your light out here." He hesitated, indicating her flashlight. "But I didn't realize it was you. I thought it might be a reporter."

He stood in front of her, his hands in the pockets of his khakis. He had hard features, his nose a little hooked, his thick hair, sprinkled with gray, was slicked back. He allowed her to study him, knowing it wasn't anything more than it was. He'd known from the beginning where her interests were. Hank had blamed Tom for not telling him the truth about the woman he took as his wife, and for a while it had looked as though Tom's position was in jeopardy. But he managed to survive because of his talent for massaging Hank Tudor's ego, and Hank depended on him for so much.

Not to mention that Tom Cromwell knew where all the bodies were buried.

So to speak.

"Why so late?" she asked.

"What do you mean?"

"Why did you have to check on something over there now? It's the middle of the night."

Tom gave a low chuckle. "Are you worried about me, Anna? I can assure you that no one's going to take off my head without a fight."

She shouldn't have even asked. Why would she think he'd tell her anything?

"Why don't I walk you home?" Tom asked.

Anna glanced around. Where was Will?

He sensed her hesitation. "I already sent him back."

A bubble of anger rose in her chest. Will worked for *her*. Tom had no business giving him orders.

"I assured him you were safe with me," Tom said.

Anna thought about the scratches on his hands. *Was* she safe with Tom? When she got back to the house, she was going to have to talk to Will.

Without a word, she began to walk again, albeit even more briskly now. It wasn't far; the sooner she got home, the better she'd feel. Tom fell into step beside her as the moon slid out from behind a cloud and illuminated the marsh, where Caitlyn's body had been discovered just yesterday. She froze for a moment, the shadows playing with her imagination.

Tom moved closer, leaning in, his breath hot against her ear.

"So close," he whispered. "Didn't you hear her scream?"

24

CATHERINE

Catherine anxiously tapped the sides of her laptop. She'd been trading but forced herself to stay away from any Tudor Enterprises stocks. She'd already done the damage she set out to do, and others were picking up where she left off. Still, she found herself compulsively checking stock prices. They couldn't go back up. Not yet.

This would drive Hank crazy. He couldn't control it, and he always had to be in control.

Catherine wished she could see him, see his reaction to what was happening. She wanted to be a fly on the wall of his boardroom when he met with the shareholders, the board of directors. There was a time when she might have donned a disguise and made an effort. But now, she saw the world only through her laptop.

Catherine poured a cup of coffee. Lourdes had brought in some croissants and jam, so she fixed a quick plate and carried it, along with the cup, into the den. She set everything down and turned on the TV to see the morning shows. One channel was showing an interview with Alex Culpepper, the new James Bond. The one who'd been involved with Caitlyn Howard. The interviewer, a pencil-thin woman wearing a skintight dress, blonde curls cascading over her shoulders, was lobbing softball questions at him, nothing about the girl. Maybe he'd cut a deal to do the interview as long as no one asked him about her. It wasn't as though that wasn't done.

Catherine felt almost sorry for him. He had seemed to love that girl. It had been bad enough when their affair had been splashed all over the media, but something had happened, and as suddenly as it had started, it stopped. She was certain that strings had been pulled—either by Hank or Tom Cromwell. More likely Cromwell, since Hank wouldn't want to get his hands dirty.

Cromwell was all about getting his hands dirty.

Catherine felt the bile rise in her throat as she thought about him. Cromwell allowed himself to represent the worst of Hank. He was Hank's so-called fixer, the one who would take care of all the unpleasantness that might surround Hank. Catherine had done some digging, back when Cromwell began negotiating the affair with That Woman. It hadn't been easy. Cromwell seemed to have come out of nowhere. The man had no background that could be traced; he'd spent some time in the military, but Catherine had been unable to discover where or what he'd done because his service had been highly classified. He claimed to be a lawyer, but there was no record of him attending any law school. The only thing Catherine could find was a wife, but she'd died the year before. No obituary, no details about their marriage except a buried police report of a domestic disturbance that he'd clearly been unable to expunge.

He was just the kind of man Hank Tudor would embrace.

Cromwell had come to work for Tudor Enterprises after That Woman had already cast her spell on Hank, so Catherine had had no chance to get to know him as she would have liked. In another day, another time, she might have appreciated Cromwell's talents as Hank did. She'd been as ruthless as her husband at one point, enough so that she'd been able to stall the divorce for seven years.

Of course, Catherine had her own fixer, but no one had paid enough attention to notice. *She* had suspected in the days before the affair, but it was soon forgotten when she was caught up with Hank.

The phone rang next to her, and she froze for a moment before she recognized the number on the caller ID. She picked up the handset.

"Mummy, it was Caitlyn Howard. The body. They've identified her."

Catherine took a deep breath. It was only a matter of time. It wasn't like before.

"Who?" she asked Maril. "Who identified her?"

"Daddy."

She pictured Hank, his shoulders sagging with grief, his head in his hands. But then she felt her anger rising. Why didn't she know about this? She certainly shouldn't be hearing this news from her daughter.

Maril shouldn't still be at Anna's, but Catherine hadn't been certain how to convince her to leave without her getting suspicious. Her daughter had to think that she wanted any and all information she could gather about what was going on with the investigation. She had no idea that Catherine was being kept more than informed on the situation.

"Mummy? Mummy?"

Catherine took a deep breath, composing herself. "Yes, dear, I'm here."

When all was well with Hank, before That Woman came into their lives, he'd had big plans for his daughter. She'd gotten her MBA at Harvard after her undergraduate work at Yale and interned during the summers at each of her father's businesses. He'd told her she could choose any of them, and it would be hers.

Yet just like that, it was over. Hank wasn't so cruel as to leave Maril with nothing, but he gave her a position that certainly didn't give her any power. Catherine's reminder about his dreams for their daughter fell on deaf ears.

"I don't owe you anything," he'd told her. "And I don't owe her anything. She's had everything she's ever wanted, so you can't say that I haven't been generous."

Catherine wanted to tell him that he *did* owe her. He owed her for all the years she gave him, all the work she did beside him, building those companies. But she bit her tongue. Telling him that wouldn't change his mind. It had to be done subtly. Maril didn't understand.

"He promised," Maril had said over a glass of red wine. "Maybe I should find another job."

"It will be okay," Catherine had said. "Do the best job you can. See if you can't do something that catches his eye." It was all she could say; Maril would benefit in the end, but she couldn't yet know that.

Maril had scowled. "Where I am, there's nothing I can do."

Catherine blamed herself. She'd raised her daughter to feel privileged, entitled, and now that her father had demoted her—in more ways than one—it was extremely difficult for her. Maril was a Tudor, like Hank, and she deserved so much more.

"Do you want me to come over there?" Maril was asking, interrupting her thoughts.

"No. I'm fine."

"Is there *anything* I can do for you?" Her daughter's voice was soft, almost inaudible.

"You could do something," she conceded. "Why don't you offer to help with the children a little longer? See if you can find out whether the police have any suspects." This would keep her busy.

"I'll see what I can find out," Maril promised. "Please take care of yourself, Mummy. Leave it all to me."

Catherine had barely hung up when the phone rang again. Maril must have forgotten something, but when she looked at the display, she didn't recognize the number.

"Yes?" she asked tentatively when she answered it.

"Catherine?" The voice was familiar, an old memory resurfacing. Once upon a time, she and Margaret Pole had been good friends. Until That Woman bewitched Maggie the same way she'd bewitched Hank. Catherine hadn't talked to Maggie since. She was puzzled why the woman would call her now, after all these years.

"What can I do for you?" she asked coldly.

"You know why I'm calling."

"I don't believe I do." And she honestly didn't.

Silence for a few seconds, then, "It's happened again. Don't tell me you didn't have anything to do with it."

"What's happened again?" But a tickle of anxiety tugged at her. Margaret couldn't know anything; she never did. She'd always been convinced of Hank's guilt, which had been convenient.

"It was a mistake to do it the same way this time. Lines will be drawn."

There was no proof of anything. Nothing could be traced back to her.

"I know you're waiting for him to come back to you. But you have to know that's not going to happen. He's gotten married again. She's young, she's beautiful."

Catherine had been young and beautiful once. She stared at the pictures that sat all over the room, pictures of her and Hank, his arms around her, his smile only for her. Pictures of the two of them on their wedding day, Hank in a tuxedo, she in yards of white tulle and lace, making her look like a princess. One of these days he *would* come back to her. It was their destiny.

Catherine held her breath for a moment, then let it out slowly. "Don't call me again."

"Where is her head, Catherine? What have you done with it?"

December 7

Her name is Elizabeth, but we call her Lizzie. She is beautiful and perfect and the most amazing thing that's ever happened to me. She's curious about everything, and sometimes I worry that she's going to be too serious. But then she breaks out into a smile or laughter, and it melts my heart. I love Hank, but the love that I feel for this tiny person is beyond anything I've ever experienced. I hold her close, feel her little body next to mine, and I know I would do anything for her. I would kill for her.

The divorce finally came through, and Hank and I got married three months before she was born. I was big as a house, but he didn't mind, told me that he finally had everything he'd ever wanted. I traveled with him throughout my pregnancy. He didn't want me out of his sight, wanted to take care of me, make sure I had everything I needed. We went to London, Paris, Shanghai, Dubai. He had business everywhere, but he didn't have crazy hours, we spent every evening and night and morning together. He said that was one of the perks of owning his own companies.

He didn't want me working. I told him I was perfectly capable of it, that my pregnancy didn't mean I couldn't think, but he said he was old-fashioned and wanted me to take care of myself in every way. And now I'm still not working, because he wants me home with Lizzie. My initiative is on hold; he said I can get back to it in a few months, when Lizzie is a little bit older. I worry, though, *that because he wasn't completely on board with it in the beginning, this is his way of making sure it never happens. It really would be ridiculous to head up an initiative that helps women advance in the workplace if I, as a woman, am not allowed by my husband to go back to work after having a child. I said that to him once, and we had a big fight about it. I have to remember to keep my head and not provoke him. I've learned the hard way that's not the way to get what I want. He does talk about the businesses with me, and he usually seems to value my opinions, so that's why I don't hold back. I have to push for what I believe needs to happen in the companies, especially now that we have a daughter. She has to have the same opportunities that a man would.*

Don't get me wrong. The more I'm with Lizzie, the more I love being a mother. I feel like I'm at my best with her. But I want to make a difference in other ways, too. I figure I'll wait until she's a year old before I go back to work.

I've started to talk to Lizzie in French when we're alone. I want her to be bilingual so we can have our own language together. Our special thing. I'll take her to Paris, bring her to the museums and sit at the outdoor cafés, walk through the Tuileries gardens, day trips to Versailles. Hank thinks it's a little silly, but he's indulgent. He asks if he can come along, and I always say yes. Even though I might want time alone with Lizzie, to have her all to myself. Is that selfish? To want a special bond with my daughter?

Hank really is a wonderful father. He wants all the best things for our girl. He tells me that he's going to make up for everything that went wrong with Maril and Catherine. That we are his life and nothing will get in the way of that.

He's just a little old-fashioned. I'll work on that.

25

Kate woke up feeling discombobulated. She'd spent the night tossing and turning, the bed next to her cold and empty, alternating between wishing she'd comforted her husband more after he'd told her he'd identified Caitlyn's body and upset about Caitlyn's pregnancy, which was still shrouded in mystery. He hadn't reassured her that he hadn't slept with the girl.

The police made a statement that the body of the woman found on Hank Tudor's property was his ex-wife—although the fact that she'd been pregnant had not been part of the release. Thank goodness for small favors. Kate stayed up too late, flipping from channel to channel, scrolling through the internet, unable to look away, the talking heads discussing the similarities, the "coincidence" of two headless bodies, the disappearance of Nan Tudor, the death of Caitlyn Howard. They'd interviewed the police chief on Martha's Vineyard, but he hadn't been chief eight years ago, taking over when the previous chief died of a heart attack. The insinuation that the former chief's death might have been to keep him quiet was typical of the games the media played. She found herself taking notes like she would've if she were still Hank's assistant, her fingers itching to pick up her phone and call her contacts to see how damaging this might be.

But there was nothing she could do. Nothing at all. The thought terrified her. Because without anything to do, her thoughts continually drifted to Caitlyn Howard, the young woman she'd spent so much time trying to control. She may have been a train wreck, but Kate never doubted for a moment that Caitlyn loved Hank for a while. She wouldn't have married him if she didn't. Caitlyn never did anything she didn't want to do. She'd been so full of life—sometimes maybe a little too much, but it was what Hank had loved about her. Until it exhausted and frustrated him and he turned to Kate for a little more stability.

How had that girl ended up the way she did—and in such a vicious way?

Underneath it all lurked the stock sell-off. There was no way this wouldn't affect the stocks even more. Shareholders were a skittish bunch. The word "bankruptcy" was tossed around a bit, and for a moment she wondered what it would be like to be married to a Hank Tudor without the billions, a Hank Tudor who lost it all because of a body found on his property. She'd grown up in a middle-class family, in a suburban, nondescript town. She worked summers and afternoons after school at the local diner, serving up BLTs and coffee and ice cream sundaes, scraping together enough money to go to the movies, concerts with her friends, putting a little aside every paycheck to help defray college costs. She knew how to live like that; she wasn't afraid of it. Hank had grown up with money, though. He didn't know what it was like to struggle financially.

She imagined the two of them settled into a small house somewhere. She could go back to work, and Hank could start a new business. They could have home-cooked dinners and Sundays in front of a fire, reading and just being together. No media hovering outside the door, no need for security teams.

Was that what she really wanted? She sighed. No. Life with Hank would never be like that. It was a scenario that was unfathomable. If she truly wanted that, she wouldn't have married him. That man wouldn't be the man she loved.

Kate pulled on a pair of leggings and an oversized sweatshirt and made her way downstairs, the rest of the house quiet.

Anna was in the kitchen making coffee.

Kate slid onto one of the island stools. "Did Hank tell you about Caitlyn?" she asked.

Anna nodded.

"It's only a matter of time before the police come around again," Kate warned her, aware that she was using her public relations voice. "Now that they know it's her, they're going to question all of us all over again, and it'll be more intense than before. Not to mention it will be a media frenzy." While Kate had done her share of crisis management during her career, this was going to be on a different level. She was married to the murder victim's ex-husband.

Anna was quiet as she poured them each a cup of coffee, her face drawn. Kate realized she'd been insensitive. She probably wasn't the only one who hadn't slept well. After all, Caitlyn had been here and then disappeared, only to show up dead in the marsh next door.

"How are you doing?" she asked.

Anna shrugged. "I'm fine." But she didn't seem fine.

"It's not your fault," she tried to reassure Anna. "You didn't know."

"She was too young to die. I know she was difficult at times, but there was just something about her that made it hard to dislike her." Anna shook her head. "Who would've done something like this?"

Kate thought about Alex Culpepper. Could he have killed her? She didn't want to think so, but domestic disputes were violent; men killed their girlfriends, their wives. In that moment in her apartment, she'd seen the anger in his eyes, the possibility of violence. He'd been angry with Caitlyn about the baby, angry with Hank. Alex might be young, he might be at the cusp of an extraordinary career, but who really knew the man? The only ones who ever knew what really went on in relationships were those directly involved. "What about Alex?" she asked.

"No. He loved her."

"A lot of women are killed in the name of love," Kate reminded her, remembering her ex-husband and how easily he could have turned from a stalker into a killer. He knew everything about her, knew where she was at all times. He left flowers at her doorstep, notes declaring his undying love for her, but it wasn't love. She'd left him and he couldn't accept that. He'd wanted to control her. She'd bought a gun, learned how to use it, because she'd been that concerned about her safety.

"I don't believe it. He couldn't do it. He has a gentle soul," Anna said.

"Even the most gentle of souls can have a temper."

Anna shot her a look that immediately made her feel guilty. "This was more than a temper, Kate. My god, she was beheaded."

Kate didn't want to think about that.

"Where did Hank go last night?" Anna asked.

Kate hadn't heard anything from him. She'd checked her phone, but there were no messages. It was the longest they'd gone without communication since she'd started working for him. "He said he had to go to Frankfurt for an emergency meeting." She wasn't ready to share the fact of Caitlyn's pregnancy—or the fact that they'd had a fight about it.

The floor creaked overhead, reminding her that they weren't the only people in the house. Joan, the children, Maril. Tom. He hadn't gone with Hank. Kate wondered if it was because of her meeting with Alex yesterday. Hank didn't trust her, so he left Cromwell behind to keep an eye on her. Speaking of trust . . .

"You trust Will Stafford? Do you think he would have told anyone that he took me into the city to meet with Alex? Do you think he would've told Hank or Cromwell?"

Anna shook her head. "Absolutely not." To her credit, she didn't ask why Kate suspected Will of telling Hank, but Kate could see her putting it together.

"*Someone* told Hank that I met with Culpepper at my apartment. He knew that I did," Kate said. She wondered about Cromwell, who always seemed to know everything somehow. "Those scratches on Tom's hands . . ." Her voice trailed off as she remembered the lame rosebush excuse.

"Why would Tom kill her?" Anna asked, knowing what she was thinking. "Hank divorced her. He married *you*. He moved on."

"The diary." Caitlyn might have tipped her hand. "What if she told *Tom* she had it?"

Anna was quiet for a few seconds. "Tom arranged my marriage. He wanted Hank to have the newspapers, and somehow, he knew the only way I'd let go of them was if I was married to him. He saw the state I was in then and took advantage of it. Hank was hurting after Jeanne and needed a mother for his children. Tom played us both. If he thinks it will benefit Hank in some way, he'll go rogue. Caitlyn might've told him about the journal, and he might've taken matters into his own hands and kept Hank out of it."

He's going to kill me.

The words written in Nan Tudor's diary came back to her. What if . . . No, Kate pushed the thought from her head. Like Caitlyn, Nan had been prone to the dramatic; at least that's what everyone always said. Those words didn't have to mean anything. Diaries were not reliable; emotions were involved. Kate remembered her own diaries from her youth: anger at her parents for silly things like not letting her go to a party. *I hate her,* she'd written more than once about her mother. She hadn't really meant it.

Anyway, that body eight years ago hadn't been Nan. Her DNA had proved it.

He covered it up. Money will do that, and there's plenty of that to go around.

Margaret Pole's words swirled in her head. She pushed them away, unwilling to give the woman any credibility.

What was more concerning than what Nan wrote was the fact that Caitlyn was planning to blackmail Hank with the diary—and Culpepper knew it. Kate had no doubt he'd tell the police about why he'd gone to see her at the rehab center. He'd seemed eager to blame Hank for something.

And if he told the police what Caitlyn was planning, it would point a finger at Hank.

Maybe they should get rid of the journal. If it didn't exist, Alex couldn't prove anything. The police would have nothing, no evidence that what Alex might claim was true. Kate was sure Anna wouldn't tell, and since she hadn't told Joan, all the better. *What journal?* It was only a little white lie.

But first, she wanted to read it. The whole thing, to see what Nan Tudor had written about her marriage. She had an opportunity now since Hank had gone and wasn't expected back for a couple of days.

"Can you bring me the journal? We have to figure out what to do with it."

Anna bit her lip, an odd look crossing her face.

"What is it?" Kate demanded.

"It's gone."

PART III

26

Kate had promised Hank she'd go to the city and start packing up her apartment, but it was the last thing she wanted to do. Instead, she took her cup of coffee and went out to the pool, settling down on one of the chaise lounges, and considered a swim to clear her head.

Anna had kept the diary in a shoebox in her closet and claimed no one knew it was there. And yet someone did know. Someone found it and took it. Was it Joan? Maril? One of the children?

This last thought gave her pause. What if Lizzie had found the journal? Kate wouldn't put it past Lizzie to snoop, and if she'd discovered her mother's diary, she most likely wouldn't tell anyone about it. Kate had no doubt Lizzie knew how to keep secrets.

"Mrs. Tudor?"

His voice startled her. Kate twisted around and held her hand up to shield the sun from her eyes, the better to see Trooper Pawlik standing over her. He'd crept up quietly, which didn't seem right. If the police came, they should be announced, shouldn't they?

"Ms. Klein told me you were out here."

Anna could have warned her first.

He didn't wait for her to respond. "You weren't here when I spoke with Ms. Klein yesterday. I've got a few more questions."

Not a surprise, considering. But she couldn't talk to him without Tom. Where *was* Tom? She realized now she hadn't seen him all morning. Kate took her phone off the small table next to her and texted him, explaining to Pawlik what she was doing.

Pawlik's eyebrows rose. "You don't need a lawyer," he argued.

"I don't agree."

He sighed and sat down on the edge of the lounge next to hers. His legs were too long and the seat too low, but he didn't indicate he was uncomfortable. "Can you at least tell me where we might be able to find your husband? We have been trying unsuccessfully to get in touch with him." His words seemed too formal for the casual way he was sitting, his elbows on his knees, his hands clasped together.

"He's in Frankfurt on business." It wasn't as though it was confidential information. Or so she hoped.

Pawlik's mouth tightened into a grim line. This was not the answer he was looking for. Kate was aware that Hank told him he would be accessible, but Hank wasn't about to adhere to anyone else's rules. This trooper should know that. He'd met Hank, and it wasn't as though he wouldn't know his predilections. Hank had a reputation.

Kate checked her phone, but still nothing from Tom. Damn him. He was always lurking, except when you might need him. "My husband told me he spoke with you yesterday. When he identified . . ." Her voice faltered.

"I'm sorry about Miss Howard," he said, not unkindly.

"Thank you." Where *was* Tom? Her phone was silent.

"It's come to our attention that you met with Alex Culpepper in Manhattan yesterday."

Kate forgot about her phone. "How on earth—"

Pawlik held up his hand. "We have our ways," he said.

Jane Rocheford must have told the police. Kate wouldn't put it past her. Jane didn't know how to keep her mouth shut, an unfortunate trait in someone who was supposed to protect her celebrity clients. And then she wondered if Jane was the one who told Hank about the meeting. She didn't have time to ponder that, though, because Pawlik was still talking.

"It seems Alex Culpepper is a popular man these days. Your husband paid him a visit last night at his hotel."

Kate tried not to react. Why would Hank go see Alex?

Pawlik cocked his head and met her gaze. "And shortly thereafter, Mr. Culpepper left the hotel. He was supposed to be on his film set today, but no one's seen him. He's not at the hotel, either."

"I don't know what you're looking for here. I told you, Hank is in Frankfurt," Kate said, hating that her voice wavered slightly and hoping he hadn't noticed.

"How well do you know your husband?"

Alex had asked her the same thing.

"Ms. Rocheford has made some serious accusations." Pawlik was trying to bait her into saying something that would incriminate her—or Hank.

Kate snorted. "Jane doesn't like Hank. I wouldn't put any stock in her opinion." She paused a moment, then added, "I think this conversation is over. What happened to Caitlyn has nothing to do with my husband."

"But what if it does?" His question hung between them.

"It doesn't," she said, more confidently than she felt, doubts swirling in her head. Hank couldn't have had anything to do with Caitlyn's murder, could he? No, of course not. He was only ruthless in the boardroom. Even when he'd discovered Caitlyn's affair with Culpepper, he had shown little emotion, withdrawing to his London apartment, calling lawyers, and setting the divorce in motion.

But Alex was a different story. He had frightened her. Maybe she could turn the tables and get Pawlik to focus on *him*. "Alex told me Caitlyn was pregnant," she said. "He said she told him he wasn't the father. He was angry about that."

Pawlik's eyes widened slightly, taking in this information. "How angry?"

Kate remembered how Alex pinned her to the kitchen island, his face close, dark. Maybe the idea that he killed Caitlyn wasn't so off base. "He was very angry," she said, her eyes meeting Pawlik's.

"Do you think Alex Culpepper could have killed her?"

Did she? Did it matter, as long as the police stopped looking at Hank? Kate had spent the past couple of years protecting Hank Tudor, taking care of things for him so he wouldn't have to. This was what she was good at, why he'd hired her in the first place. And, she hoped, one of the reasons he'd married her. Caitlyn had been a loose cannon; she was the opposite.

"Yes."

"You're aware of what happened eight years ago, right? A woman was murdered in the same way, her body found on your husband's property. In a marsh."

Why would he bring this up? "She wasn't identified," Kate said. "Even though the police had DNA."

Pawlik nodded. "That's right."

"It could have been anyone."

"Yes."

"But you don't think so."

"It's interesting how similar Caitlyn Howard's murder is to that one eight years ago. That's when your husband's second wife disappeared, isn't it?" He knew damn well when Nan left.

"The DNA proved that it wasn't Nan," she said. "Maybe whoever killed Caitlyn wanted to frame my husband by setting it up to look like that other murder."

Pawlik leveled his gaze at her. "Maybe," he said after a moment. "But there was one thing about that murder that was never reported. It wasn't just that the victim was found beheaded on your husband's property." He hesitated a moment, then added, "*She* was pregnant, too."

February 5

I'm pregnant again, and I can't be more happy! Lizzie is a wonderful little girl, but she needs a sister or a brother. Lizzie has her father's red hair and my eyes. She also has a temper to her, but that could come from either of us. I think having a sibling will help with that, it will keep her a little more grounded. She also might not get so spoiled. I worry about that, spoiling her too much. She will make a good big sister. Even though she's headstrong, she can be kind and gentle. And she is so smart. She's only three and she knows the alphabet and I've taught her some French.

Sure, it's going to be a little harder with two kids and working, but it's easier for me than for other women. We have money. We have help. And I finally have my women-in-management initiative back up and running. I don't want to abandon it again.

It wasn't long after Lizzie was born that I wanted to begin trying for another baby. I didn't tell Hank, just never started back with birth control and, like a man, he didn't even ask about it.

I didn't think it would take too long to get pregnant, since I'd gotten pregnant the first time we'd ever had sex. But this time wasn't as easy as the first. Months went by, and every month I got my period like clockwork. Not even a pregnancy scare. Catherine had a couple of miscarriages, I know that, but at least she could get pregnant.

I finally told Hank that I wanted another baby. He wasn't convinced that I should get pregnant again so soon. He told me I should be happy with Lizzie and enjoy her. I was back at work, wasn't I? Wasn't this all I wanted? I was enjoying her, and yes, I was happy to be back at work, I reminded him, but I wanted her to have a sibling. Didn't he want a son? Hank laughed when I asked him that. He said he didn't care, that he already had two daughters, he didn't need more children.

I couldn't stop thinking about it, though. Every month, it was like my own body had betrayed me when I saw the blood. I made a doctor's appointment so I could find out if something was wrong with me. But nothing. No one had an answer to why I'd been able to get pregnant once but I couldn't get pregnant again. The doctor told me to relax, that I was too stressed. Maybe I should quit my job and stay home. Like I was some sort of delicate thing.

Hank didn't complain at first because I wanted to have sex all the time. I figured the more sex, the better the chances I'd get pregnant. I bought a kit that would tell me when I'd be ovulating, and I showed up in his office in the middle of the day and fucked him on his desk with the door locked. I'd send Lizzie out with the nanny so when he came home from work, I'd be naked and ready for him. I even flew to Paris when he was there on business and surprised him in his hotel room. He started calling me a nympho, but I didn't care, as long as I got pregnant.

But I didn't.

I know it was crazy, that I was going crazy. That I should have been content with my life the way it was, but another baby would make it so much better. Lizzie was getting older; sometimes she pulled away from me when I wanted to hold her. I started staring at babies I saw when I was out. I wanted to cradle them in my arms and smell their smell and know that they were mine.

I tried to explain it to Hank, but he had a hard time understanding. I could tell he was humoring me, but he refused to be tested. He said he had two daughters, nothing could be wrong with him. We had a huge fight over that, but I still fucked him that night even though I didn't want to.

The drugs were a natural next step. The doctors told me that they'd help me ovulate, that my chances were good, especially since they didn't find anything wrong with me. I didn't like the shots. I hate needles. Hank wasn't happy. He told me that if it would make me happy, he'd try it, but only for six months. He worried that I'd end up having twins or triplets or even more than that. I didn't want more than one at a time, either, but I agreed to the time frame, figuring that I could push it because he wouldn't pay attention to how long it had been anyway.

I didn't realize how it would be when I was on the drugs, though. They made me crazy. My emotions were up and down and all over the place. I picked fights when I didn't want to. It's almost as though I've had another person living inside me, another person who wants to make him as miserable as I am. I've been like a manic depressive: really high and happy and then in a blink of an eye, I'm in a dark, angry place and I lash out—mostly at Hank, because he doesn't want sex anymore. And I guess if I'm honest, neither do I. The fun of it is gone. There's no more passion, no more sweet caresses, no more explosive orgasms, no more whispering and giggling under the sheets, sweaty and satisfied. It's always over so fast, and then I have to lay there with my legs in the air, hoping that his sperm will meet up with one of my eggs, while he disappears to who knows where.

Where is that man who wooed me? The man who spent years divorcing his wife so we could be together? We went through so much together. I still love him. I want him to hold me, like he used to. Talk to me, spend time with me.

I want him to want a baby as much as I do.

But I'm scared.

Because I saw him with her. With Jeanne, my former assistant. While I was out on maternity leave with Lizzie, she'd moved to another department. I didn't even try to bring her back when I returned to work. Maybe I should have. I might have seen it earlier. Instead, it was so random. They were walking down the sidewalk near the Midtown office. His arm was around her, and they suddenly stopped. I couldn't see her face, but I saw his. His eyes were full of desire—I've seen that look, he used to look at me like that. And then he leaned over and kissed her, his fingers tickling her neck, kissing her like he used to kiss me. I wasn't that far away, but they only had eyes for each other; they had no idea I was there.

I don't see what he sees in her. She never had a mind of her own, which is good for an assistant, but I don't care for it in someone I'd be friends with. I didn't think he'd go for someone like her. He likes to be challenged. She's not even pretty. She still hasn't made herself over. Her hair is thin and stringy, and her eyes are too big for her face. She's still wearing frumpy clothes. But he's staying out late, saying he's working. I can smell her on him when he comes home.

Now that I'm pregnant again, he'll have to give her up. Won't he?

27

There were too many coincidences. A beheaded pregnant woman found on Hank's property. When Hank said he was the common denominator, he was right on target.

Was Pawlik suggesting that the body on Martha's Vineyard really had been Nan?

Kate didn't like where her thoughts were taking her. She couldn't believe that her husband could kill anyone, especially a pregnant ex-wife. And what was Hank doing, going to see Alex at his hotel? Kate would have thought he'd be smarter than that, but he'd been so angry last night. Had he confronted Alex about the baby? About Caitlyn? About seeing Kate at her apartment?

It could be any of those things.

"I think you should go," Kate said, standing up and walking around the side of the house, not waiting for Pawlik. He fell into step beside her, silent. Kate sensed he wanted to say more, ask more questions, but he didn't, perhaps knowing she was done talking.

Just as they reached the police cruiser in the front drive, Tom's Mercedes careened toward them and slammed to a stop.

"What's going on here?" he demanded of Pawlik as he got out of the car, frowning at Kate. "We answered all your questions yesterday."

Pawlik touched the brim of his hat and nodded at Kate before turning to Cromwell. "I assure you, Mr. Cromwell, that Mrs. Tudor did not say anything incriminating. I do need to reach Mr. Tudor, however. Perhaps you can help with that?"

Tom shot Kate a look and cocked his head, indicating the house. She bristled a little. It wasn't so long ago that she'd be in on conversations like this. It wouldn't be worth Tom's ire to argue, though, so she turned on her heel and went up the stairs. Joan opened the screen door for her. It was obvious Anna's wife had been standing there longer than a few moments, and Kate wondered if she'd overheard any of her conversation with Pawlik.

"You'll have to answer to Cromwell, you know, for talking to that cop," Joan said. "Hank Tudor likes to keep an eye on his wives, and when he's not around, he's got that Cromwell doing it for him."

Joan wasn't telling her anything she didn't already know. "Does he keep an eye on Anna?"

"What do you think?"

Kate was intrigued. She knew precious little about Anna and Hank's courtship and marriage, which had ended in record time. She'd always chalked it up to the fact that they were clearly not compatible sexually, but was it something else as well? "Do you know why they split up?" she ventured.

Joan smiled. "You know why they split up."

So much for that. Kate wondered if Hank was embarrassed about it, but then decided that his ego would be happy that it wasn't *him*. That was very possibly why he was so generous with her. Anna had been discreet, too, in that the tabloids never really paid attention to her, since Caitlyn had captured Hank's attention right away and she was much better fodder.

The screen door squeaked open, and as Tom stepped into the house, Joan disappeared toward the kitchen. Kate could see Pawlik's cruiser making its way down the drive.

"Mrs. Tudor," Cromwell said, "you shouldn't have talked to him without me present."

She made a face at him. "I texted you. Where were you?"

Tom ignored her question. "Hank said you were going to go into the city to start packing up your apartment. I'm heading that way, so I thought I could give you a ride."

Kate suddenly couldn't breathe. "Is there any way I can keep it? I've had that apartment a long time. It's rent-controlled." It was a weak argument now that she was married to a billionaire. "What about putting it in the name of an LLC or something like that?" she asked, grabbing at straws. "No one has to know."

"You must've known that you would have to give it up," Tom said. "If you don't, then people will talk. 'Why does the new Mrs. Tudor have her own apartment? Why doesn't she live with her husband?' The tabloids can't get a hold of that. You should know that more than anyone."

She did.

He leveled his gaze at her, and she squirmed before she could stop herself. "Hank wants you out of your apartment in two weeks. He wants to know that you're completely committed to him. Caitlyn Howard kept her apartment in LA. And look what happened to her."

Kate glanced at Tom's hands. The scratches that he casually dismissed had faded, but she could still see their faint lines.

"You know what I mean," Tom said. If he noticed her looking at his hands, he didn't indicate it. "She and Culpepper. Meeting there. And then you meet with him at *your* apartment. It doesn't look good."

No, it didn't. Asking Alex to meet her there had been a mistake.

Still, she wasn't ready to go pack up her apartment. Not today. Tom saw her hesitation.

"Don't worry, Kate. I'm not your babysitter. I'm only your escort." He attempted a smile, but it came out more like a grimace.

"It's not that," she said, hoping he didn't hear the lie. But before she could pull together an excuse, she heard Anna's voice behind her.

"I asked her not to go. Not today."

Tom's expression didn't change. "Why is that?"

Anna glanced at Kate, then looked back at Tom. "Maril has an appointment today that she can't cancel, and I asked Kate to spend some time with the children while Joan and I get some work done around here. Since we don't have guests at the moment, it gives us an opportunity we don't normally have." She hesitated, then added, "Hank has spoken to me about how he'd like Kate to get to know his children better."

Well played, Kate thought.

Tom sighed. "Okay." He leveled his gaze at Kate. "But you can't put this off too long."

"No, of course not," she said, trying to keep the relief out of her voice, but not sure she succeeded.

"I'll see you all later," Tom said. He pushed the door open and went down the front steps to his car.

Kate and Anna stood silent, watching through the screen until the car was out of sight.

"Thank you," Kate said. "Does Maril really have an appointment?"

"So she says."

"She's probably going to see her mother."

Anna chuckled. "Probably."

The convenience of Maril taking over the role of babysitter the past couple of days meant they'd had to turn a blind eye to her propensity for reporting everything back to Catherine.

"Are you okay?" Anna asked.

Kate smiled. "I am now."

Anna bit her lip as though debating what to say next.

"What?" Kate asked.

"Was Caitlyn pregnant?"

"Yes." It didn't matter how she'd found out, but if she were to hazard a guess, it would be that Joan *had* been eavesdropping.

"Who was the father?" Anna asked, as though she knew there was a question about that. When she didn't answer, Anna pressed. "Kate?"

Kate shook her head. "I don't know. Alex told me it wasn't his."

"Could it have been Hank's?"

Kate forced a smile. "You know better than that, Anna." She paused, then added, "None of this leaves this house."

"The police know she was pregnant. The media's going to find out. Someone will leak it."

Anna was right. It was inevitable. Kate hoped Lindsey was up to the challenge, since it was clear she wasn't going to be playing any role in crisis management. Except maybe as the supportive wife.

28

The day stretched out slowly, even though Lizzie and Ted kept Kate busy. Anna had been true to her word to Cromwell that Kate would play babysitter in Maril's absence.

She hadn't anticipated questions from them, though, about Caitlyn, underscoring her inexperience with children.

"Caitlyn's dead, isn't she?" Lizzie had asked in the middle of a croquet game on the back lawn, startling Kate with her frankness. "She's the woman the police found next door."

Ted had stopped running around the wickets and was as still as she'd ever seen him, staring at her with wide eyes. Having to explain about Caitlyn shouldn't be left to her—or even Anna or Maril. This was Hank's responsibility. But from what she'd seen, he wasn't here for the hard parts. The everyday life of his children was not his everyday life.

"That's right," Kate said. "It was Caitlyn."

"Do the police know who killed her?"

Lizzie's gaze was steady and unblinking. Kate glimpsed a force to be reckoned with. Hank should be on guard. The girl was eleven going on twenty-five.

"Not yet."

"I liked her. She was silly, but she let me try on her makeup." Lizzie flashed a sad smile.

"I liked her, too," Ted said. "She let me have ice cream for supper."

Kate wondered if she should give them a hug, but it felt awkward. Instead, she said, "It's good you have fond memories of her. I'm sure she liked you, too."

"Did you like her?" Lizzie asked, her eyes narrowing as though daring her to be honest.

"Yes," Kate said. "I liked her."

Lizzie's expression changed slightly, not believing her. Kate didn't think she'd believe herself, either.

To her relief, Lizzie turned back to the croquet game, deftly hitting the ball through the wickets, the conversation forgotten—for the time being, at least.

⚬━┿━⚬

The house was quiet and dark when Kate stepped into the hall early the next morning. She made her way soundlessly down the stairs in her socks, her sneakers in her hand. She was restless and hadn't slept well, tossing and turning all night, the empty spot in the bed next to her a reminder that the honeymoon phase was definitely over. She'd left a couple of voicemails and texts for Hank, but he still hadn't responded. Even though his anger had seemed to pass—*We're going to be so happy*—the radio silence was enough to justify her reluctance to start packing up her apartment.

She had to work out her stress.

Anna's gym was on the lower level of the house in the back, and to get there, Kate had to go outside, so she slipped her shoes on. The air was cool as it wrapped itself around her, belying the heat wave expected later in the day. A thin line of pink danced on the horizon above the water, the moon still bright in the sky.

Kate punched in the code to open the door. To her surprise, the room was brightly lit, a TV mounted on the far wall was on, and someone was running on one of the two treadmills. She recognized Will Stafford's back.

He was wearing earbuds, so he didn't register that she'd come in until she stepped up onto the treadmill next to him.

If it startled him to see her, he didn't indicate it, merely slowing down and pulling one of his earbuds out, his eyebrows raised.

"Can't sleep," she said simply as she started up the machine. The treadmill wasn't her preferred way of running, but it would have to do.

He got the message that she didn't want conversation, replacing the earbud and focusing on the TV in front of them. Kate felt her muscles burn as she pushed herself faster, her thoughts drifting away. It had been a while since she'd gone running—or worked out at all. It had been since before the wedding a little more than two weeks ago now. Hank had been giving her a different kind of workout, and she felt herself blushing, glancing over at Will, but he wasn't paying attention to her.

He was wearing shorts and a wifebeater, tattoos on his shoulders bleeding down underneath the shirt. If she had to guess, he was about her age.

He caught her looking and grinned. Now she was embarrassed; she hoped he didn't get the wrong impression. She certainly wasn't flirting, although if she were to be honest, she was curious about him. Their conversation in the car had piqued her interest in his background, but not enough to interrupt a much-needed workout. She turned her attention to the TV. The sound was off, the closed captioning on. The local weatherman was talking about the heat wave on its way. Temperatures would rise into the low nineties by the end of the week.

Sweat dripped down between Kate's breasts and she wished she'd worn a simple tank top and a pair of shorts instead of the short-sleeved T-shirt and long leggings. Suddenly, she felt a little lightheaded, and she slowed her pace. A tap on her arm, and she glanced over at Will, who was standing next to her with a bottle of water. She came to a stop and took the bottle.

"Thanks," she said, chugging it.

"Water's over there," he said, pointing to a small fridge in the corner—Anna thought of everything, didn't she? "I didn't expect to see you here," he added.

She walked the bottle over to the recycling bin and dropped it in. "You neither," she said.

"Have to get an early start. Lots of media attention. More now."

"Anna said you saw Caitlyn the night she was here."

Will nodded. "Yeah. Cops wanted our video from that night. She was crazy drunk when she left and nearly hit a tree as she drove out. But the car didn't go toward Tudor's house. She went in the opposite direction." He hesitated. "I shared our video of the road for the next three days and nights. To get to Tudor's house, you have to pass this place, since it dead-ends down there. She didn't come back. I don't know how she ended up over there."

Kate mulled that over for a few moments. "She could've been in a different car."

"Yeah, I thought about that. But our camera setup out there is top of the line. Ms. Carey insisted on it. It's the paparazzi problem. We were able to give the cops the license plates of every car that passed in those three days. I'm sure they're checking out each one."

It would certainly be like Joan to invest in such high-quality security. Anna was lucky her wife was so savvy. And he was right: Pawlik was going to follow up on any possible clues to Caitlyn's murder. Maybe he'd be able to find out who was in that Rolls that Anna had seen at Hank's house, too—Mary or someone else.

Kate turned these new facts around in her head, wondering what Pawlik was discovering, if anything. She caught a flash on the TV out of the corner of her eye. Footage of a fire from the day before, the closed captioning telling them that the body found in the rubble this morning had been identified.

Not another one.

And then she saw the name of the victim.

Margaret Pole.

29

A fire. She died in a fire.

Kate couldn't shake the thought that this was too much of a coincidence. A chance meeting with the woman on the beach. The woman's words, an ominous warning. Her mention of Catherine. It had to be a coincidence, didn't it? It was a sad, unfortunate accident. Yet now Margaret Pole, who seemed to know *something*, was conveniently dead.

Margaret told her that money covered it up. Was she talking about Nan Tudor? Kate was starting to have a bad feeling about this. Nan had written in her journal that *he* was going to kill her. Who was *he*?

How well do you know your husband?

Pawlik's question pinballed around in her head. No, Hank couldn't have had anything to do with Nan's disappearance. DNA doesn't lie. But money could buy any result, as long as there was enough of it. By thinking this, was she admitting that her husband—maybe Tom?—could've been responsible for a woman's brutal murder?

Kate wondered again how Anna knew Margaret Pole. She'd called her Maggie but acted like she didn't know who Kate had been talking about.

"Are you okay?"

Kate had forgotten that Will was there.

"I'm fine," she said with a tight smile. "See you later." She made her way to the door, pushed it open, and went upstairs to find Anna in the kitchen pouring hot water into a French press.

Anna didn't seem surprised to see her. "You're up early."

Kate slid onto one of the chairs at the island, wiping her forehead with a towel she'd snagged from the shelf in the gym. "Margaret Pole is dead."

Anna froze. "What?"

"It's on the news. There was a fire. She died in the fire."

Anna's face went white, but she didn't say anything, just finished up with the coffee press.

"You knew her," Kate said.

Anna set out two coffee mugs. She took her time in responding. Finally: "Not really. She came here. Once. She made me promise not to tell anyone. She said she'd made a promise to look out for Lizzie. Make sure she was doing well, that she was happy." She hesitated a moment, then added, "She told me Nan was dead."

Kate was quiet, processing what Anna said.

"Who did she make that promise to?"

Anna shrugged. "I don't know. She didn't tell me. I didn't ask," she added quickly.

"Weren't you curious?"

"Maybe. Not really. I was getting my business started. I didn't have time to wonder about anything."

"You never talked to her again?"

Anna shook her head. "No. I see her sometimes, in town, when I'm with the children. She's never approached me or them. She keeps her distance."

But the other day, Margaret Pole had come to the beach to talk to her, to Kate, to see the children close up. She'd managed to circumvent security somehow.

She remembered Margaret mentioning Catherine. What did Catherine Tudor know?

"Maybe we should talk to Catherine after all, like Margaret suggested," Kate heard herself saying. She'd dismissed the idea as crazy, but it crept back now. She didn't want to spend her life looking around corners, afraid of what her husband might have done. Because that's what this was about. The possibility that Hank might have done something—even if it were through someone else.

If he had, what would she do?

No. She couldn't think about that now. It was premature.

Kate didn't want to think what Hank would say if he found out she'd sought out his first wife for anything, much less answers about a decapitated body. They were already on tenterhooks.

Still, the idea wouldn't go away.

"Are you sure?" Anna asked. "I mean, you might learn something you won't want to know."

"If we find out first, we can make sure no one else does." It wasn't until she said it that Kate realized that despite her suspicions, she was still willing to protect her husband at all costs. She stood up a little straighter, a little more confident now that she had made up her mind.

For a moment, she worried that Anna wouldn't understand, but the other woman nodded and put her hand on Kate's arm. "I have something I need to share with you first. I wasn't sure what to think of it, but now . . ." She held up a finger, indicating Kate was to wait, and she left the room.

Kate had no idea what was going on. She got up, pushed the plunger down on the French press, then poured the coffee into the two mugs. By the time she'd added a little milk to hers, Anna was back, holding an envelope.

"What's that?"

Anna handed it to her. It was addressed to Anna, no return address.

Kate pulled a single piece of paper out of the envelope and read:

Watch out for yourself and the new one. You're both in danger.
Maggie

30

ANNA

She'd gotten the note the day before in the mail. She hadn't mentioned it because she didn't take it seriously. Maggie was a harmless old woman. Wasn't she? Maybe Anna should've paid more attention to it after all.

"First she's talking about money covering things up, telling me to talk to Catherine because she knows something, then she sends you a warning, and now she's dead," Kate said. "And not from natural causes."

"You think someone set that fire?"

"Not out of the realm of possibility." Kate hesitated. "I tried to find her online, but I couldn't find anything about her. It's like she never existed. Mary told me she knew her, but nothing more."

"Mary? You talked to Mary?"

A sheepish look crossed Kate's face. "Yes. I called her the other day. I was surprised she answered. She said I shouldn't tell anyone I'd talked to her. It was right before Hank came back and told me he'd identified Caitlyn."

Anna remembered how Tom told her not to tell anyone she'd seen Caitlyn. What was with all the cloak-and-dagger stuff? Who was everyone protecting? Could it be Hank? *Could* he have had something to do with this—and what might have happened to Nan? Anna wished she'd read more of that diary before it went missing.

When Maggie had told her with certainty that Nan Tudor was dead, Anna hadn't questioned it; there was something about the way she'd said it that made Anna believe her. Maggie knew something all right. And Anna had left it alone. It was easier not knowing.

"I'm going up to get changed," Kate announced, sliding off the stool. "I'd like to see Catherine before lunch. Catch her off guard."

Anna wasn't sure about Kate's idea to talk to Catherine, but she could tell that Kate had latched on to it, desperate to believe that her husband was innocent and wanting to protect him at all costs. That had been her job, after all, protecting Hank Tudor.

But wasn't that the job of all his wives? Anna was still protecting him, too. Granted, legally she had to. Those papers she'd signed had all but guaranteed her continued silence. No one was ever to know about their life together, anything about Hank Tudor's personal life. She was sworn to secrecy about his children, the money, her business. She wasn't even allowed to tell Joan. Their finances were completely separate. Joan had readily agreed; she had her own accounts and didn't want any ties to Hank's. Every once in a while, Joan dropped a comment that if Hank "got into trouble" she didn't want to be entangled in it.

Anna couldn't let Kate go see Catherine alone. Kate was a bundle of nervous energy, anxious to believe that her new husband was only a man who loved his wives until he didn't—and he had nothing to do with any who ended up dead.

It was going to be tricky, especially since Cromwell was lurking around somewhere. It wouldn't be easy to get past him. She was also going to have to figure out how to get out of here without the paparazzi catching on to their destination. That would be a disaster in more ways than one, if they discovered she and Kate were visiting Hank's first wife. Will Stafford might be helpful, as he was when Kate went to the city to meet up with Alex Culpepper, although Anna was still upset that he'd abandoned her with Tom the other night. He'd seemed contrite when she confronted him, vowed it wouldn't happen again. But a little bit of her trust in him had eroded.

Anna was in the middle of making breakfast for the children, who would be down soon, when Joan came into the kitchen.

"Penny for your thoughts." Joan sidled up to Anna, her arm making its way around Anna's waist.

Anna leaned into her, resting her head on Joan's shoulder. "Mmmm," she whispered into her wife's neck. "Maybe we need a vacation. Go somewhere. An island, maybe, somewhere tropical where we could be alone and forget all this for a little while."

Joan chuckled. "Problem with owning a small business like this is it's hard to get away."

"No kidding." Anna straightened up. "I guess I should've known what I was doing when I signed on to this."

"You love this."

"I love it when my ex-husband's ex-wife's body isn't found next door." She tried to keep her voice light, but as she said it, the weight of her words pressed against her chest and a rush of sadness overwhelmed her.

Joan was gesturing to the ceiling. "Is she okay?" she asked.

Anna knew she was asking about Kate. "As well as she can be."

"He was angry when he left the other day."

Anna nodded. "I know."

"Do you know where he went?"

"Kate said he was going to Frankfurt on business."

"That's not where he went first, though," Joan said.

"What do you mean?"

"All I know is, I overheard Hank telling Cromwell that he had to 'take care of' what he called 'the Culpepper situation,'" Joan said, using air quotes.

That could mean any number of things, and Anna didn't like any of them.

"And that cop, the one who's hanging around? He told *her* yesterday that your ex-husband went to see Culpepper and now Culpepper is missing."

Kate hadn't mentioned that. But Anna hadn't mentioned Maggie's note, either. While they had formed an odd bond the past couple of days, it was clear neither of them completely trusted the other.

"How do you know all this?" Anna didn't know whether to be upset with Joan for eavesdropping or impressed that she managed to get all this information.

A smile played at the corners of Joan's mouth. "It's like I'm invisible around here. The lesbian who married the famous Hank Tudor's ex-wife."

Invisible, maybe, to Hank and Tom, but to the media that was always lurking at the perimeters of their lives, definitely not. Although it was much easier for Joan to go out on her own. They didn't follow her if Anna wasn't with her.

Anna gave her a playful slap on the arm. "Don't tease me."

"I like teasing you. You're far too serious all the time."

Anna fidgeted, impatient now.

Joan chuckled. "Okay, okay. I know something else. Cromwell's not coming back here. At least not today."

"And you know this how? More invisibility?"

Joan chuckled again. "No. He called to let us know, to be *courteous*. I talked to him a few minutes ago."

That seemed a bit out of character. But it would mean that she and Kate could go see Catherine without worrying about Tom's watchful eye.

"Hank should have taken *her* with him," Joan was saying.

"Who?"

"Her. Upstairs."

Joan never used Kate's name. Why not? It was usually "her" or "Wife Number Six."

"You don't like her, do you?" Anna asked. "Why not?"

Joan shrugged. "It's not that I don't like her. It's just that she seems too smart to marry him. She should know better. It's not like she didn't know his history."

"I knew his history and married him," Anna said.

Joan stepped back and studied her face. "He'd had only three wives then, and the last one had died a tragic death. He'd loved her."

"He loved all of them." Anna was taken aback by the sharp tone of her voice.

"Did he? Did he love *you*?"

Before Anna could even think of a way to respond, Joan said, "You were a business merger. Caitlyn Howard was his midlife crisis, and that one upstairs, she's the one who will get him back the respect that he wants after that last disaster of a wife."

"He loves her," Anna said, biting back her anger.

"Does he? That man only thinks about himself and what pleases *him*. She's only the latest, and she won't be the last." Joan shook her head. "He should have stayed with Catherine. Would have saved all of you a lot of grief."

March 12

Tonight was the first time I was truly afraid of him. We spent so much time falling in love that it surprised me, the ferocity of his anger. I wasn't completely innocent. I wanted to see how far I could push him. I wanted to see if he still wanted me, even a little bit. I haven't told him I'm pregnant yet, and I'm not showing. Not that he would notice any change in my body anyway, since he hasn't touched me or seen me naked in over a month. He's been spending nights at the office. I know he's with Jeanne. I don't have to see them together to know.

I decided to throw him a surprise birthday party. I hired extra help in the kitchen, waiters, bartenders, a band. Jeanne wasn't invited, but she came anyway. She flounced in, wearing a dreadful green dress that hugged her in all the wrong places. She's pale, her hair is too short, and she has an unusually high voice. But men were watching her, vying for her attention. I don't see it. The attraction. Maybe it's in the way she pretends to be inferior. Hangs on the word of every man who speaks to her. She doesn't challenge them. Doesn't have a mind of her own.

Is that what he wants? We've spent hours debating politics, religion, social issues. I never noticed that he'd tired of it, that our banter slowed to a halt so now any evening we spend together is spent in silence.

But I digress. This was about me. About my plan to see if I could reclaim my husband from someone like her. Even though I noticed him watching her from *across the room, that look on his face that he used to have when he looked at me. His wife.*

Charlie Brandon was easy. He drinks too much and doesn't have a filter. He'll fuck anything that pays him any attention. When I touched Charlie's arm, grazed his lips with mine when he arrived, something I never do, it took him by surprise, but I could see the interest. He knows about Jeanne. About how my husband doesn't want me.

It makes me fair game.

I don't care about Mary, his wife, Hank's sister. She's hated me from the beginning. And she's had to put up with more than her husband doing a little flirting at a party.

At least that was the plan. I didn't think it would get out of hand, but when I saw Jeanne adjusting her dress after a trip to the bathroom, him following, tucking in his shirt, their faces flushed, something snapped inside me. I know the way he is, that he won't actually fuck her before they're married, but that doesn't mean he's a complete monk. He likes to take it to the edge; he likes foreplay.

Charlie is a terrible kisser, but I let him kiss me. I let him grope my breasts. I tried not to cringe; I had to make it look good. I had to make him think that I liked it, that I was enjoying myself like he was enjoying himself.

No one noticed. No one saw us. Charlie gave me a grin and a sloppy, wet kiss and went to get another drink.

So I grabbed the guy with the band. The young one with the face like a movie star who played bass. He didn't have time to react before I kissed him. For a moment, he kissed me back, my eyes closed, and I remembered what it was like to kiss like that, before Jeanne, when Hank was still with Catherine and wanted me.

What was I doing? I didn't want this guy. I wanted my husband. I wanted my husband to want me, not only because he might get jealous. I was being stupid. There were other ways. I blamed this on my hormones, being pregnant, desperate. It was fortunate that it seemed no one noticed this kiss, either. I straightened myself out and began to mingle, making small talk, trying to meet Hank's eye. In the early days, we'd go to parties and share smiles and winks and nods, eager to be alone and gossip about our guests. Maybe we could do that tonight, I thought. Maybe Jeanne would go home and Hank would stay and I could make this work.

They began to leave, the guests, the people I'd invited to be my audience but who'd let me down. Fortuitously. Finally, I was alone with the one person I'd wanted to hurt.

There had been a time when we'd argue, shouting at each other, but instead of turning us against each other, it brought us together. We'd make passionate love for two days after, I would be sore with pleasure, and he would call me every hour to tell me he loved me.

This time, it was different. We weren't those people anymore. And my behavior hadn't gone as unnoticed as I'd thought.

He grabbed me by the hair and shoved his hand up my dress, forcing his finger inside me. "Is this what you want?" he asked me. His voice was low, measured, as though he were asking me if I wanted wine with dinner. And then he took me from behind like a farm animal.

Afterward, he told me to clean myself up, that "next time" he wouldn't be so gentle. That I was still his wife and he expected me to behave like I was, that if he ever saw me kissing another man, he'd kill me.

I believed him. I saw the hate in his eyes, and for a moment his hand shook, like he wanted to hit me. Or worse. I forced myself not to start shaking, to look him in the eye even though all I wanted to do was curl up in a ball and cry. I wouldn't give him the satisfaction, though. I stood my ground, hiding my fear.

And then he called her. Right in front of me. Told her he'd be right over.

He didn't say goodbye.

He just left.

31

CATHERINE

Catherine had committed every word to memory. She ran her hand across the handwriting, tracing the bold penmanship of the woman who'd replaced her, the woman who'd had too much confidence—and then not enough. She'd been stupid for what she'd done. She should have known better.

Catherine pushed herself up from the chair, letting the diary fall onto the cushion, its pages closing over Nan's pain.

Catherine went upstairs and into the bathroom. She shook a Xanax into her palm and swallowed it with a glass of water. Never mind that it was ten o'clock in the morning. She would need it to get through the next few hours.

They were coming, and she had to be ready.

She dressed carefully, putting on a pair of black slacks and a white blouse from her life before the divorce. She'd put on weight, so it tugged against the extra pounds, but a light cardigan covered it up. She'd blown her hair dry, happy that she'd had the hairdresser in last week. The gray was camouflaged by a soft reddish-brown, the same shade her hair had been when they'd met. Her complexion was like porcelain because of her confinement, and she considered and finally rejected blush. She brushed mascara on her lashes, accentuating her large brown eyes, and a light pink lipstick was the final touch.

Catherine surveyed herself in the full-length mirror in the bedroom. She could have been the woman after, instead of the woman before.

The clock ticked audibly from across the room. Catherine sat stiffly, perched on the sofa for fear of wrinkling her outfit.

The doorbell startled her, even though she'd been expecting it. She heard Lourdes come through from the kitchen to the foyer, the light from the open door stretching all the way in here.

She didn't stand up. They had to come to her.

She studied the taller one first. This was the new one. Kate Parker, her name was. She was all angles, her hair swept up into a loose bun against her neck, a white sheath dress with a simple green scarf. She could see what Hank saw in her, an elegance, a grace, but at the same time there was a visible nervous energy that she couldn't hide. This wouldn't be to her advantage with Hank, if she couldn't conceal her anxiety. Hank would pluck at her weakness until there was nothing left.

The other one, this Anna Klein, she was a different sort. How Hank hadn't seen it in her, he who was usually so observant. It hadn't been love that had kept the truth from him. More likely he'd been too consumed with greed for her wealth, her company, to notice. She was curvy in beige linen slacks and a white T-shirt, her long chestnut hair plaited back, but it was the serenity in her face that Catherine found herself envying.

These two women couldn't be more different, yet here they were, together. She felt that adrenaline rush she used to get before a meeting, when she was in control.

"What can I do for you?" she asked, not bothering with niceties. If they were surprised that she wasn't surprised to see them, they didn't indicate it. She had to admit her curiosity was piqued, unsure why they'd paid her this visit. But instead of keeping her off-balance, she liked this game, to see if she could continue to stay ahead of them.

"Hank doesn't know we're here," Anna Klein admitted.

Catherine gave a short snort. "I wouldn't think so."

"It would be best if he didn't find out," she added.

Catherine met Anna's eyes and, after a second, nodded. "I see."

This wasn't a scenario Hank would find at all comforting. He'd immediately suspect that they were up to no good—and he'd be right. If he found out about this, it wouldn't end well for any of them. She would keep their secret, but they would have to make sure that there was a reason for her not to tell Hank.

Despite her first impression of Kate Parker, the woman leveled her eyes at her, a steely gaze that Catherine had to force herself to meet. Now she knew why Hank had married her. Her strength was palpable, not dissimilar from the second one.

"We'd like some information."

Kate Parker hadn't spoken. It was the other one, Anna Klein, who sank down onto the end of the sofa to her right, hands folded neatly in her lap, a kind smile. Catherine didn't trust her.

"Information about what? I can't imagine what I can help you with." She thought about the stories she could tell.

Kate Parker now sat on the other side of her, at the other end of the sofa. They were tag-teaming her, and for a few seconds she was impressed by their moxie, as though they were employees looking for a raise or promotion.

"Margaret Pole."

Catherine kept her expression neutral; she'd learned in the corporate boardroom how to do that. Never let them see your weakness—or your fear. "I haven't seen her in years," she said truthfully.

"Why not?" Anna Klein asked, her tone sincere. She truly wanted to know.

"I haven't left this house," Catherine said. "I've secluded myself here."

"But you must have spoken to her." This from Kate Parker. Catherine didn't like that they were on opposite sides of her. She had to swivel her head back and forth. She'd made the wrong decision by not sitting in the chair across from the sofa. She hadn't figured that they'd play it this way.

"Why on earth would you think that?"

"She told me to come talk to you," Kate continued.

"About what?"

"She told me to ask you about the body that was never identified."

Relief rushed through her. They weren't here about the girl. "Ask me what, exactly?"

"Do you know what Maggie was talking about?" Anna asked, her voice soft yet firm at the same time.

"There was something about a body, but no one ever discovered who it was," Catherine said. "I believe it was on Martha's Vineyard. It was unfortunately near Hank's home. Very sad." She wasn't telling tales out of school. She wasn't saying anything anyone else wouldn't be able to find out.

"You don't know who it was?" Kate prodded.

Catherine smiled patronizingly. "How on earth would I know? I certainly wasn't there at the time. Since I haven't seen Margaret in years, I have no idea why she would have said anything like that to you."

"Margaret said that money covered it up."

"Covered what up?" Catherine kept her tone measured. Maggie hadn't been a threat for a long time. She'd taken the money and kept quiet. Yet the phone call the other day had been Maggie's mistake. Somehow Maggie had pieced it together, saw that it all came back to her, not Hank, after all. Maggie might not have allowed herself to be bought off this time. How long would it have been before she spoke to the police? Maggie had sealed her fate by underestimating her. Catherine couldn't take any chances. Maggie had to die, her secrets with her. So it was arranged. But *had* her secrets also died? What, exactly, did these two wives know?

Kate leaned forward. "Margaret is dead," she said.

"Yes, I know. I saw it on the news. I'm sorry about that, of course, as anyone would be."

"You were friends?"

"I wouldn't say friends."

"What, then?"

"I really don't think I can help you."

Anna shifted forward now, leaning her elbows on her knees. "I think you can," she said softly.

Catherine had had enough. "I'm not surprised Margaret was murdered. She was always on the wrong side of things. What I *am* surprised at is that it didn't happen sooner."

Anna frowned. "No one said she was murdered."

32

Catherine knew she'd made a mistake the moment she'd spoken. Kate noticed the slight tic of her eyebrow.

"That's right. Margaret died in a fire." Her tone was steady, not too soft, not too loud. "But someone on the TV said it might have been arson."

Kate and Anna exchanged a look.

"We hadn't heard that," Kate said.

Catherine shrugged. "Maybe it's true, maybe it's not. I'm just saying what I heard."

"You said she was on the wrong side of things. Wrong side of what?" Kate pressed.

Catherine sighed, as though she were being put out. "I don't have time for gossip."

"We're not looking for gossip, only the truth."

"The truth isn't going to help you," she said.

It was a curious thing to say. "We're not looking for help, per se," Kate said. "We just want to know what you know about Margaret."

Catherine gave her a small smile. "You're better off not knowing. You have to know that by now."

She did, but she couldn't let it go. "Do *you* think it was arson? Did she have any enemies?" Kate persisted.

"We all have enemies, my dear, and some of them are closer than we think." Her gaze wandered to Anna, settled on her face.

"If you know anything," Anna said, "maybe you should talk to the police."

Catherine cocked her eyebrow. "Of course not. I never speak to the police about anything. And you shouldn't, either." She paused. "I'm curious why you're so worried about Maggie when that poor girl was murdered on your doorstep." She was talking to Anna. "You ought to watch out for yourself."

Curious that she was giving them the same warning Margaret Pole had, Kate thought. But before either she or Anna could respond, the woman who'd answered the door when they arrived came into the room. She was carrying a tray with a china teapot and cups. She set it down on the coffee table in front of them.

"Thank you, Lourdes," Catherine said, but her tone was icy. She hadn't wanted to entertain, it was clear, but Lourdes hadn't gotten the memo.

As Lourdes began pouring the tea, Kate stood. "Bathroom?" she asked Catherine.

Despite her clear annoyance, Catherine waved her hand in the air and said, "Down the hall and to the left."

As she left the room, Kate took a deep breath. She needed to get out of there for a few moments, regroup. Try to figure out how they could get anything at all out of Catherine, who didn't have any intention of telling them anything about Margaret Pole. Anna was right, and Kate should have listened: this was an exercise in futility.

She found the small half bath, but instead of going inside, she spotted another open door just beyond it. Kate glanced around behind her, as though Catherine—or Lourdes—might be lurking, but no one was there. She stepped inside a large room lined from floor to ceiling with built-in bookshelves overflowing with books. A marble fireplace was at one end, plump cushioned chairs and a coffee table in front of it. This was the kind of library Kate had always dreamed of having, she thought, as she scanned some of the books. A whole section for US history, another for British history. Pulitzer winners lined up together. Biographies. Rows of mystery novels. Kate could spend days here. Was this what Catherine did, sequestered in her home, read all day in this cozy space? Because despite its size, the room felt small, lived in.

An array of framed photographs sat on the fireplace mantel. Even though she should get back, Kate was drawn to them, curious. She peered at the faces: a much younger Catherine, a much younger Hank, their arms intertwined, looking at each other with obvious affection. Maril, dressed as a princess in pink, her parents holding her hands, a happy family. And Catherine and Hank's wedding picture: Catherine swathed in a cloud of tulle and lace, Hank in a tuxedo. That couple looked so happy, so *in love*. Kate thought about her wedding, the blue dress, Hank's business suit. Should she have held out for this, a royal wedding?

What was she doing? This wasn't right. Kate turned but, in her haste to leave, bumped against the coffee table. She leaned down to rub her knee and saw it. A small brown leather-bound book that looked vaguely familiar. It was facedown on the table, as though someone had been reading it and was interrupted. She picked it up and saw the familiar handwriting.

Nan Tudor's journal. How did Catherine end up with it? It certainly couldn't have gotten here by itself. Someone had taken it from Anna's and brought it here.

It had to be Maril. That would make sense. Maril had been at the inn the whole time, except yesterday, when she'd had an errand to run. Anna had even speculated that she might be visiting her mother. She could have found the diary in the shoebox and brought it with her. That was the most likely scenario.

Kate had thought the book was gone, that Nan Tudor's secrets had disappeared before she'd had the opportunity to peer inside these pages and see what happened to her. What happened between her and Hank. Now that she held it in her hand, she didn't want to let it go. Couldn't let it go.

But she couldn't exactly take it. She had no way of concealing it. And then she had a thought. She pulled her phone out of her pocket and started taking pictures. Because she didn't know how much time she had, she couldn't photograph every page but randomly chose entries in order starting with the first one. While she wished she could read every one, this would have to do, although she did make sure to get the last few. When she was done, she turned the book over the way she'd found it, returned her phone to her pocket, and went back out to join Anna and Catherine.

They were sipping tea without conversation. Lourdes was nowhere to be found. Kate wondered if she'd been spying on her from somewhere, but it was too late now if she had been. Catherine didn't seem to notice how long she'd been gone, and if she did, she didn't say anything.

As she sat, Kate was struck by how surreal this was. Three of Hank Tudor's wives having tea together.

"Did you ever meet Caitlyn Howard?" Kate asked, to break the silence, curious to hear what Catherine would say.

"Yes, poor girl."

"You *did* meet her?"

Catherine sipped her tea before answering. "Once."

She was so guarded. Kate couldn't really blame her, considering what she'd gone through. Catherine had fought long and hard for her right to be Hank Tudor's wife and was still fighting.

"When was that?" Kate asked, trying to keep her tone casual. She could see Anna frowning, wondering what she was up to.

Catherine waved her hand in the air. "I can't remember."

Kate was pretty sure she did.

"She was pregnant when she was killed."

Catherine's lip twitched slightly, and then she abruptly stood. "It's time for you to go. You can find your way out yourselves." With that, she left the room.

"What was that about?" Anna asked.

Kate grabbed her bag and shook her head. "She's right. It's time to go."

The car was parked in the front drive, and they climbed in. Anna's knuckles were white as she gripped the steering wheel and the car moved out into the road, leaving Catherine's house behind. As Kate looked back, she saw Lourdes on the front step, staring after them.

They'd only gone a block or so when Kate said, "Catherine has Nan's diary."

"What?"

Kate told her how she'd found it in the library.

"How on earth did it get from my house to Catherine's?"

"I'm thinking Maril."

Anna nodded. "You're probably right."

"I took pictures. Of the pages. I wanted to take the journal itself but couldn't figure out how. This was the best way."

"Why did you do that?"

"Because I want to know what it says."

Anna snorted. "Caitlyn had it and she ended up dead."

"You think it has some sort of curse on it?" Kate chuckled nervously.

"No. I don't believe in curses." Anna was serious. "But I do believe that there are some things we shouldn't know."

"But it could hold the truth about Nan."

"That's exactly right."

"And possibly the truth about Caitlyn."

"Do you really want to know what happened to her, Kate?" The question hung between them, and Kate weighed her answer carefully before answering.

"Yes."

"Why?"

Kate bit her lip and looked out the window. "Because I have to make sure it doesn't happen to me, too."

Anna gave a low chuckle. "What happened to Caitlyn won't happen to you. Hank loves you."

Until he doesn't, Kate thought, and he might have already started down that road. Her phone vibrated in her pocket, and she wiggled to pull it out.

A text.

From Alex Culpepper.

I need to see you. It's important.

33

CATHERINE

She'd planned on leaving the room like that. It would send the message that they couldn't control her, that she held all the cards—until Lourdes said she saw Kate in the library.

"She was taking pictures of a book."

Lourdes didn't have to tell her anything more. She'd made a mistake, leaving the journal there instead of securing it safely upstairs in her room with the computers. But she'd had no way of knowing that Kate Parker would snoop like that.

"I am so sorry, Mrs. Catherine," Lourdes kept saying.

"Don't worry about it," Catherine told her. They would wonder how she got it, come to their own conclusions.

Maggie must have wondered where it had gone when it went missing. Catherine was surprised the woman hadn't put *that* together, too. But maybe she had, just hadn't gotten around to confronting Catherine about it yet. In the larger scheme of things, the theft of a journal wasn't nearly as important as the death of two women.

It hadn't been easy reading, seeing the demise of her own relationship with Hank and the rise of That Woman after all she'd done for her. Catherine had liked her, saw her ambition. In the beginning, before she saw the threat, she even began to groom her. She'd been particularly impressed with how she'd planned that masquerade event. She'd had talent, and if she'd continued to reject Hank's overtures, she might have been able to run one of the businesses in her own right—and still be running it. That women-in-management initiative had been brilliantly executed and was still being used at Tudor Enterprises. Hank may discard wives, but he knew enough not to discard good ideas.

She should have gotten rid of the diary, but after a few days of digesting its contents, she realized it could give her leverage someday—if it ever came to that. Enter Caitlyn Howard.

When they started asking her if she'd met the girl, she should have known that Kate discovered the journal. But Kate didn't know that she'd given it to Caitlyn.

The more she thought about it, the more it didn't bother her—that the new wife had found it. It wasn't as though she could do anything with the knowledge. She couldn't tattle on her to Hank.

No, she wasn't concerned about the diary. But she *was* concerned about their questions about Maggie. She'd made a mistake bringing up the arson. It hadn't been in the news—yet.

Curious that they hadn't seemed to know what Maggie's connection was. And while Maggie had told them to come see her, she hadn't explained why. Maggie might not have told them anything else in the end. But Catherine had no regrets. Things had been put in motion long before Maggie caught on.

And now it was time for the next move.

Catherine punched the familiar number into her phone.

"Yes?"

"It's time," Catherine said.

Hesitation.

"It seems too soon."

"No. Now." She didn't have to explain herself or her decisions. She was as sure of this as she'd been when she ran Hank's companies. She trusted her instincts. They were telling her that she couldn't wait any longer. "Are you ready?"

"Yes. You know I am."

"Then get it done."

She hit END.

34

Kate's gut reaction was to ghost Culpepper. Delete the text and pretend she'd never heard from him. But before she could, another text came through:

You might want to know what your husband's up to.

He wasn't wrong. She *did* want to know, even if it wasn't just so she wouldn't get caught off guard with the police again.

OK

He wanted Kate to meet him at a small hotel on the East Side.

Kate didn't like that idea, not wanting to be alone with him again. She didn't know for certain that he *hadn't* killed Caitlyn. She thought about the most public places she could meet him.

Central Park. Bethesda Fountain. Two hours.

He texted back a thumbs-up emoji without any argument.

Kate didn't want to share her plans with Anna. Instead, she asked if she could drop her off at the train station. "I want to go to my apartment. I need some time alone."

"That's not a great idea," Anna said. Will Stafford was waiting for them at the inn. She'd called him when they started back, as arranged, so he could manage the paparazzi.

"I don't care," Kate said. "We weren't followed." At least as far as she knew. "I'll be able to get on the train and no one will be the wiser."

Anna must have sensed she wasn't going to let up, so she reluctantly agreed.

"Thank you," Kate said as Anna pulled up in front of the station.

Anna reached over and put her hand on Kate's arm. "Be careful," she said, reminding her of Maggie's note.

Kate gave her a smile. "Of course." She climbed out of the car and felt Anna's eyes on her as she walked toward the station.

Once she settled in on the train, she began thumbing through her phone. Nan's diary was in here. She opened the first image, the handwriting a little hard to see on the small screen. She stretched it out with her thumb and finger so it was larger. And then she started to read.

⋄

When the train stopped at Grand Central, Kate was happy to put her phone away. She needed a break from the diary, to process what she'd read. She wasn't sure if she could finish it, didn't know if she wanted to know what happened to cause Nan to disappear. She'd resisted the impulse to start with the end, wanting to see how their relationship had progressed. Nan gave her insight into her husband, but she didn't like it. She could say he'd changed, but he hadn't, not really. Hank was Hank, and the man Nan had married was the same man *she'd* married.

What did that mean for *her*?

Kate had been so confident that she and Hank could make it work, that there wouldn't be a Wife Number Seven. But when he'd put Caitlyn's ring on her finger, well, that had been cruel. He'd seemed to enjoy watching her squirm. And the silence ever since he'd left that night didn't bode well.

After those first two magical just-married weeks together, it felt as though their marriage was already falling apart.

She checked her watch. She had enough time to catch a cab to her apartment before heading on foot to the fountain to meet Alex. She wanted to change out of her dress and put on a pair of jeans, a T-shirt, sneakers, something less formal. When the cab came to a stop in front of her building, she got out, pushing open the door and welcoming the familiarity as she climbed the stairs. She slid her key into her door lock and stepped inside. She didn't notice the boxes until she'd shut the door behind her. They were piled up neatly next to the bookshelves, taunting her.

Someone had been here. Someone had been inside her apartment.

She shouldn't be surprised. She'd told Hank she was going to start packing. He'd probably had the boxes delivered to make it more convenient for her. But she still felt violated. And angry.

And that's when she spotted the small rectangular box with the red ribbon tied around it in the middle of her kitchen island. She put her bag down and picked up the box, a small piece of folded paper fluttering to the floor. She ignored it, tugged on the ribbon, and opened the box. Inside was a diamond pendant in the shape of a heart. It was small and tasteful and exactly what she would have chosen herself. She reached down and picked up the paper.

"Darling Kate," it read, "let's not fight. Hank."

Kate closed her eyes and took a deep breath. She put the necklace around her neck, the cold diamond settling against her skin, reminding her that Hank loved her—and that he was pulling all the strings.

The buzzer startled her. She hit the intercom and said, "Yes?"

"Kate, it's me, Alex."

"How did you know I was here?" she asked warily.

"I was walking to the park to meet you, and I saw you come in. Let me up, Kate. It's important. Seriously important."

"Go on ahead, and I'll meet you at the park. Give me fifteen minutes." Her voice sounded unnaturally calm, while her stomach was doing jumping jacks.

"Come on, Kate. Please?" His tone was frantic, desperate.

"No," she said. Didn't he understand that she couldn't let him back in? Someone—Cromwell, Hank—would find out and she couldn't risk that.

Silence. Good.

She crumpled Hank's note in her palm and went to the other side of the island, tossing it in the trash can under the sink. But then she heard the doorknob, and she froze as the door opened. She hadn't locked it.

Alex Culpepper walked in.

The last time she'd seen him, he'd been his movie star self, tall, confident, good looking. But today his hair was tousled, his eyes bloodshot, his cheeks blotchy, and he hunched over as though in pain.

"What do you want?" she demanded. "I didn't invite you in."

"Kate," he pleaded, lunging toward her, trapping her against the counter, her arms behind her.

Panic rose in her throat. She felt around and her fingers closed over one of the knives in the block.

He leaned in closer.

She could smell the liquor on him, his breath hot against her face. "You shouldn't be here, Alex." She tried to keep her voice calm, but her entire body was shaking with fear.

Suddenly, he stepped back.

"I'm not the father of Caitlyn's baby. Your husband is."

35

Kate gripped the knife, and the sharp blade sliced into her thumb. She let go and looked at her hand. Blood dripped along her palm.

"Are you all right?" Alex asked, his tone anxious, his gaze settling on the blood.

Was she? No. Not at all.

His face had gone white.

"Are *you* all right?" She grabbed a dish towel and wound it around her hand.

"It's embarrassing, but I might faint." He was looking everywhere except at her hand.

"Don't like blood?"

"No."

She gently pulled the towel off her hand and peered at her thumb, glad for the distraction. "It doesn't look too bad." She went to the sink and turned on the faucet, putting her hand underneath the stream of water. She flinched when the water hit the wound, but the pain subsided quickly. "Can you get me a bandage? There's a box under the sink in the bathroom." Was that her voice? Calm, soft. Not at all matching how she felt.

Alex walked around the corner, then came back with the box of Band-Aids. He fumbled with it, but she didn't try to help him. The wound had begun to bleed again, so she stuck it under the faucet, welcoming the initial pain, happy to have the momentary distraction. He turned his back again while she patted it dry and managed to get the bandage around it. "I'm all set now," she said. "All clear."

He turned around. "I'm sorry." Was he sorry for not being able to help with her first aid—or was it more that he was sorry about telling her that Hank was the father of Caitlyn's baby?

Even though she desperately wanted to deny that her husband could have slept with his ex-wife while wooing *her*, Kate had no reason to believe Alex was lying. It wasn't as though she hadn't considered the possibility once she'd found out about the pregnancy. Caitlyn may have been a lot of things, but she wasn't a slut, despite the rumors. She'd stepped out on Hank, but only with Alex. She'd loved him. But she'd also loved Hank. And Hank had most definitely loved her.

She absently twisted the diamond engagement ring on her finger, the ghost of Caitlyn's still haunting her. When had Hank actually gotten it back? After they'd had sex? Had she willingly given it to him, like he'd said? Kate had been so oblivious those last months Hank was married to Caitlyn. They'd begun their courtship, their attraction growing. He hadn't wanted to sleep with her, but was that because he "respected" her like he'd said, or was it because he was still sleeping with Caitlyn?

"How did you find out?" she asked Alex.

He knew what she was asking. "He told me. He came to my hotel room the other night."

Pawlik was telling her the truth, then, that Hank had gone to see Alex. He must have known he was the baby's father when he left her at Anna's. But when did he find out?

"How far along was she?" she asked. Her voice sounded far away, like it was someone else speaking on the other side of the room, the other side of the building.

Alex stared at her as though he didn't understand the question.

"How far along?" she repeated. "Do you know?"

"She said three months."

Her heart was pounding so hard in her chest that she had to take two deep breaths, trying to make sense of all of this. "What did Hank want when he went to see you? At your hotel, I mean." She had a suspicion and wasn't sure it was wise asking, but she had to.

He gave a short snort. "He offered me money to disappear for a little while. He said if anyone asked, I should lie and tell them I was the father." He shoved his hand into his pocket and pulled out a crumpled piece of paper, tossing it on the island. "I don't know why I took it, but I don't want it. It's blood money."

Kate picked it up. It was a check. A check from an LLC that she'd never heard of, made out to Alex Culpepper for fifty thousand dollars.

"He said there'd be more where that came from, if I did what he asked."

While Kate wanted to believe this was Cromwell's idea, she knew better than that.

"What about DNA? Wouldn't the police know?"

"He said he could take care of that."

Money covered it up. Is that what had happened the last time, too?

"Did he threaten you, I mean, if you refused?"

Alex raised his eyebrows at her. "What do you think?" He hesitated a moment, then said, "The police want to talk to me. I've been holed up in Brooklyn with a friend. No one knows where I've been. But they need to know about him. That he tried to buy me off."

Kate's breath caught in her throat. "No," she said. "Don't talk to the police."

Alex snorted. "You're still trying to protect him? I guess I shouldn't be surprised. You're the one who bought me off with the Bond gig to get me to stay away from Caitlyn. I was a fucking idiot for agreeing to it." He hesitated, then added, "The irony is that's when they started fucking again, and you didn't even know it. If you hadn't done what you did, she wouldn't have gotten pregnant by him."

But Hank had filed for divorce then. He told her he couldn't trust Caitlyn anymore. That Kate was who he wanted to be with. A thunderous noise filled her ears. Alex's mouth was moving, but for a moment, she couldn't hear him; if she let herself, she wouldn't be able to ignore it.

"He killed Caitlyn," Alex was saying. "I know it. You have to save yourself. Get out of it while you can. Before he can destroy you, too—or worse."

Kate struggled to regain her composure. She'd deal with her emotions later. For now, she had to convince Alex not to go to the police. "You know that Hank couldn't possibly have killed Caitlyn. He was with me the past two weeks. If you go to the police, you will only look like a jealous lover. You can't prove anything." She hesitated a moment. "The police have been looking for *you*. They think *you* killed her." At least that's what Anna had told her. Alex didn't have to know that Pawlik was looking at both him *and* Hank.

She glanced down at the check in her hand. In a swift move, Alex grabbed for it, and it tore in half, the pieces floating to the floor.

Her cell phone rang, startling them both. Kate swung around and spotted it on the kitchen counter, the face lit up with Hank's number. So now he was calling her. The irony didn't escape her. Should she answer it, or should she let it go to voicemail? She looked at Alex, as though he'd give her the answer.

Instead, he said, "I can't keep letting you and Tudor run my life." He picked up the pieces of the check, stuffed them in his pocket, and went to the door. As he opened it, he turned around and looked her in the eye. "Be careful, Kate. He's dangerous." And with that, he left, the door shutting behind him, leaving her alone, wondering how long it would be before Pawlik came knocking again.

Her phone pinged with an alert that a voicemail was waiting.

Kate picked it up and worried the corner with her fingers. She put the phone to her ear and listened to Hank's message: "Tom's coming to pick you up. The apartment can wait."

36

K ate's first thought was: *How does he know I'm here?* He'd also known when
she met Alex here the first time, too. Was he tracking her through her
phone? A few taps on the screen, and she discovered that, yes, Hank was
tracking her location.

A surge of anger rushed through her. Marriage was supposed to be based
on trust, but clearly there were no boundaries where Hank was concerned.
Another couple of taps and Hank would have to guess where she might be.

She paced back and forth in front of the kitchen island to calm herself
down, taking deep breaths in and out. She'd told Alex that there was no
proof that Hank was involved in Caitlyn's murder, but he had a torn check
that was more than incriminating.

Her phone pinged again, and she glanced at it.

I'm downstairs.

Cromwell.

She thought about refusing. She could pretend she didn't get Hank's
voicemail. She could pretend she didn't get Tom's text. She could stay in
her apartment, keep the curtains drawn; no one would have to know she
was here. But Hank *did* know. And ghosting him would be cowardly, not

to mention that she wanted answers. She wanted to know why he'd slept with Caitlyn when he was supposedly in love with *her*.

While Alex might think Hank killed Caitlyn, she wasn't convinced. Alex was angry, and Hank had truly loved the girl, despite everything, once upon a time.

Maybe it was more that she *couldn't* believe it. Couldn't believe that the man she'd married would kill his ex-wife—and in such a barbaric way.

Resigned, with her anger ebbing, she packed a small bag, since she couldn't assume Cromwell was taking her back to Anna's. It was always good to be prepared.

When she stepped out onto the sidewalk, the limo was idling by the curb, and Cromwell was leaning against the door, his hands in his pockets, as though he didn't have a care in the world. Without a word, he reached over and opened the back door.

Tom climbed in after her, the door slamming shut, leaving them alone. The glass was up between them and the driver. This wasn't unusual. Tom hadn't taken off his sunglasses, so she couldn't see his eyes. He was almost too relaxed, the way he was sitting, his elbow on the armrest and his legs crossed. This *was* unusual.

"Where are we going?" Kate asked.

"Don't you know?"

It wasn't an answer. Not at all. Kate pulled her phone out of her bag. Tom held his hand up. "Hank's not available now."

Not available? He'd just left a voicemail for her. "Is he flying?"

"No." The answer was too short, too cryptic.

"A meeting?" Kate was grabbing at straws, although the stocks had continued to tumble and the shareholders were probably more than rabid right now.

Tom shook his head as he took off his sunglasses and stared at her. Kate forced herself not to look away. That's what he wanted.

"I'm not going to tell him about Culpepper," Tom said, his voice low and conspiratorial.

"I don't care what you tell him," Kate said, her tone belying the anxiety that was ripping her apart. "There's nothing going on. You know that. And Hank knows that. He's my husband."

"He was Caitlyn's husband, too, but that didn't matter."

"I'm not Caitlyn."

Tom was quiet for a moment, then, "No, you're not. And that's why you should be smarter than she was." His phone buzzed, and he put it up to his ear. His eyes skirted from Kate to the window. "Yes?"

Kate waited for him to say something more, but after a few seconds, he ended the call and put the phone next to him on the seat. What was that all about? Was he getting instructions from someone? Hank. It had to be Hank. He didn't want her to know where he was, but he still communicated with Tom. She could still see the faint scratches on Tom's wrist. Kate shifted a little, even more uneasy now. While she didn't believe her husband was a murderer, Tom was a different story. She'd ridden alone with him in this limo more times than she could count, but this was the first time she was afraid.

He caught her looking and held out his arm so she could see more clearly.

"Rosebushes, Kate. I have rosebushes. Do you want to see them? We can make a stop." His tone was taunting.

Did she believe him? Should she call his bluff? "Yes. Let's." The words were out before she could stop them.

For a second, Tom looked as though she'd slapped him, but he quickly recovered and forced a grin. "Okay." He leaned over and tapped on the glass, which slid down. He murmured something to the driver, and the glass went back up. Was it going to be that easy?

It couldn't possibly be.

As the white farmhouse came into view, Kate sat up a little straighter. She'd watched the signs, and they were in Connecticut, but past Hank's Greenwich home—and Anna's bed-and-breakfast—near the shore but not close enough to see the water.

The driveway wasn't very long, and she spotted what looked like an authentic English garden to the side of the house—complete with rows of rosebushes.

Tom hadn't been lying.

He gave her a nod, and when the car stopped, he opened the door, waiting for her to get out first. The scent of the roses became stronger as they got closer. Kate marveled at the white, pink, and red blossoms.

"I took up gardening after my wife died," Tom said, sounding remarkably human.

"I thought—" Kate started, before she could stop herself.

"I know what you thought." Tom sauntered along the edge of the garden, his hands in his pockets. "I found gardening was a good way to deal with my grief."

Kate kept in step with him, curious despite herself. As he reached out and lightly touched the petals, it was as though he was a completely different person than the man she'd known for the past three years. He seemed so relaxed—gentle, even—yet she knew she couldn't let her guard down. He was still *Tom*.

"How did she die?" Kate found herself asking.

Tom stopped, his eyebrows rising slightly. "I know there are rumors."

"So tell me the truth," she challenged.

A flicker of a smile, then it was gone. "She had breast cancer." Something akin to pain crossed his face, and Kate again was surprised by how human he seemed. "Roses were her favorite. She planted these gardens. It wasn't until after she was gone that I decided I couldn't let them die, too."

"How long were you married?"

"Ten years."

It was perhaps the longest conversation she'd ever had with him. At least the longest *civil* conversation. She leaned down and drank in the scent of one of the pink roses. Maybe things would be all right. Maybe all of her suspicions about Tom were just that—suspicions, unfounded. Hank hired him to be ruthless in business. She hadn't seen him in any other role before today. Not as a grieving widower, a man who kept his roses alive to commemorate his wife's life.

The tension began to ease out of her shoulders.

"You made him angry." He said it so softly that she wasn't sure she heard him right. "You questioned him."

The tension crept back in. "He has Caitlyn's ring," she said, aware that her tone was too defensive but unable to stop it.

"It's his property," Tom said. He hadn't turned away from the roses; it was almost like he was talking to them and not to her. But she wasn't fooled. He had his eye on her, and she'd become aware of the driver behind them, standing by the car. "You know what your responsibilities are as his wife, don't you?"

Did Tom know about the baby? Did he know Caitlyn's baby was Hank's? She couldn't push the anger down. "Who are you to tell me what my 'responsibilities' are?" she demanded, using air quotes.

"No need to get upset, Kate." A small, amused smile tugged at Tom's lips. "It's my job to remind you. In case you forget."

"Did you remind Caitlyn, too?" She couldn't stop herself.

He faced her. "Yes. Yes, I did. But she didn't listen to me. And look what happened to *her.*"

April 18

Hank left me. I know he's never coming back. He won't return my calls. He won't speak to me.

I can't say I'm surprised. After the party, when he threatened me, it was clear it would never be the same again.

I still haven't told him I'm pregnant.

I managed to get through to Cromwell, who said he was drawing up divorce papers. When I said I wanted my own lawyer, he came back to me the next day and said if I stayed quiet, if I didn't tell anyone about the divorce, if I didn't get a lawyer, Hank would let me stay on at the company and finish my initiative. Six months, he said, that's the time he was giving me. He felt it was more than generous.

I agreed, or so I let him think.

There wasn't a prenup. We'd joked about it at one point, a couple of years before his divorce from Catherine was final. But he told me that we'd never get divorced, that our marriage was a true one, that I was his only love and he would never want another woman.

I wonder if he's going to make Jeanne sign a prenup.

Because we don't have one, I can take him for quite a bit. Cromwell has already outlined Hank's terms. They're less than what he gave Catherine. I want to hold out for at least as much. I've got six months to work on it, to plan my next moves.

All this time I thought this affair with Jeanne was going to pass. We're a family. Hank, Lizzie, me, and the new baby. Granted, he had Catherine and Maril. He left them, too.

I wonder how long it will take him to leave Jeanne.

I'm staying at the Vineyard house for a couple of weeks while I sort things out. Cromwell is still here.

He's watching me. His job is to convince me to let Hank go. His survival depends on his success. I told him today that if I go, then he goes, too. He didn't like that. Tom has nothing outside of Hank. He had a wife once, but the story of what happened to her is murky. He doesn't have any emotions, no ties to anyone except Hank.

That's why he can do Hank's bidding with no remorse. Getting rid of a couple of wives is nothing for him. He's done worse. Much worse. Maybe with a little encouragement, I could be convinced to tell tales. I know things. Things that could be very damaging. Catherine knows things, too, but he's not threatened by her. She'd never tell anyone anything because she's as guilty as he is. That's why she stays in that house and never leaves.

Of course, if I do tell what I know, then I'd have to leave. I'd have to disappear and never come back.

37

ANNA

Hank was leaning against the porch railing at the inn, a drink in his hand, when Anna got home. She hadn't rushed back, instead found a small café and had a sandwich and a coffee. She had shut off her phone after texting both Will and Joan to tell them she'd be a little while longer.

Enjoy! was Joan's response. *I'll hold down the fort.*

She hadn't needed the permission, but it felt good to get it all the same. She savored the alone time, something she rarely had. She wandered in and out of shops, small art galleries, and considered buying an abstract painting that Joan would hate but she felt drawn to. In the end, she decided against it.

She wondered vaguely what it would be like to be Catherine, confined in that house by choice.

"Have a nice outing?" Hank asked as she came up the front steps, and Anna caught a whiff of sarcasm. She knew better than to answer. He was in a mood, and it was better to stay silent.

He leaned toward her and asked, "What am I going to do with you, Anna?"

She caught her breath, and butterflies began fluttering in her stomach.

He reached out and touched her cheek, his finger cold from the glass. She forced herself to stand still and not flinch, looking him in the eye.

214

"I'm not sure what you mean," she said, her voice calm, steady.

"I can't have you conspiring with my wife."

"We're not *conspiring*." Anna hated that he was putting her on the defensive.

"Why did you go visit Catherine?"

Anna had crossed a line. It was too late now. Maril must have heard about it from Catherine and told Hank, or maybe it was Lourdes. She wouldn't be surprised if Hank got regular updates from Catherine's aide. Either way, it didn't matter. He knew. But she didn't have a response prepared. Why *did* they go visit Catherine? Because an old woman said Catherine knew something about—what exactly? They should have stayed home, stayed out of it.

"You and I have an unspoken agreement, Anna," he reminded her. "You do as you're told, and I will do what I can to make sure you're comfortable."

Anna took a deep breath and stared at the house across the marsh. She was concentrating on it so much that when she felt his hand tighten around her arm, it startled her and she instinctively tried to break free.

"I don't give second chances." His breath was hot against her ear as he whispered his threat, his grip growing even tighter so she winced with pain. "Promise me you'll stay out of my business."

Anna nodded, unable to speak. She'd never been afraid of him before, but at that moment, she knew he was capable of anything.

He let go of her. "Good girl," he said, draining his glass and putting it on the railing. He cocked his head in the direction of his house. "Could you go back in that house after what happened?" he asked.

Curious, since Caitlyn was found in the marsh. No one had indicated where she'd been killed. Was Hank implying that she'd been murdered in the house and then brought outside? Her imagination was going places it shouldn't. She was on edge because of what had happened in the past few days.

"I don't think so," she said. "Is Mary coming back?"

"My sister is not a sentimental person," Hank said, not answering her question.

It wasn't until she went inside that she realized he didn't ask where Kate was.

The house was quiet. Hank seemed to be the only one here. Upstairs, Anna paused at Lizzie's room, gently pushing the door open and peering inside. The bed was carefully made, a favorite unicorn stuffed animal perched on the pillow. The rest of the room was neat and orderly. Lizzie liked things just so. A rush of love for the girl hit her. They shared no blood, but she'd come to think of the girl as her own these past years.

What had happened to her mother? Despite what Hank told Kate, was *she* the body found on Martha's Vineyard?

Anna had never doubted Hank before. She'd never believed that he would do any harm to any of his wives, not physically, anyway. Yet the moment she'd seen those words—*He's going to kill me*—in Nan's journal, a tickle of doubt began to nag at her. Hank was ruthless in business; would he be as ruthless with a wife who might not obey the rules? She thought about Maggie's note. Her warning to Anna—and Kate—resonated, despite Anna's initial dismissal of it.

A quick glance in Ted's room—this one not so neat—and then the room where Maril was staying confirmed that none of them were in the house. Anna made her way back downstairs to the kitchen, expecting to find Joan getting dinner ready. Everything was in order, the stainless steel appliances gleaming with Joan's usual elbow grease. But her wife wasn't there. She peered around the corner into the great room, but that, too, was empty. She went back upstairs and poked her head into every room again. No one here.

Anna stepped out onto the second-floor porch. She could see across the expansive lawn, down to the beach, and the side yard that butted up against the marsh between her house and Hank's. No Lizzie, Ted, Maril, or Joan to be seen anywhere.

Anna went back downstairs, perplexed. Hank was heading into the den, and she stopped him.

"Where is everyone?" she asked.

Hank shook his head. "No one was here when I arrived. I texted Maril and she said she'd brought the children to some sort of rock-climbing gym." He snorted. "They've got so much here. I don't know why they have to go somewhere else to play."

Despite being a father, Hank had little understanding of children. Anna chose not to say anything.

"What about Joan?"

Hank frowned and shrugged. "Maybe she went out on an errand. Maril didn't say anything about her."

What he didn't say was that he didn't miss Joan, that her wife was inconsequential to him and he didn't bother asking about her. She shouldn't have expected more.

"I'm going to make some phone calls," Hank announced. "If you don't mind, I'll need some privacy."

He didn't wait for a response—not that he expected one—and disappeared into the den and shut the door behind him.

The fear that lingered from Hank's unexpected visit grew as Anna returned to the room she shared with her wife. The bed was neatly made. Nothing was out of place. Where was she? Her car had been in the garage when Anna pulled in, so she certainly couldn't have gone far.

Anna took a deep breath. Joan was a grown woman perfectly capable of taking care of herself. Maybe she was tending the gardens somewhere on the property. She made her way outside and circled the house, the silence almost unbearable, as with every step it was becoming clear that Joan simply wasn't home. But then, why was her car there?

Joan hadn't made friends in town. She'd spent all her time at the inn with Anna.

"I don't need any more friends," she'd scoffed when Anna asked her about joining a book club at the library or the local women's business association. "I've got all I need right here."

The idea of being Joan's whole world had never worried her before; she'd enjoyed it. But now, as she mulled over where Joan could be, her thoughts inevitably drifted to the house next door, to Caitlyn. She'd always felt safe here—she had a good security team—but what if she wasn't? What if Joan wasn't?

She forced herself to slow down. But the desire to hear Joan's voice, to be reassured that her wife was all right, was overwhelming. Anna's phone was still in her pocket, so she pulled it out, hitting Joan's number. It took her a few moments to realize that while she could hear the phone ringing in her ear, the familiar ringtone also was coming from somewhere nearby. The kitchen window was open, and it was coming from inside. Anna pushed the door open and moved toward the sound. She yanked open the drawer next to the stove. Nestled inside was Joan's phone, with "Anna" on the screen, indicating who was calling.

Wherever she'd gone, Joan had left her phone behind. And how did it get in the drawer? That wasn't like her at all. Joan had her phone in her pocket even when she was gardening.

Anna's hands started to shake as she called Will Stafford, but he didn't pick up. It went straight to voicemail. She dialed Murphy's number.

"Hi, Murph," she said, trying to keep her tone light. "I was wondering if you know where Joan is."

"Joan? No, sorry, I don't. We had a little incident with some kids getting onto the beach, so we've been tied up with that. Is everything okay?"

"I hope so. Check in when you're done, okay?"

"Sure thing."

Anna took in big gulps of air to keep the anxiety at bay. She couldn't explain it, but she sensed that something was wrong. Very wrong. She spotted Pawlik's card next to the phone. He'd given it to her on his first visit to the inn, written his cell number on the back. Her fingers closed over its corners as she debated for a second. Should she call him and tell him that Joan was missing? Would he take her seriously? Someone had to be missing for twenty-four hours, right? She didn't know if that was a television thing, but it seemed right.

Maybe she was being paranoid, but she decided to call him anyway on his cell, not patient enough to go through official channels.

It rang four times before he answered. "Pawlik."

"It's Anna Klein."

"Yes? What's wrong?" She could hear his concern.

"I was out for the afternoon and Joan's not here. I don't know where she went." Her thoughts were all over the place, jumping in front of one another. Should she tell him Hank was here, that he had threatened her, that she'd been afraid? No. Only if it seemed relevant to Joan's disappearance would she reveal that. She wasn't stupid.

"Take a deep breath and start at the beginning. You were out?" He wasn't telling her that she shouldn't have called. She didn't know if that was good or bad. But he was taking her seriously.

"That's right. I was gone, I don't know, about three hours?" Why was she questioning herself, the time she was gone? It had been three hours. "When I got back, Joan wasn't here. She's not anywhere. It's not like her. Her car is still here. And her phone, too." The panic rose into her throat, and she choked back tears.

"Hang up the phone, Anna."

The voice came from behind her. She swung around and saw Cromwell standing in the doorway.

"Tell him everything's fine and then hang up." He took three steps toward her, held out his hand.

Didn't you hear her scream?

"No," she said. "Everything is not fine."

"Ms. Klein, are you all right?" she heard Pawlik asking.

"The police can't help you," Cromwell said, his hand closing over the phone, shutting it down. He shook his head at her. His face was close to hers, his breath hot against her skin. "Anna, Anna, Anna. What am I going to do with you? You know the rules."

"Where is Joan?"

Cromwell shrugged. "I'm not her keeper. I thought *you* were."

"She's not here." Anna's imagination had been taking her to places she didn't want to go. What if the next body that washed up in the marsh was Joan? Where was Will Stafford? Why didn't he answer his phone?

"We don't need the police. We can find Joan for you."

"How?"

"We have resources. You know that," he snapped.

She always did as she was told. But now Joan was missing, Caitlyn was dead, and Anna didn't want to end up in that marsh. Was that where Joan was? Had he gotten to her, too?

"Did you kill Joan like you killed Caitlyn?" she demanded.

38

Kate wasn't eager to go inside Anna's, so she lingered in the driveway as the limo made its way back out through the gate. Tom had looked at her expectantly when they'd arrived, anticipating that she'd follow him into the house, but Kate turned away, uncertain how she was going to face Hank. Her husband was here, Tom had told her, and he wanted to see her. But did she want to see him? Was she ready to see him? Alex Culpepper's revelations had stung. She fingered the pendant Hank left for her, still around her neck. Would it send the wrong message to him, that she was wearing it and thus possibly willing to forgive and forget? She wished she had more time to mull it over, but when Hank came down the front steps to meet her, it was too late.

"You were the father of Caitlyn's baby," Kate blurted out. She immediately regretted it. She hadn't wanted to do it this way, but there was no taking it back now.

Hank took a deep breath. "Yes, I know."

"When did you find out?"

Hank leveled his gaze at her, and she couldn't look away. But he didn't answer her question.

"You slept with her. While you were divorcing her."

"And while I was courting you. That's what you're angry about, isn't it?" Kate nodded.

"It was a moment of weakness. She came to me, vulnerable. I loved her once, Kate. You know that. You and I, I didn't know if you loved me for the right reasons. If you weren't involved only because of my money."

"You know better than that!" Kate snapped.

"I do now." He hadn't made any move toward her, kept some distance between them.

Despite Hank's protests—excuses—as to why he'd slept with Caitlyn, he'd still done it and she felt betrayed. The ghost of Caitlyn's ring wrapped itself around her finger, and she shivered.

Hank was watching her, as though he could read her mind, as though he knew she was wrestling with herself. Did she want to make it easy for him to say he was sorry and then all would be forgiven? Would it be that easy for *her*?

But before either of them could say anything more, movement caught Kate's eye.

The police cruiser came through the gate, and Trooper Pawlik got out.

"What's going on?" Kate asked anxiously as Pawlik approached.

"Anna called me about Joan."

"What about Joan?"

"Anna thinks she's missing," Hank said. Doubt tinged his words, as though *he* didn't think Joan was missing.

"Why?" she asked Pawlik, ignoring Hank.

"Because she's not here. Because her car is here, and so is her phone, but she's not." Anna came down the steps toward them, Tom right behind her, her voice louder than it should be. Had she heard Hank?

"She could have called a car service. Maybe there's something wrong with her car," Kate suggested.

"I suppose that's possible," Anna conceded.

"Do you have any thoughts as to where Joan would go if there was an emergency and she didn't have time to tell you?" Pawlik asked.

"No," she said, her voice catching on the word. Her face was streaked with dried tears, worry etched into her forehead. "She would have brought her phone. She would have texted me."

Kate spoke up. "She mentioned she had a couple of adult children. Where are they? Maybe one of them is in trouble."

"I never met Joan's children. They were upset about me. About us. They were estranged."

"So you know nothing about them? Where they are?" Pawlik asked.

Anna shook her head. "No."

"Where was she from?"

"She always said she was from everywhere. She was an Army brat, apparently, and they moved all over the world."

"Did she talk about any other family? Any friends?"

"No. She said her parents were dead; there was no one else." Anna hesitated. "She always said I was her family," she whispered, a tear slipping down her cheek.

Kate put her arm around Anna's shoulders. Hank stood to the side. Tom was hovering near him, as usual. They were keeping an eye on her. On Anna.

"What was Joan's profession before this?" Pawlik was asking Anna.

"She was in finance. She worked at Tudor Enterprises for Catherine for a while."

"Did she ever work with your ex-husband?"

"She never worked for me." Hank stepped out of the shadow. He addressed Pawlik. "When Anna met her, I had a private investigator look into her."

"What?" Kate and Anna asked at the same time.

Hank nodded at Anna. "I wanted to know more about the person you were getting involved with."

Kate knew what that meant. He was checking up on Anna, intervening in Anna's life because he still owned her. He wouldn't have any hesitation to do that with anyone in Kate's life, either, she thought grimly. She also understood that he'd want to know if Joan was using Anna to get to him, because in Hank's eyes, it was all about him.

"As it turns out, yes, she did work with my first wife but left the company to work for a competitor. I found nothing that would have raised any red flags." Hank hesitated. "I did not know she had children. My investigator said she'd never been married and found no relatives."

"But she told you she had children?" Pawlik asked Anna, a curious tone in his voice.

"Yes," she said, her voice barely a whisper.

Kate could see the anguish on Anna's face. Why would Joan tell her she had children if she didn't? That didn't make any sense at all. Why had Anna never pressed to meet her wife's children? Had she merely trusted everything Joan had told her about herself, much like how Kate had trusted Hank's devotion without any questions, not knowing that he was still sleeping with his soon-to-be ex-wife?

"If necessary, can you turn that investigator's report over to me?" Pawlik was asking Hank.

"Absolutely," he said. "I want to help as much as I can."

He sounded sincere, Kate had to admit. But he was so good at sounding one way and being another.

"Kate, why don't we go in and make some coffee?" Hank had taken her elbow and was already leading her into the house. She could still hear Pawlik asking Anna questions.

"What are you doing?" she asked Hank once they were in the kitchen, yanking her arm from his hand and whirling around to face him.

"He needs to ask Anna questions, and we all need some coffee. It may be a late night."

She peered into his face. "It may be a late night? What do you know about it?"

Hank's face grew dark. "Nothing. I know as much as you do. Anna's wife is missing. Or not. That's for the police to find out."

He had conveniently left Tom out there, though, to monitor the conversation.

"I'm sure Anna's security team will be able to provide the police with whatever they need as well," Hank continued.

Anna's security team. That's right. Where was Will Stafford?

"Will you come back to the city with me when this is over?" Hank was asking, interrupting her thoughts.

When this is over? He made it sound as though Joan missing was insignificant. A mere blip in their lives to be skipped over to get to the next part.

"I'm not sure that this is the time to have this conversation," she said.

"I just want to know if we'll be all right."

Would they? Kate studied her husband's face. The man she'd married only two weeks ago. The man who'd promised to love her until death. A mere twenty-four hours ago, she had believed him, but Caitlyn's pregnancy changed things. It forced her to take a harder look at Hank and whether she could trust him. If Caitlyn was three months pregnant, he'd slept with her far more recently than she was comfortable with. And then there was the fact that he'd given Alex a check for fifty thousand dollars to lie about being the baby's father, if it came to that.

"I don't know," she said truthfully. They stared at each other for a few moments, uncertain what to say next. Neither made a move toward the coffee maker.

"Daddy?"

Lizzie's voice startled them both. Hank turned to his daughter, who stood in the doorway with her brother and Maril. They must have just gotten back and come through from the garage.

"What's going on?" Maril asked. "Why are the police here?"

"We're looking for Joan," Hank said. "She seems to have left, and no one knows where she is."

Lizzie glanced at Kate, then back at her father. "She went for a walk," she said matter-of-factly, as though they should have known this.

"A walk?" Kate asked. "You saw her?" She looked at Maril, who shook her head.

"I didn't see her."

But Lizzie was adamant. "Maril was driving, so she wouldn't know. We were going to the rock-climbing gym. I saw Joan walking. She was on the phone."

But her phone was here, in the house.

"Where, exactly, was she?" Kate persisted.

Lizzie looked at Kate, then her gazed settled on Hank. "She was going to *your* house."

39

ANNA

Anna sat on one of the wicker chairs on the porch and held a mug of coffee, breathing in its scent but not bothering to drink. If she did, she was afraid she'd throw up. Kate sat stonelike next to her, deep in thought. Anna had barely said anything when Kate had handed her the coffee.

Where was Joan?

She wanted to be out there with them, with the police, looking for her, but Pawlik told her to stay at the house, in case Joan showed up. It made sense, but she wasn't naïve enough that she didn't realize he wanted her out of the way.

If she wasn't so worried, she'd be furious at Hank for hiring a private investigator to look into Joan. It was one thing to know everything about her life, but another to investigate her wife as though she were some sort of criminal. He didn't trust her, didn't trust that she would honor the nondisclosure agreement even with her spouse.

Although truth be told, she was now embarrassed that she seemed to know so little about Joan. Everything had been so easy between them; they had clicked so perfectly that it had never seemed to matter what had happened with either of them before they'd met, only how it was while they were together. Joan told her that she'd quit her job at Tudor Enterprises because she was tired of working in the corporate world, never mentioning working for a competitor, like Hank said. And what was that about not having children? Why would Joan lie about that? Hank's private investigator must have made a mistake. He must have.

"Anna, where's Will?" Kate asked, breaking the silence.

That was a good question. He hadn't picked up his phone when she'd called, and Murphy hadn't mentioned Will when she'd talked to him earlier. She'd assumed he was busy helping Murph with the trespassers on the beach, but was he? She hadn't asked. The whole team—minus Will—were now out helping the police in their search, and she'd been so distracted that Will's absence hadn't registered.

"I don't know. Hank was here when I got back, but no one else was. Will's phone is going to voicemail." It dawned on her that it seemed almost too convenient that no one could reach Will at the same time Joan was missing. "You don't think he had anything to do with this, do you?"

Kate shook her head. "I don't know." She didn't seem surprised at the question.

Anna was suspicious of everyone. And there was Hank. Hank said he hadn't seen Joan, but was he lying? She remembered how he'd frightened her. Had he frightened Joan, too?

Because Lizzie had seen Joan going toward Hank's house, police were back over there, searching the house, the grounds. It was the same scene as a few days ago when Caitlyn's body was found. Anna gave them Joan's laptop, and they had her phone. They were searching the inn, too, for anything that might tell them where Joan had gone. She and Kate had come out here, onto the porch, to stay out of their way. But she was antsy. She needed to do something. She couldn't just sit here, nursing her fears. She got up, and Kate got up, too.

"Where are you going?" Kate asked.

She forced down irritation. She didn't need a babysitter. "I'm going out to the garage. That's where the security offices are, on the second floor."

"Will said he's been staying overnight out there," Kate said.

"That's right."

"I'll go with you."

"I can go by myself," Anna snapped.

Kate looked as though Anna had slapped her, but Anna didn't apologize. She started down the steps as Pawlik came up to meet her.

"I'm going to look for Will Stafford," Anna explained without waiting for him to ask where she was going.

Pawlik gave her a funny look. "He checked in with Tom Murphy a few hours ago and said he was going home." He paused a second. "We're not sure where he is now. His phone is still going to voicemail. I've sent an officer over to his place."

Anna frowned. None of this sounded like Will. "You don't think . . ." Joan had hired Will. She'd known him from, well, where, exactly? Anna couldn't remember now. Had Joan ever told her?

"We don't know. He could just be sleeping and has his phone turned off," Pawlik said.

That would make sense. Will had been putting in a lot of hours the past few days. She forced herself to be reasonable.

"He's been staying over the garage," she offered.

Pawlik nodded. "Yes, we know. We were over there to look at the security footage from today but he's cleared out." He hesitated, then added, "We didn't see anything on the security footage except that your daughter was right. Your wife left the property and was walking toward your ex-husband's house. But that's all we've got."

"What about the security cameras at Hank's house?" Kate asked.

"Nothing," Pawlik said. "The system was down when Miss Howard went missing, and apparently there have been glitches with it since."

Anna didn't like the sound of that.

"We're doing what we can to find her," Pawlik said.

Anna nodded. "Thank you."

"Anna, let's go inside," Kate said.

She turned to Kate, about to tell her that she didn't need coddling, she needed something to do so she wouldn't feel so helpless, when Cromwell approached.

"You're wanted out there," Tom told Pawlik, who glanced briefly at Anna before heading across the lawn.

Anna hadn't seen Tom since earlier, when she'd asked him if he'd killed Joan.

"No, Anna. I don't know what's happened with Joan," he'd said. His face had been a mass of shadows and light, so she couldn't read his expression, see if he was lying. But he was Tom. Even if he was lying, he'd be able to mask it. That was how he'd gotten where he was.

Without a word to Tom, Anna followed Kate into the house. Kate pulled a pair of slippers out of the basket, which reminded Anna of Maggie. She now remembered the note, that Maggie warned them they were in danger. A deep sob caught in Anna's throat. *She* hadn't been in danger. Joan had.

The wood floors were cool against the bare soles of her feet. She could hear Ted laughing somewhere upstairs.

"Hank's with the children," Kate said.

Surprising, but Anna was glad for it.

"Anna?" Kate held out the slippers.

If Joan were here, they would be having a glass of wine and talking about their day, what to feed the guests for breakfast, arguing playfully about when they could close the house for a few days so they could get away themselves.

Joan had to come back. It had to be a mistake. She'd walk up the driveway and the police out there would all feel like fools and they'd have a good laugh about it.

Anna was about to take the slippers from Kate when she heard shouting. She pushed the screen door open and stepped back out onto the porch. It was louder now, and figures that had been spread all across the property moved in tandem toward one spot near the marsh that separated her property from Hank's. The place where Caitlyn had been found.

She couldn't breathe. Not bothering with her shoes, Anna flew down the stairs and ran across the lawn, the grass wet underneath her feet.

Pawlik looked up when she approached. He was holding a stick, and on the end of it dangled a shoe. A sneaker. A red sneaker.

Joan's.

PART IV

40

ANNA

There was blood on the sneaker.

Anna crumpled to the ground. All of her worst fears were coming true.

"Did you find her?" she sobbed.

"Not yet." Pawlik handed the stick and shoe over to one of his troopers. "Come on, Ms. Klein, let's go back to the house."

He shouldn't be babysitting her. He should be looking for Joan. Anna got up and wiped her hand across her eyes. She had to pull it together. She had to be strong. For Joan.

She needed to show him Maggie's note.

"I got a note yesterday. From a friend. It said that I was in danger. Kate, too," she told him.

Pawlik frowned. "Where is this note? And who is the friend?"

"Margaret Pole," came Kate's voice from behind her. "She's the woman who died in the house fire."

If he was surprised, Pawlik didn't show it. "Where is this note?" he asked again.

"Come on, Anna," Kate said, "let's get the note and show it to him."

If Pawlik wanted to scold her for not telling him about this sooner, he kept it to himself. Anna was relieved that he wasn't going to blame her for not telling him. She pulled the note from the top drawer in the desk in the office off the kitchen. He took it and stared at it for a few minutes.

"When did you get this?"

"Yesterday."

"She died in the house fire yesterday."

Anna and Kate nodded in unison.

"How did you know her?"

"She came here just before I opened," Anna said. "She told me that she wanted to keep an eye on Lizzie. That she made a promise to her mother. She told me Nan Tudor was dead."

Pawlik was quiet, still staring at the piece of paper.

"Do you know who she was?" he finally asked.

"She was my ex-wife's divorce lawyer." Hank's voice startled her, and she turned to see him come into the room. "Nan wanted full custody of Lizzie. I was fighting it. But then Nan disappeared."

And so did the custody battle, Anna thought.

"That was convenient." Pawlik said out loud what Anna—and probably Kate, from the look on her face—was thinking. "She said that Nan Tudor was dead?" he asked Anna.

"Yes."

"Did you ask her how she knew that?"

Anna shook her head. "No." How to explain that curiosity was not part of the deal? How, if it came down to it, she really didn't want to know details.

"I don't know how that would pertain to Joan's disappearance," Hank interjected. "Perhaps we should stay focused on finding Joan." He spoke with authority, like he always did, but Pawlik wasn't having it.

"A note warning your wife and ex-wife to be careful, that they were in danger, is pertinent," Pawlik said. "There was a threat."

"A perceived threat by an old woman who had dementia," Hank said, annoyance lacing his tone.

"How do you know she had dementia?" Pawlik asked, his surprise evident.

Hank looked from Anna to Kate and back to Pawlik. "Because I've been paying her medical bills for the last few years. I've also been paying her mortgage. You'll probably find that out in your investigation, which is why I'm being up front about it."

"Why would you take care of a woman who was defending your wife in a divorce settlement?"

Hank hesitated only a second. "Because she was distraught when Nan disappeared. She had been a family friend. I wanted to help her. Nan shouldn't have left all of us the way she did."

Anna watched Kate's expression; it was full of disbelief. What had Kate said? Maggie told her that "money covered it up." Had Hank been buying her off all these years so she wouldn't pursue any legal action against him? So she would drop any suggestion that Nan was dead, leading the police to his door?

"Like I said, I'm not sure how any of this will help you find Joan Carey," Hank added.

Pawlik was quiet, but Anna saw something in his expression that she couldn't read. Amusement? Irritation? A mixture of both?

"I'm going to take this note, if that's all right with you," he said to Anna.

"Certainly. Do you think this will help?"

"I don't know, but right now, anything might."

Anna wasn't so sure. How would a note from a dead woman help? It wasn't as though they could go to Maggie and ask her why she felt Anna and Kate were in danger. Maggie's suggestion that they ask Catherine didn't come to anything. If Hank was right and Maggie was suffering from dementia, the note meant nothing but an old woman's delusions.

"Are you staying here tonight?" Pawlik was asking Hank.

Hank's eyes moved from him to Anna to Kate. "I have to leave in the morning."

"Is Mrs. Tudor going with you?"

"I'm heading to Dubai for a meeting. So, no. My wife is not coming with me."

Kate's expression changed slightly. She didn't know about this meeting, and she wasn't happy.

"The only people here will be your wife, Ms. Klein, and your children? What about Mr. Cromwell?"

"He'll be coming with me," Hank said.

Anna saw where Pawlik was going with this. "You think that because we're women we won't be safe here alone. But we will be. I have a good security team."

"Your head of security is unresponsive, and your wife went missing under their watch." Pawlik's tone was stern.

"I can't leave. What if Joan comes back?" she said.

"They could go to my house on Martha's Vineyard," Hank suggested as though Anna hadn't spoken. "I have a top-notch team I can pull together on short notice. They can go tonight."

Pawlik nodded. "We can't let the media find out or everyone will know."

"Don't worry about that."

They were talking as though no one else was in the room. Making a decision without consulting her—or Kate, whose face was dark with anger.

"But—"

"I think you'll be safer," Pawlik told Anna.

But she didn't feel she'd be safer. The moment Hank mentioned the house on Martha's Vineyard, all she could think about was Nan Tudor. That was the last place she'd been seen. It was also the place where another headless body had been found.

"What if Joan comes back here?" she tried again.

"Your security team is here, not to mention that she has your phone number," Pawlik said. "I have your phone number. You'll be the first person we contact when she shows up."

"I'll have Maril pack up for the children," Hank said. "She can go, too, to help with them." He didn't seem aware that neither Anna nor Kate were jumping up and down with enthusiasm for the plan. He was being Hank, and he never considered that what he was proposing might not be welcomed.

"I'm not leaving," Anna said, straightening up so she was eye level with Hank. "You can't make me. If you want to take Maril and the children to the Vineyard, then do so. Kate can go, too. But I am not leaving my house." She turned to Pawlik. "I am safe here. As safe as I'll be anywhere."

She clutched her hands together to keep them from shaking. She'd never stood up to Hank like this, but she had to be here for Joan. Pawlik had said "when" she showed up, not "if." Anna was going to hang on to that; there was hope Joan was still alive somewhere.

Hank stared at her, realization growing that she meant what she said. He finally nodded. "All right. But I'm going to talk to Stafford when he gets here to make sure you're well protected."

"He's not coming," Pawlik announced. He was looking at his phone.

"What do you mean?" Anna asked.

"I sent an officer over to his place. It's cleared out. Nothing there. No furniture, no clothes, no sign of him." He hesitated a second. "He's gone."

41

Kate never completely trusted Will Stafford, but she wasn't going to say "I told you so" to Anna, whose entire life had crumbled within a matter of hours. Still, she thought about her few conversations with him and she would never have imagined he might actually be behind Joan's disappearance. But it certainly seemed that way now.

Since Will had intimate knowledge of Anna's security system, Hank insisted that none of them could stay here.

"Who knows what sorts of back doors he put in place in case he wants to get back in here? Your team doesn't have time to completely rework the system," Hank had argued when Anna protested. "Caitlyn was murdered, and now Joan is gone. Who will his next target be?"

Pawlik had agreed with him. So that was why Kate was helping pack the children's bags. Hers was still packed, untouched since Tom had brought her back.

"Anna's been crying. I've never seen her cry."

She turned to see Lizzie in the doorway. She stopped folding the girl's clothes and faced her.

"She's sad because Joan didn't tell her where she was going," Kate said.

"Is Joan dead? Like Caitlyn?" Lizzie asked. The bluntness of the question startled her. But the girl was serious; she wanted to know.

"We don't know." It was the truth, and Lizzie seemed to accept that.

"Are you coming with us?"

"Yes."

"Are you going to take care of us now?"

Good question. "I don't know." She didn't know a lot of things at the moment, did she?

"I'm not interested in a new mother again. I don't have a mother." It was said matter-of-factly.

"Fair enough," Kate said.

"I like it here. With Anna and Joan. What if Joan doesn't come back?"

"Then I suppose your father will figure out what to do."

"My father is too busy." She narrowed her eyes at Kate and announced, "I'm going to grow up and run my father's companies. He thinks Ted's going to do it, but Ted's not smart enough."

Kate couldn't help but chuckle. "Ted's seven."

"Old enough to know he's not smart enough."

Kate had the sense that there was a very old soul inside Lizzie Tudor and she wouldn't doubt that the girl could do as she said.

"Lizzie."

Cromwell's voice echoed ominously off the walls. Lizzie's head snapped back.

"Why don't you go help Maril with Teddy's packing?"

Kate couldn't help but admire the defiant look Lizzie gave Tom as she swept past him. The girl probably *would* be running Hank's companies someday.

"Change of plans," Tom said. "At least for you."

She frowned. "What?"

"You're going back to the city with Hank."

"What about Martha's Vineyard?"

"Hank thinks you'll be safer at the penthouse."

"Does it matter what *I* think?"

Tom chuckled. "Actually, no. Not under these circumstances."

Kate tried not to let her frustration seep into her voice. "Anna needs me. She shouldn't have to deal with Maril and the children alone."

"You and Anna . . ."

"What?"

"No fraternizing between wives. It doesn't look good."

She got it then. "It's about Catherine, isn't it? That we went to see her?"

"Give the girl a gold star." He hesitated, then asked, "Why *did* you go over there, anyway?"

She might as well tell him. She was sure he—or Hank—would find out eventually, and if she admitted to it now, she could be in control.

"It was Margaret Pole. She said Catherine knew something."

Tom's eyebrows rose. "Knew what?"

Kate thought about her conversation with Margaret and Hank's confession that the woman was Nan's divorce lawyer. "Something about Nan," she said. What else could it have been?

Tom gave a short snort. "Nan was going to take Hank for everything he had. Or at least, that's what she thought." He hesitated. "She was volatile. Nan, I mean. It was the drugs."

"The infertility drugs."

Tom's eyes widened, and he took a step backward. He was rattled, something Kate had never seen before, but he quickly recovered. "How do you know about those?"

Kate shrugged. She wondered if Tom or Hank even knew Nan had kept a diary, and if so, they certainly couldn't know that Kate had seen it. That she'd read it. But something told her that they didn't. That this was a secret Nan had kept.

"Did Catherine tell you about it?" Tom asked.

Kate frowned. Catherine? Is that what Margaret Pole had alluded to? That Nan couldn't get pregnant without drugs? It was clear from Nan's own words that she and Catherine had no contact after Nan stopped working for her and married Hank, so Catherine couldn't have found out about the infertility drugs if it weren't for the diary. Unless they had had some contact that Nan hadn't recorded. Contact that Tom would know about—because this didn't seem a surprise to him, that Catherine might have told her.

"Yes," she lied easily.

If Nan was telling the truth in the journal, Tom hadn't known she'd actually gotten pregnant. Neither had Hank.

And then Kate remembered the unidentified dead woman found on Martha's Vineyard.

She'd been pregnant, just like Caitlyn.

Just like Nan.

May 2

I'm still at the Vineyard, my favorite place on earth. This house is the one that I feel the most at home in. I spent months decorating it, getting it exactly the way I wanted. He doesn't love it like I do, but he doesn't have attachments to any of his houses, so it's not surprising. He's more at home on his jet, going from business meeting to business meeting. That's what keeps him going, what makes him feel alive.

It used to be me. I was the one who made him feel alive.

I can't let myself get distracted.

Jeanne's sly. She's smarter than she looks. I hear things. I've got my spies. She won't sign the prenup. She was a little loose with him in the beginning, teasing him into thinking she'd fuck him, but now that she knows he's discarded me, she's holding out for marriage and won't even let him near her. He's going crazy for her. This is right out of my own playbook. I did this with him and it works. Like I said, she's not stupid. She knows what she's doing.

I don't want Jeanne in this house. I don't want her touching my things, sleeping in my bed.

I don't want her near my daughter.

She's beautiful, my Lizzie. And smart. So smart. She's already talking in full sentences. Her smile lights up the room. I love feeling her little arms around my neck as she nuzzles her head on my shoulder and I can smell her little girl scent.

I bundled her up in a thick coat and we went to the beach this morning. She collected shells and presented them to me like they were the queen's diamonds. When I brought her back in and got her ready for her nap, I tickled her belly and she giggled, the best sound in the world. I wrapped us both up in a cashmere blanket and I read to her in French. She already understands a lot, and I'm trying to give her the confidence to start speaking it to me.

Afterward, I watched her sleep for the longest time. Her red curls cover her cheeks in little wisps. Her eyelashes are so long, and when she sleeps, she flexes her fingers like she's going to start playing the piano. I want her to take music lessons, dance lessons. Is that too girlie? Maybe she could also play soccer or field hockey, or both. Whatever she does, she'll be the best. She's got my genes. His genes. Together, we made one amazing little girl.

Hank has been sending messages through Cromwell. I hate that man. I hate the way he looks at me, like I'm the enemy. Did he look at Catherine like that, too, when he was trying to get her to agree to the divorce?

Cromwell has threatened that he'll take me to court if I don't do everything Hank wants. He'll say I'm unfit and I won't be able to see her. He'll have full custody, and I won't be able to do anything about it.

The only reason he wants full custody is to hurt me.

I wonder about Maril. How she got through the divorce. She was an adult, though, and knew what was going on. I'm ashamed now that I never thought about her, how our affair would affect her. I only thought about me and my happiness. Maril was collateral damage. Sometimes I want to fix things with her, but she hates me. She does send presents to Lizzie, though. I think she could love her little sister, even if she doesn't like me.

I think Maril might take care of Lizzie if the court says I can't see her. Maril knows how he can be. She can protect Lizzie. Keep her safe.

I haven't told anyone about the baby growing inside me. No one needs to know about her yet. She's mine, I don't have to share her with him. I've been wearing a lot of loose clothing so if anyone sees me, they might not suspect anything but a little weight gain. At some point everyone will know, but until then, she's my secret.

42

Kate had spent the two weeks after her wedding in the penthouse, but that didn't mean she liked it. It was too modern, too white, too much marble. The windows overlooking Central Park offered up a spectacular view, but they only contributed to the coldness of the place. Hank had hired a designer who commissioned paintings of splashes of color that looked like Rorschach inkblots. When she had been Hank's assistant, she had the vague feeling that she was going to be psychoanalyzed if she voiced an opinion about what they actually reminded her of. So she kept her mouth shut. Like she was doing now.

The only spot that felt warm was the terrace, decorated with planters sprouting colorful flowers and comfortable plush sofas and chairs under a striped awning. She'd talked to Hank about bringing that warmness inside, and he'd seemed open to the idea: "You live here now, too. I want you to feel at home, so whatever you want to do, go ahead." But the phone call about the body had interrupted any plans for redecorating.

Kate stretched out on a chaise lounge, overlooking the park. She had dropped her bag in the front foyer and gone straight to the terrace, unwilling to engage in conversation with her husband.

But now he stood in front of her, obscuring her view.

"Why don't we go out and get some dinner?" he suggested. "It's time to stop this silent treatment."

He was acting as though she didn't notice Pawlik pulling him off into the den before they left Anna's, a dark look on the trooper's face. She wondered if Alex had contacted him about how Hank had attempted to buy him off. Even if he had, Pawlik must have been satisfied with his conversation with Hank, because he let her husband whisk her away after saying goodbye to his children and Anna, who looked at Kate with such an imploring expression that Kate asked Hank if she couldn't stay with her.

"It's best if you don't," he'd said. "She'll be safe."

But that wasn't all she was worried about. Anna was being sent away and still had the responsibility of the children, despite Maril's presence.

"They'll find Joan," Kate had whispered to Anna as she gave her a hug. "Pawlik will find her."

Anna had clung to her for a moment, then let go.

"I'll call you later, okay? And you call me when Joan gets back, okay?" Kate had said.

"Okay."

As she thought about Anna, hoping that her optimism about finding Joan would prove right, Kate fingered the pendant around her neck. She hadn't taken it off, but it felt like an albatross. Perhaps she should have left it on the kitchen island in her apartment and not given Hank the satisfaction of seeing it on her.

He kissed me where each pearl kissed my neck.

Nan Tudor's words came back to her like a gut punch. She studied her husband's face. She could see the annoyance in his eyes. She wasn't behaving like she should, like he expected.

"I'm not hungry," she said, aware she sounded petulant but not caring.

He sank down in the chair next to her, his elbows on his knees as he leaned forward. "It didn't mean anything," he said.

Kate swung her feet around so she was sitting up, facing him. "She got pregnant. It meant something."

"No, it didn't."

She studied his face, looking for the lie. But she couldn't see it. He was too practiced at hiding it. "Why did you go to Alex's hotel room?"

"He told you I offered him money, didn't he?"

"I saw the check. He ripped it up."

"It seems we've both been keeping things from each other," Hank said. "You've met him twice now without telling me."

"And you slept with Caitlyn and got her pregnant. I think that's the bigger problem."

He reached over and took her hand. "I'm not perfect, and I never said I was."

"You cheated on Catherine. On Nan. On me." She thought about what Will Stafford had said, how everyone's a cheater. "Alex told me you knew about the baby, that it was yours."

He dropped her hand and stood, pacing back and forth in front of her for a few seconds before he stopped to look at her. "Do you want a divorce, Kate? If you do, this is the time to do it. I don't want it, but it seems you might not be able to move past this."

He was giving her an out. Could she trust him after all of this, after reading Nan's diary? She wasn't naïve enough to think that he'd change. Men never did. It didn't get past her, either, that he hadn't denied knowing the baby was his.

When she didn't answer, he sat again. "I'm going to Dubai in the morning. I'll be gone two days. Think about what you want." He touched her cheek, and she felt the familiar electricity. He felt it, too. His breath quickened, and he leaned in and kissed her. She didn't resist. She was ashamed that despite everything, she still wanted him.

She heard his phone buzz, and he pulled away, reaching into his pocket. He stuck the phone to his ear and walked away from her, farther down the terrace, his voice drifting across the park.

She shifted back onto the chaise, and when he came back, his face drawn and serious, she knew what he was going to say.

"You're leaving," she said before he could.

"Emergency meeting."

"The stocks again?" They hadn't talked about it.

"Seems that someone leaked to the press that Joan is missing." He frowned. "But the odd thing is, the stocks had started to go back up and began to fall again *before* the news hit."

He didn't seem to hear the implication of what he was saying.

"Before the press got hold of it or before Joan went missing?" Kate asked.

"Before she went missing," he said.

"Just like with Caitlyn. The stocks started to fall before the body was even found."

They stared at each other, both thinking the same thing now. Whoever killed Caitlyn and possibly Joan was manipulating Tudor Enterprises's stocks.

"We should let Trooper Pawlik know about this," Kate said. "He might be able to find out who's doing this."

Hank shook his head. "I have people I can put on it. I'd rather keep it quiet until I know what's going on. First, though, I have to get to this meeting. Stay put, order something in for dinner. I can't promise I'll be back. I might have to go to the airport from there." He gave her a quick kiss on the cheek and disappeared inside. How easy it was for him to dismiss her.

This was what her life would be like now. She'd seen how he was when he was married to Caitlyn. Why had she thought her marriage would be any different? Because they'd had such a close working relationship, because she felt as though he trusted her as his assistant and, therefore, even more so as his wife? Maybe her friends were right. Maybe she *was* crazy for marrying him. She considered what Hank had asked. Did she want a divorce?

She'd wanted this marriage, wanted Hank. She had never been so sure about anything.

Kate had a sudden and unexpected urge to talk to Anna. Anna, who would understand more than anyone how she was feeling. But Anna was dealing with Joan's disappearance—and her possible death. She couldn't lay her problems at Anna's feet.

Kate waited until she was sure Hank was gone. She didn't like being in the penthouse; it felt like she was imprisoned. At least Cromwell wasn't lurking. He'd gone with Anna and Maril to "settle them in" before joining Hank in Dubai.

She got up and went through the penthouse to the bedroom. She sat on the bed, running her fingers over the soft cotton duvet, remembering how gentle Hank had been at first, as though she were too delicate and might break under his touch. She'd taken the lead, surprising both of them, not wanting him to hold back. No, there had been no doubts. None—until she found Caitlyn's ring in his bag.

Her eyes strayed to Hank's dresser. She wasn't one of *those* wives, who checked up on her husband or searched his things for clues of infidelity. But if Hank had Caitlyn's ring, what else was he keeping secret? Before she could stop herself, Kate was flinging clothes out of his drawers until the floor was littered with them. From there, she moved to the walk-in closet, shoving her hands into the pockets of his suit jackets and trousers. Nothing. She sat on the floor of the closet and took a deep breath. What was happening to her?

She spotted the carryall Hank had with him at Anna's. He must have taken a larger bag with him for Dubai, one that could accommodate an extra suit. Absently, she unzipped the carryall, but a glance told her it was empty. As she began to zip it back up, she felt something in its side pocket.

No, not the pocket. Inside the lining of the bag. She inched her fingers around until she found a hole in the seam. Unless she'd been looking for it, she would never have found it. She slipped her fingers inside and felt something smooth. She managed to grab it and pulled it out.

A phone.

She hit the side button to power it up.

Within seconds, the lock screen appeared: the date, the time, and a photograph of Caitlyn and Alex Culpepper, their arms around each other, grinning.

It took her a second before she realized what she was holding.

Caitlyn's cell phone.

May 5

The house is on the market. Cromwell tells me that it has to be sold, that I have to move out within two weeks. I know it's because I told him I'm going to fight. I told him it will be worse than Catherine. I have a lawyer. Her name is Margaret Pole. She goes around in the same circles as Catherine and Hank, but they're not friends. I met her at a few functions, and we hit it off. I didn't know who else to call, so I reached out. She's tough, and she says she can stall a divorce a long time, maybe even longer than Catherine's lawyers stalled hers. Long enough so I might be able to ruin him. Crush his reputation. At the very least, he won't be able to marry Jeanne. He'll tire of her, too, anyway. And then when it's all over between them, I can walk away.

Maggie tells me that he can't get custody of Lizzie. That's my main concern. Even though I love this house, I'll let it go if I can keep my daughter. Maggie said he doesn't have any basis for divorcing me, except irreconcilable differences. He's claiming adultery, but he can't prove it. That one night at the party doesn't count. A lot of people saw it—that was the idea—but there's no trail showing that I'm having an affair with anyone. It was a drunken indiscretion. Maggie doesn't see any problems with that.

I've threatened to use his affair with Jeanne, but he's stopped seeing her—at least for now. I can't prove the affair. I hired a private investigator, but he hasn't been able to catch them. I asked Maggie if we should tell him about the baby.

He'll find out soon enough, but she says to keep quiet about it for now. It probably wouldn't sway him either way. She's right about that. He wants to be rid of me, of our marriage. I want to destroy him. A baby would get in the way.

I don't have access to our finances anymore. He's hidden them away. He gives me an allowance, but every month it gets smaller. He did this with Catherine, too. But it won't work on me like it didn't work on her. We are both smarter than he is. I've got money socked away; I have access to it. He doesn't know. I knew I had to be prepared. Just in case. Of course, I didn't seriously think it would come to this, but I'm glad I made the arrangements anyway.

Cromwell has been threatening me with financial ruin, taking Lizzie away, spreading stories that would keep me from ever working again. These threats come from Hank, although it's easier for him to send his messenger. Then he can claim down the road that it wasn't really him. That Cromwell acted on his own. Even though everyone knows Cromwell doesn't do anything if Hank doesn't approve it.

I've been recording my conversations with Cromwell. He doesn't text me or email me or send me letters, because he knows I'll save them. Maggie told me to try to get some of the threats in writing, because legally I shouldn't be recording without his consent. But I have to have some backup. In case something happens.

Cromwell probably knows about the recordings. He's evasive on the phone, not outwardly threatening, but I can hear it in his voice. I can't use the apartment in the city or the house in Greenwich. All the locks have been changed. And now this house is for sale. To challenge any of this, I have to agree to the divorce immediately. I'd rather be homeless and living on the street before I let Hank go without getting what I want.

It's killing him.

43

K ate fiddled with the phone, but it was locked and she didn't know the password. She tried Caitlyn's birthday, Hank's birthday, Alex's birthday, but none of them worked. She turned the phone around in her hand. Hank had Caitlyn's phone hidden in his carryall. How had he gotten it? She didn't want to go there, but her thoughts were taking her there anyway. No one gave up their cell phone, just as it wasn't believable that Caitlyn would have given up that ring.

Had Hank had something to do with Caitlyn's disappearance? Her murder?

She hadn't seriously considered it before, since she and Hank were honeymooning and he couldn't possibly have killed her. What about Tom? Did his rosebushes really back up his story about the scratches on his hands?

On a whim, Kate opened the lock screen and punched in the simple 1-2-3-4-5-6, and shockingly, it unlocked. It figured Caitlyn wouldn't have set her own pin.

Dozens of texts appeared on the screen, from Alex, from Jane Rocheford. She saw her own, asking Caitlyn to call.

There were almost as many voicemail messages. Kate scrolled through the list, and Hank's number caught her eye. It was left on the same day Caitlyn had visited Anna's. Kate hit play and listened:

"Tom will pick you up tomorrow at ten for the appointment."

Kate hit the button to play the message again. And again. And again.

What appointment? Caitlyn had been upset at Anna's, drunk and crying. And she was pregnant.

If this was about the pregnancy, then Hank lied to her. He'd known. Caitlyn must have told him. How far would Hank have gone to make sure Caitlyn didn't have that baby?

She had no proof of anything. The message didn't really say anything. But why would Tom be picking Caitlyn up? And for what kind of appointment?

Kate put the phone down on the floor next to her, her hands shaking. Caitlyn left the rehab center and went to Anna's after Hank left this message. And then she disappeared into the night; no one saw her again. Except the person who killed her.

Hank had her phone.

Why hadn't he gotten rid of it? It would be easy enough to do.

Her thoughts were pinballing all over the place and landed in one place: she'd turned on the phone, which meant that anyone—the police, Pawlik?—who might want to locate this phone would be able to track it. Her fingers found the power button and shut it down again.

She sat on the floor of the closet and debated what to do. Put the phone back where she found it? Put it in her own hiding place? Toss it in a dumpster? Destroy it?

Using a safety pin, Kate removed the phone's SIM card. She turned the little computer chip over and over in her palm. And then she slipped the phone itself back into its hiding place in the carryall.

In Hank's den, she found a small padded envelope with the other office supplies she'd had access to when she was his assistant. Putting the SIM card into a white letter envelope, she stuck it inside the bigger one and filled out the address on the front.

Hank might be back tonight—or he might not be. Kate glanced around at the mess she'd made in the closet, in the bedroom. Leaving everything as it was, she walked through the penthouse and grabbed her bag from where she'd dropped it on the living room sofa, tucking the padded envelope inside. She didn't want to stay in the penthouse. She didn't want to be alone with Hank, in case he came back. She had to sort out her thoughts, figure out what she wanted to do.

She rode down in the elevator and spotted the bodyguard in the lobby. He wasn't supposed to engage, but he would follow her. She tried not to focus on that as she approached the desk.

"Can you post this for me?" she asked the concierge in a low voice so as not to be overheard, a twenty-dollar bill on top of the envelope she took from her bag. She stood in such a way so the bodyguard, at a distance, might not be able to see the transaction.

The concierge smiled. "I'll keep an eye on that for you," he said cheerily, his eyes flickering over her right shoulder as he slid the envelope underneath a pile of newspapers on his desk. "Have a nice evening."

She gave him a smile. The doorman opened the door for her, stepping aside as she moved past him with a nod.

Kate quickly moved along the sidewalk, acutely aware that the bodyguard was following her. She also knew, however, that he wouldn't get too close. When she reached the subway stop, she scurried down the stairs and to the turnstile. She pulled her phone out of her bag and tapped it to the turnstile's screen. She hurried through to the subway platform, looking around behind her, but she didn't see the bodyguard. Kate checked her watch, but she didn't have to wait too long before the train rumbled toward her on the track. The doors opened, and she stepped inside the air-conditioned car. She found a vacant seat, so she sat, staring out at the platform as the doors closed.

That was when she saw the bodyguard standing outside, a puzzled look on his face. Before she could stop herself, she lifted her hand in a wave and then he was gone.

⊶──⊷

Kate still wasn't certain that she wasn't being followed. She might have left that bodyguard back at the station, but it didn't mean Hank hadn't hired more than one. She took the train to Times Square and made her way through the maze until she was aboveground again, her eyes darting around, suspicious of everyone and anyone. The sidewalk was thick with pedestrians, and she weaved her way around them, letting the city with its scents and sounds envelop her. The penthouse had felt claustrophobic, but here she could breathe again, clear her head.

She thought about checking into a hotel, but she really only wanted to go home, to her apartment, where she was surrounded by everything that comforted her. Hank would be able to find her—it wouldn't be hard for him to guess where she'd gone—but if he showed up, at least she'd have the home-turf advantage.

The cab dropped her in front of her building. She was climbing the stairs when her phone rang.

She fished it out of her bag and stared at Hank's name as she let herself into her apartment. No doubt he'd received the report that she'd left and lost the bodyguard. When she got inside, she put the phone on the island. He could talk to her voicemail.

Kate took a wineglass out of the cupboard. She had a bottle of white in the fridge. She shouldn't drink without something to eat, so she found some crackers and settled in on her couch. She felt numb, the wine further anesthetizing her. She didn't want to think about Hank, how happy she'd been until a few days ago, how her future seemed as though it had so much promise. So she drank and nibbled her crackers, staring at the pictures of her parents and her travels, thinking about how much she missed them and wanted to ask their advice. The sky outside faded to dark, streetlights splashing against her walls, not unlike the paintings at the penthouse. She finished the bottle of wine and stumbled to the bedroom, stripping down and pulling an oversized T-shirt over herself before falling into bed.

The sound of shattering glass startled her awake.

44

ANNA

Anna wasn't used to first-class travel. Even when she ran her family's company, she flew coach and took public transportation. The private jet to the island and car that picked them up at the small airport belonged in another world, one she hadn't lived in long enough to make it part of her everyday life. Maril, on the other hand, was nonplussed. She, of course, was used to traveling this way.

Anna wasn't happy—not at all—about leaving her house. She felt as though she were abandoning Joan. She could imagine her saying, "You really want to trust the police to find me? You should know better than that." But she'd been outnumbered. Everyone—including Kate—thought that staying would not be safe.

"It won't do Joan any good if something happens to you, too," Kate had argued. Anna could tell Kate wasn't happy, either, because she had to go back to the city with Hank and there was trouble in paradise. Anna suspected Kate was having second thoughts about marrying him. Hank certainly wasn't doing much to change her mind, either, although Anna had noticed the new diamond necklace around Kate's neck that she kept fiddling with.

Spending time with Kate had been interesting on a lot of levels. They both knew what the rules were, and despite their differences, they had a bond. Joan would never completely understand. Not really. She could walk away at any time, but Anna and Kate would forever be Hank Tudor's wives. They'd shared so much in the past few days. An odd relationship: one wife, one ex-wife.

Hank certainly couldn't be happy about that, which was probably why Kate had been whisked off to the Central Park West penthouse and she found herself on Martha's Vineyard.

Anna kept checking her phone, anxious that she'd miss a call from Joan. Or from Pawlik, telling her they'd found Joan.

She couldn't let herself believe that anything had happened to her wife. That Joan wouldn't come home to her. She had to have hope—or she wouldn't be able to go on.

Joan should have been sitting next to her. She would have relished this, "an adventure," she would have called it, if she hadn't been the reason for the banishment to Martha's Vineyard. Joan had a curiosity and an animosity about Hank. She didn't like the way he "took advantage" of Anna, but at the same time, she followed all the news about him. She'd taken some pleasure in the stock sell-off after Caitlyn's body was discovered, said it was his "comeuppance." Anna hadn't liked that but kept her mouth shut. She'd had a lot of practice and it was second nature to her now.

What would Joan say, to see her with Maril and the children, no allies to speak of? Her wife would say something caustic, urging Anna to stand up for herself and not allow Hank to tell her what to do. But if Joan were here, Anna wouldn't have been sent away at all.

Where was Will Stafford? Anna had had no reason to suspect him of anything except loyalty. She shivered, thinking of how many nights she was alone with him on her nocturnal walks. Joan was the one who found him, who hired him, but now that Anna thought about it, she didn't really know anything about him except his military service. She'd told Pawlik everything Joan told her about Will, but as she did, she realized he'd never volunteered any information and she hadn't asked. She'd always figured he didn't want to talk about what happened in Afghanistan. Now she found herself wondering if he'd even been there at all. But why would Joan lie? The question brought her back to one that had been hammering at her ever since Hank admitted hiring a private investigator: Why had Joan lied about having children?

She didn't like having doubts about her wife, but they crept into her head and wouldn't budge.

The Vineyard house was fairly modest, as Hank's houses went. It was similar to the one in Greenwich, with gray clapboard siding and white gingerbread trim, but it was larger. While some of the typical island houses were a little too frilly for Anna's taste, Hank's house had an elegance about it. Anna, Maril, and the children climbed out of the car—no gate, but Anna suspected the security cameras were capturing everything that was happening on the secluded property. If they were working. Hank had been especially apologetic about his "glitchy" cameras at the Greenwich house, said heads would roll because they still weren't working properly even after Caitlyn's body had been discovered.

They were herded in through the kitchen, and Anna was immediately taken by the six-burner, stainless steel gas range with a colorful Italian tile mosaic backsplash. The rest of the kitchen was equally as tasteful, with a porcelain farmer's sink and a quartz countertop that looked like marble. She thought about her own kitchen, now a little worn around the edges, and wondered if, once Joan returned and they were back home, they could do some updating.

Maril didn't give her much time to ruminate, however, as she led them up a back stairwell to the second floor. No one said a word, not even Ted, who was usually not prone to keeping quiet. Lizzie took everything in with those large gray eyes of hers, missing nothing. Maril, who knew her way around this house, assigned bedrooms. The one chosen for Anna had wallpaper with tiny pink-and-blue flowers, and the bed was covered with a large white goose-down comforter.

"Nan redecorated the house. She didn't like the way it was when my parents were married," Maril said, finally breaking the silence after Lizzie had been deposited in her room and was out of earshot. "Daddy never changed it after that."

"What about Jeanne?"

"He never brought her here."

So there had been no wives in this house since Nan.

Hank must have had someone open the house, air it out, before they left, because there was no sign of dust or dirt. It was impeccably clean, as though it had been expecting them.

As Maril went to check on Lizzie and Ted down the hall, Anna ran her fingers along the bedcovers and the edge of the carved wooden dresser. An oval mirror set in a gold frame hung over it. Anna peered at her own face, wondering about Nan Tudor and if there were answers about her here among the ghosts.

The window was open, a soft, warm breeze kissing her cheeks. The ocean spread out beyond the house. A couple of sailboats moved across the water.

Tom Cromwell appeared in the doorway. He'd escorted them from Greenwich, but he'd spent the time rifling through papers in his briefcase, stabbing messages on his phone. Distracted.

"You've never been out here, have you?" he asked.

Tom knew very well that she'd never been to the Vineyard house, and she resented him pretending otherwise. But she forced a smile and said, "No, I haven't. It's beautiful."

He reached over then and touched her arm. Instinctively, she recoiled.

"I'm not going to hurt you, Anna," he said in a soft tone she'd never heard before. "I lost my wife. I know how it feels."

And for a moment, Tom Cromwell seemed human, but as his words settled, she took a deep breath, tears springing into her eyes. "*Your* wife is dead. Joan is—isn't—"

"I know," he said, still in that unfamiliar tone. "We'll find her."

"I'd like to be alone right now," Anna said firmly, channeling Joan.

Tom narrowed his eyes at her, as though debating whether she *should* be left alone, and then said, "Certainly," and stepped backward out of the room, shutting the door behind him.

Anna sat on the bed and waited a few minutes. She pulled her bag up onto the bed and unzipped it, feeling underneath the clothes, her fingers finally touching the hard surface of the tablet.

She and Joan shared it for inn business: guests, vendors, housekeeping staff, chefs they hired for special events, landscaping. It was all here. Pawlik had taken it for a short time but returned it, saying there was nothing of interest, nothing that could lead them to Joan's whereabouts.

Maybe not. But holding it and scrolling through the files and spreadsheets was somehow soothing. It made her feel close to Joan, wherever she was. It felt *normal* at a time when nothing was normal. It gave her hope that Joan was alive somewhere and would return and they could resume their lives.

She opened a few of the spreadsheets with information about their past guests. Joan had been meticulous with recording their likes and dislikes—and her impressions of them. Some were difficult, demanding. Some were relaxed and delightful company. Anna remembered all of them—and how she and Joan had gossiped over glasses of wine after they'd left.

Except one.

Anna frowned as she tried to recall this particular guest. But the name John Dudley didn't ring a bell. According to the date on the file, he stayed at the inn two years ago, not long after Joan became a part of her life and the inn. Curious, she opened the spreadsheet.

The only thing on it was a phone number.

Before she could think about it, Anna picked up her phone and punched in the number.

It went straight to voicemail.

Hi, it's Will. You know what to do.

45

ANNA

It wasn't Will's phone number, at least not the one she had. But it was his voice. Unmistakably.

Anna fumbled with her phone. She'd put Pawlik's number in her contacts, and she found his name and hit CALL.

"Is everything all right?" Pawlik didn't bother with greetings and pleasantries.

"I, um, might've found something, but I don't know what it means." Anna told him about "John Dudley" and the phone number.

"Let me look into this. Give me the number."

She did. "I didn't leave a message. I was too stunned, honestly, to think of it. Should I call back?"

"No," Pawlik said. "I'll take care of it."

"He'll know I called, though, right? He'll have a missed call. He knows my number." Anna felt a small panic attack rising.

"He doesn't know where you are," Pawlik said, his smooth baritone calming her. He hesitated a second, then added, "We haven't been able to find anything on Stafford. It's like he doesn't exist. But let me look into this other name. It seems he could have been using an alias with you."

"Do you think he did something to Joan?" Anna asked.

"We can't speculate right now," Pawlik said, although Anna could hear in his tone that he was doing just that. "Did you find anything else in that tablet that we may have missed? Any more about this Dudley?"

"Nothing else," Anna admitted. "I can take another look through it, if you think it might help."

"It might. That would be helpful." Again he hesitated, before saying, "You said you found this in your tablet that you shared with Ms. Carey?"

"Yes, in the spreadsheet of guests we've had the last two years."

"Does anyone else besides you and your wife have access to it?"

Anna understood what he was asking. If she and Joan shared the tablet, then one of them would have entered the information—and it wasn't her. "No one else has the password," she said. She didn't like what that could mean. Joan had hired Will, brought him in early on, vouching for his skills, his background.

"I'll take care of this," she'd assured Anna, who didn't know the first thing about hiring a security team.

There must be a good explanation. Although what that might be, Anna had no idea. By putting "John Dudley" into the spreadsheet, what did Joan know about him that she hadn't shared with her? And why wouldn't she share it?

"There's no news about Joan?" She didn't want to ask but had to—even though if there *was* any news, she was sure he would have called her already.

"Nothing, I'm sorry."

At least they hadn't found her body—or any other evidence that would point to Joan being harmed in any way. Thank goodness for small favors. It meant Joan could still come home to her.

She hung up with Pawlik and went through the tablet again, but nothing else jumped out at her. Her finger hovered over the spreadsheet for John Dudley and opened it once more. She stared at the phone number, wondering what was going on. She switched over to the search engine and typed "Will Stafford" and "John Dudley." A quick scan of the results told her nothing.

She tried both names on social media platforms, but nothing. No one who looked remotely like Will or had his background. She tried both names with the phone number, but since it was likely a cell phone, there were no results.

Pawlik had resources she didn't have, and she hoped he'd turn up something. As she went to put the phone down, it vibrated with an incoming call. Hank.

"Have you heard from Kate?" he demanded.

It wasn't enough that she had lost her own wife, now she was supposed to keep track of his? "No. Should I have?"

"I've been calling her and texting, but she's not picking up."

Anna sighed. "I thought you were with her."

"I had to go to the office and now I'm heading to Dubai. I left her at the penthouse, but the bodyguard said she left. Went to her apartment." He paused a moment, then said, "I really love her, Anna."

She was surprised how much emotion was in his voice.

"I don't want to lose her. I was stupid and didn't handle this well."

Anna had never heard him like this, not even in those early days with Caitlyn. "Maybe you should go to her apartment. See her before you leave. Tell her you're sorry, fix this."

He was quiet again.

"Or you could wait until you get back from Dubai. Give her a little space." Anna was irritated that she had to try to fix his relationship when her wife was missing. It was as though Hank had completely forgotten about Joan. It was always all about him, wasn't it? He was probably more upset that Kate hadn't obeyed him and stayed put in the penthouse.

"You know what, Hank," she said, not bothering to keep the anger out of her voice, "I can't deal with you right now." And she hung up.

That was probably a mistake, but she didn't really care. Anna fiddled with her phone. The recent calls popped up, and there was John Dudley's—Will's?—number again. While Pawlik said it was a good idea she hadn't left a message, she felt a strong urge to do so. Ask Will exactly where he was, if he had anything to do with Joan's disappearance.

Before she could stop herself, she hit CALL.

This time, though, instead of getting the voicemail message, she heard:

The number you have dialed is not in service.

May 18

She's gone.

He took her. He locked me in the upstairs bathroom when he did it. The bathroom that doesn't have any windows. I couldn't see her; I couldn't stop him. I screamed her name, but it's a big house and she probably didn't hear me. She probably thought I let her go.

I thought about killing myself then. But there was nothing in the bathroom that I could use. Not a towel or a pair of scissors or even tweezers. The medicine cabinet was empty. He must have planned it. He must have known.

Could I really do it, though? Could I kill myself and have my daughter know that I was dead? That I would never come back to her?

No. I had to be stronger than that.

I had to be strong for the baby inside me, too.

I don't know how long I was in there, but then the door opened. He stood there, on the other side, his arms crossed over his chest. It was the first time I'd seen him in months. Cromwell had been doing his bidding, but I suppose he'd realized Cromwell wasn't getting anywhere.

I tried to be quiet about the divorce. About our marriage. I hadn't wanted to risk losing my daughter, so I'd made Maggie promise we weren't going to leak anything about it to the media. They'd find out soon enough once it was done.

But it had gotten around that I was living here with Lizzie and that Hank was nowhere to be seen. I heard the whispers, terrified that Hank would hear them, too.

But it didn't matter now. My daughter was gone.

"Where did you take her?" I asked.

He leveled his gaze at me, his eyes full of hate. He'd loved me once. He did everything he could to have me. None of that was left in this man who only wanted to hurt me. What had I done?

What had Catherine done?

Neither of us had done anything.

"I hope you know now that I can do anything and you can't do anything about it," he sneered. "You have to fire that lawyer. You have to let Cromwell handle everything. I would have been generous if you hadn't tried to play me."

"If I do fire Maggie, will you let me have Lizzie?" I didn't want to beg, but I couldn't stop myself.

He smiled then. A mean smile that told me I had no cards to play. That he was going to do what he wanted.

He had no intention of letting me have Lizzie.

A rush of desperation washed over me, and adrenaline overcame me. I lunged at him, my fingernails ripping the side of his face. He grabbed my wrist with one hand and with the other arm caught me in a chokehold. I couldn't breathe.

"I could kill you right now and no one would ever know," he hissed in my ear. "No one would ever care what happened to you. I will never give up my daughter, and if you try to take her, I will kill you. She is mine."

He pushed me away then, onto the floor, and I coughed, rubbing my throat. His face was bleeding, but he didn't seem to notice. He turned and walked away. I waited until I heard the front door slam shut before I got up, my legs wobbly, my throat burning.

I couldn't leave her with that monster. I would find a way to get her back. I had to. If he killed me, at least I would know I tried.

HE'S GOING TO KILL ME

46

Someone was in her apartment.

Kate's eyes struggled to adjust to the darkness. She took small, shallow breaths, forcing herself to keep as still as she could.

Maybe she'd imagined it. Maybe it was a dream.

No. A musty, earthy scent of perspiration hung in the air, and the floor-boards in the living room creaked under heavy footsteps.

She shifted slightly under the covers, her heart pounding, and glanced at the red, glowing numbers on the clock. Two A.M. She reached for her phone, remembering only when it wasn't there that she'd left it on the kitchen island next to her wineglass.

Why hadn't she brought it with her when she went to bed?

Because she'd had too much to drink. She hadn't been thinking that someone might break into her home in the middle of the night and she'd need to call 911.

A light went on, its beacon stretching through the hallway and touching the bedroom door briefly before disappearing. She heard something skid-ding along the floor. Rummaging. The boxes. They were empty. He'd find out soon enough.

Did he know she was here? Was he here to rob her—or worse?

She began to shake involuntarily, aware that her gasps were audible. She held her breath for a few seconds, hoping to calm herself.

And then she remembered. The gun. It was a small Smith & Wesson .380, recommended by a friend back when her ex-husband was stalking her, when he'd left her threatening voicemails and notes at her apartment. She'd never needed it, but she'd learned how to use it. Just in case.

Right now was the "just in case."

Kate rolled over and tugged at the small drawer in her nightstand. She held her breath, but the drawer slid out silently. She slipped her hand inside and felt the small pad of paper, the pens, a vibrator, a packet of Kleenex, reaching farther in the back—but no gun.

A bubble of panic rose in her chest. It was here. It had to be.

She felt around again, sure she must have missed it. But no.

If he saw the wineglass—was that what she'd heard break?—it was likely he'd seen her phone.

And then he'd know she was in the apartment.

She had to hide.

There wasn't room underneath the bed, and that was the first place he'd look anyway. The closet? Again, not enough room.

But she did have a fire escape.

Her apartment was on the fourth floor—*No, don't think about that.* There was nowhere else to go.

Kate slipped out of bed, glad for her bare feet, barely aware she was wearing only an oversized T-shirt and her underpants. She crept to the window, her hands on the sill. As she began to lift the window, she heard the front door slam shut. She swung around and froze in place.

Was he gone?

She strained to hear anything, the silence settling over her in the dark.

Kate took two steps forward, her arms hugging her torso. She still heard nothing.

Two more steps.

Her heart was pounding. If he was still there, he wouldn't be able to help but hear it, it was so loud in her own ears.

Still silence.

She reached around on the other side of her dresser and grabbed the baseball bat leaning up against it. She should have kept this next to the bed, but then again, she thought the gun was within reach. Where *was* the gun, anyway?

Clutching the bat, Kate tiptoed through the bedroom and into the hall, passing the bathroom, and peered into the living room and kitchen area. Her eyes were completely adjusted to the darkness now.

It wasn't a big apartment, so if someone were here, she'd see him. No. She was alone. She took a deep breath and loosened her grip on the bat, but her heart was still pounding.

She stepped on something sharp; broken glass was scattered on the floor. The wineglass she'd left on the island.

And then she noticed that her phone was no longer there.

Damn.

Kate brushed the piece of glass off the sole of her foot and padded gingerly to the door to study the lock. It didn't look as though it had been tampered with. She'd put on the deadbolt, hadn't she? She remembered thinking she had to be more careful. Alex Culpepper's surprise visit had made her more conscious about securing the door, but maybe she'd forgotten. She'd been drunk, after all.

The police might notice something she didn't.

Right. The police. She needed to call them, report this. But how was she going to do that without a phone?

She locked the deadbolt and put the bat down. She reached over to turn on the light next to the sofa. She made her way around the island carefully so as not to step on the glass again and pulled the small brush and pan out from underneath the sink. As she swept up the glass, she thought about who might have been in her apartment—if, in fact, it wasn't some random burglar. Her laptop still sat on the coffee table, her TV was still across the room, and those were things that would have been taken along with the phone if it were a burglar.

She tossed the glass into the bin, and as she did, she heard something. A sort of scratching noise. She stood up, listening. Nothing.

And then she heard it again. But this time, she recognized the sound. It was the shower curtain in the bathroom. She hadn't checked in there. She'd assumed he was gone.

He's still here. He's still here.

She rushed to the door, fumbling with the deadbolt.

The light went out, bathing the room in darkness again.

Just as she flipped the lock, a glove-covered hand covered hers, and his body pressed up against her, against the door so she couldn't move, his other hand over her mouth.

"You're not going anywhere," he hissed in her ear.

The voice was familiar, but she couldn't place it. Her brain wasn't working right. She needed to get away, wanted to struggle, but it was as though she were paralyzed. She tried to scream through his hand, but no sound came out.

Kate closed her eyes and tried to push away the fear. She took a deep breath through her nose, like in yoga, and let it out slowly. She yanked her head to the right and sank her teeth into his wrist as hard as she could.

"Fuck!" he growled as he instinctively jerked back slightly.

She took the opportunity to duck underneath his arm and broke free, running down the hall to the bedroom and slamming the door shut behind her. There was no lock on the door. Why hadn't she ever put a lock on this door?

She ran to the nightstand again, pulling everything out of the drawer. Where was that gun?

She heard the door open and swung around, regretting not going out the window and wasting time on the drawer.

He stepped inside the room. He was dressed all in black, baggy pants, a hoodie covering his head, a ski mask covering his face.

"Are you looking for this?"

Kate stared straight into the barrel of her gun.

And then everything went dark.

47

CATHERINE

If she'd told someone, they probably wouldn't believe her, but Catherine was genuinely sorry for Anna Klein. Her wife had gone missing—presumed dead—and she'd been whisked away from her home and business. The press didn't know where she was, but Maril was with her.

"Anna's head of security has vanished, and Daddy's worried that it's not safe at the inn," Maril had told her yesterday when she called.

"Why do you have to go with her?" Catherine asked. She didn't like to think about Maril in that house on the Vineyard. The house had bad karma; even though Hank had bought the house for *her*, That Woman had taken it for herself.

"Because Kate is going to the penthouse, and Daddy wants someone with Anna."

"Why is she going to the penthouse?"

"Daddy's leaving for Dubai in the morning, but he wants her there. He says she's safer there." She paused a second, then added, "It's really awful about Joan. I'm afraid that she's dead, too. We all think that, but we're not saying anything because Anna's so upset."

"I'm glad you can be there for her," Catherine said. "Is it okay that you're not in the office?"

"I'm working off and on remotely," Maril said, and Catherine sensed the reluctance in her voice. Maril didn't want anyone to accuse her of slacking off because her father owned the company, but even though it wasn't a good look for her to be absent, Catherine supposed it made sense from Hank's point of view. Someone had to look after the children, and Anna probably wasn't in a state to do that at the moment.

What had surprised her was that Kate Parker wasn't going with them. That she'd gone back to the city, to the penthouse, with Hank. That wasn't part of the plan, but it made everything easier, almost like divine intervention.

"Is there any sign of Joan?" Catherine asked, curious what they knew, if anything.

"No. The only thing the police have found is her sneaker. It had blood on it," Maril said, worry lacing her tone.

When Joan Carey came to work for Catherine, they'd had an immediate connection, and she'd seen how she could use the other woman's talents. She moved her out of the office, while keeping her on payroll. Joan was the best corporate spy she'd recruited, and she proved her loyalty over and over again. There was that small misunderstanding that one time when Catherine made the mistake of showing her vulnerability after Hank had started to see That Woman. She hadn't been aware of Joan's sexual preferences until the woman had kissed her. Catherine managed to placate her ego and at the same time solidified Joan's commitment to her. This was what she was good at, why Hank should never have underestimated her.

It was too bad Joan's current assignment had to come to an end, but all good things, as the saying goes.

She hadn't heard from Maril again, except for a text last night saying they'd arrived safely. Catherine smiled at her daughter's thoughtfulness, but she was anxious. It was already midday with no more communication. She'd gotten used to daily reports, and she was riddled with regret. Well, it was too late now. Joan was gone, wasn't coming back. She wanted to reach out to her daughter, but it might look a little too suspicious. No, she'd remain patient. Maril would call her soon, she was sure of it.

Lourdes brought Catherine a tray in the library. The avocado salad and fresh baguette were a wonderful light lunch. Not to mention the glass of white wine. She didn't want to watch television or scroll through the internet, so she picked up a new mystery novel she'd preordered. But after a few pages, Catherine's gaze rested on a vase full of daisies across the room.

Daisies were the first flowers Hank had ever given her. He'd shown up at her college dorm room, four daisies in his grip. They were a little droopy, but she put them in a glass of water and set them on top of her dresser as Hank stood, awkward and uncertain. He hadn't yet become Hank Tudor. He was only Hank, the boy who fell hard for her in those early days.

"We're going to get married," he'd announced.

"I'll need more than daisies," she teased. "What about a ring?"

He took one of the daisies and broke off part of its stem, twisting the remainder around her ring finger, the petals fanning out across the back of her hand.

"How's that?" he asked, grinning. "I'll get you a proper one, I promise."

There were a lot of promises made in those days.

It was so long ago, but it felt like yesterday, even now. Even after all those wives who came after her.

Anna Klein and Kate Parker couldn't be more different, but she'd seen a strength in both of them that Hank would admire. He liked strong women, women who could stand on their own, apart from him. Even that Caitlyn Howard had had an inner strength.

None of them were a match for her, though.

The journal sat on the coffee table in front of her. She hadn't bothered to move it since Kate Parker had discovered it. What was she going to do with the pictures she took? Catherine thought about Caitlyn Howard and her blackmail proposal. Kate Parker didn't need to blackmail Hank; she had everything. Had she taken the pictures just to satisfy a curiosity about what had happened with That Woman? Possible.

Catherine picked up the book and contemplated how this could be useful to Kate Parker—and possibly Anna Klein. They had seemed unusually close despite their situation, in sync with each other. Their visit had seemed almost choreographed. She thought again how Hank would not be comfortable with that.

Catherine had leafed through the first pages of the journal after it had been returned to her, despite how painful it was. Yet, now, she felt drawn to the last entry, where That Woman described Hank taking her daughter. It had been cruel; Maril had been too old for a custody battle by the time Hank demanded a divorce. She felt a slight tug of compassion for the other woman before she remembered who had written this.

As Catherine finished reading, she flipped to the next page. The one that was blank because nothing had come after. That Woman had stopped writing and sent the diary to Maggie for safekeeping. She might have been disappointed to learn Maggie had been careless with it. Maggie had been careless with a lot of things.

But the page wasn't blank any longer.

HE'S GOING TO KILL ME

Catherine stared at the words. They weren't handwritten in the familiar bold script. They were printed, block letters, fear etched in them.

Caitlyn Howard had left this book at Anna Klein's. *She'd* written this. *She'd* left this message for Anna.

Catherine wondered if the other wives had noticed the difference in handwriting. Possibly not, because they hadn't known this page had been blank before Catherine gave the diary to Caitlyn. They would assume That Woman had written this—and they might assume Hank had something to do with her disappearance.

And if Caitlyn actually had tried to blackmail Hank with the journal, it could point to a motive for killing her. That and the fact that the girl was pregnant. Yet, even if the other wives suspected him, the nondisclosure agreements guaranteed their silence; Catherine was counting on that, on the erosion of trust.

Catherine hadn't been surprised when the wives told her about Caitlyn's pregnancy. She'd seen it, the soft curve of the girl's figure, the fullness of her breasts. But instead of being sorry about taking two lives, it only convinced her that she had no other choice. The girl would have trapped him, and Hank needed to be free.

It wouldn't be too long now before Hank would come back to her, his rightful wife. Catherine would stand by him, and he would realize what he'd almost lost and be grateful to her for never giving up on him.

She had taken only two bites of her toast when the doorbell rang. She called for Lourdes, but she didn't come, so Catherine hoisted herself up off the sofa and went to the door herself, peering through the peephole before opening it.

A messenger stood on the stoop. Catherine opened the door, and he handed her a note. She wanted to give him a tip—that was the proper thing to do—but before she could ask him to wait, he made his way back down the front walk to the waiting car.

Catherine unfolded the slip of paper and smiled when she read it.

There's only one left.

48

ANNA

Anna managed to survive by being the one who didn't rock the boat. Who kept her mouth shut. By doing whatever Hank wanted her to do. She'd played hostess to his friends, his business acquaintances. They'd stayed in her house, and she made sure that they were well taken care of. That was the deal they'd struck. That she would provide a haven for them to come and do business under the guise of spending a weekend at leisure. Hank would show up on the golf course, the tennis court, always slipping in and slipping out without anyone being the wiser.

None of that mattered now. Joan was gone, and Anna had been relegated to the Vineyard, where she encountered Nan Tudor's ghost around every corner.

Desperate, Anna called Catherine. "Is there anything about Joan that I should know that could help me find her?"

"I'm sorry I can't help you," the first Mrs. Tudor told her. "She left me to work for a competitor." She hesitated, then added, "I'm sorry for your loss."

Everyone acted as though Joan was dead.

She wasn't sleeping, but she'd stopped walking at night, letting her memories of Joan envelop her after everyone else had gone to bed as she scrolled through pictures of her wife on her phone.

Hank had left for Dubai, but he emailed her the private investigator's report, saying she could decide if she wanted to give it to the police. There was nothing in it that Joan hadn't told her—except leaving Catherine Tudor for another company and not having any children—so she forwarded it to Pawlik. She still couldn't understand why Joan had lied about having children, but maybe it was one of those little white lies you tell at the beginning of a relationship and the longer it goes on, the more embarrassing it is if you reveal the truth, so it just keeps going.

"I can hire someone else, to see if he missed something," Hank offered.

Anna realized it didn't matter. All she wanted was to have Joan back.

And maybe a little peace and quiet. Lizzie and Ted, realizing that this was not an adventure but an imposed quarantine without friends readily available, argued with her, with Maril, with each other, doors slamming, feet stomping. Anna didn't have the energy, and from Maril's expression, her patience had worn thin as well. Maril had easily agreed to come with them—another way to please her father, perhaps—but the stress of the situation was apparent in the lines around her mouth and eyes.

"I appreciate your help," Anna said to her, ignoring the raised voices from upstairs and pouring Maril another cup of coffee. As long as it didn't sound like anyone was getting physically hurt, she wasn't going to worry. Granted, it wasn't exactly fair, since Lizzie was on the cusp of puberty and going through the physical and emotional changes that went along with that and Ted was still a little boy, but as with any siblings, they would have to navigate this themselves.

Maril reached across the kitchen table and squeezed Anna's hand. "The police will find Joan. No one just vanishes."

Nan had, Anna thought. Or maybe she really *was* dead, like Maggie had said. What did that mean for Joan?

A crash overhead startled them both. Maril slid off her chair and sighed. "Stay here and finish your coffee. I'll see what they're up to." And she made her way out of the room and out of sight.

Anna took another sip of her coffee, which had started to go cold, when her phone began to trill and she saw Pawlik's name show up on the display. Her heart skipped a beat. Was it news of Joan? Besides the bloodied shoe, there were still no other physical clues as to Joan's whereabouts. But maybe . . . She took a deep breath and answered. "Yes?" She couldn't keep the anxiety out of her voice.

"I'm sorry, I'm not calling about Joan," Pawlik said, anticipating her question. "I'm calling about Mrs. Tudor."

"What about her?"

"She's in the hospital."

"What?" Anna froze, her hand clutching her phone, afraid to ask.

"First, she's going to be okay."

Anna breathed a sigh of relief. "What happened?"

"An intruder broke into her apartment in the city last night," Pawlik told her. "He shot her."

"She got shot?"

"Yes. But she's doing fine, although I'm not sure that was the intention."

Anna frowned. "You think he wanted to kill her?"

"He shot her in the head. Probably thought she was dead."

Anna let that sink in a moment. Someone tried to kill Kate. Caitlyn was murdered, and Joan was missing. Coincidence? She was dubious. But then she realized what he'd said: "She got shot in the head and she's fine?"

"The bullet didn't penetrate her skull. It tunneled under her scalp and came out the back of her head."

"That's possible?"

"Crazy, isn't it?" Pawlik asked. "But yes, it's possible. The gun was a small caliber, so there wasn't as much force, and he shot her high enough on the forehead. They told me it was a superficial wound. She was really lucky."

That was an understatement.

"You said it was an intruder? You mean like a home invasion?"

"More like a robbery. Her laptop and phone are missing, along with her engagement and wedding rings."

Anna's head was spinning, uncertain where to land. Finally, she asked, "What about the bodyguard?"

"What bodyguard?"

She gave a soft snort. "You don't think Hank Tudor is going to let his wives run around without being watched?"

Pawlik was quiet. Then: "Someone called nine-one-one, but we don't know who. When the police and EMTs arrived, they only found Mrs. Tudor and a neighbor who denied making the call." He paused a moment, then, "We're looking for Will Stafford."

"Why?"

"Mrs. Tudor's neighbor had one of those entryway cameras installed because someone was stealing packages," Pawlik said. "Stafford was there, earlier in the day. The camera caught him for a second before it went offline."

Will was technologically savvy enough to know how to dismantle a camera like that.

"You think it was him." It wasn't a question. While Anna hadn't wanted to think that Will had anything to do with Joan's disappearance, he'd vanished as completely as her wife, and it couldn't be a coincidence. And now this. But why? The engagement ring was worth a lot of money, but so was Caitlyn's, which had been in that bedroom dresser drawer where Kate had left it—until Anna stuck it in her bag, unwilling to leave it in the empty house. That one was worth a lot more, and Will had had access to the house and everything in it.

Had Joan caught him lurking around the house?

"I can see why you'd look for Will, but what if the bodyguard attacked her?" she asked. She didn't want to think that Hank's security team would be capable of that, but she hadn't expected Will Stafford—or "John Dudley"—to be anything except trustworthy, either.

"We'll look into it." She could hear the frustration in Pawlik's tone. "I'm curious about something. Did you have any contact with Mrs. Tudor yesterday or last night?"

It was an abrupt change of subject, and not one Anna was comfortable with. She bit her lip, thinking about the texts that she'd gotten late last night and dismissed. "What does it matter?"

"If she called you or texted you, it might help the investigation. She doesn't remember much."

"She texted me. She was drunk," Anna admitted.

"Can you tell me what she said?"

"She and Hank had a fight."

"She found out her husband was the father of Caitlyn Howard's baby."

"That's right."

"That's all she said? That they had a fight?" Pawlik's tone was more probing now. She would have to tread lightly.

"That's right." Should she tell him that Hank asked Kate if she wanted a divorce? She wasn't willing to make that call. It was Kate's personal business, and anyway, it might not be relevant.

"Did you know she was at her apartment by then?"

"No, I didn't. I thought she was still at the penthouse." This was becoming more of an interrogation. "I didn't know what was going to happen." Anna hesitated, then added, "It was like Caitlyn. You know, when she came to my house drunk and crying. I could picture Kate the same way. I figured she'd sober up and we could talk in the morning. In fact, that's what I told her when I responded. That's all."

Could some IT guy retrieve the messages from a cloud somewhere? Possibly. But Anna wasn't going to make it that easy.

Because Kate had also texted her the pictures of Nan Tudor's diary entries.

You should have these, too, she'd written. *Just in case.* She didn't elaborate, but now it seemed prescient.

Anna didn't want those photos on her phone—or anywhere digitally. She found a printer in the den and printed them out, hiding the pages between her clothes in the dresser. Not the safest place, but the quickest at the moment. And then she deleted all the texts from Kate.

"Speaking of your ex-husband, Mr. Tudor seems to be on an airplane heading to Dubai." Pawlik's voice pulled her out of her thoughts. "Even when he gets there, it will be a day before he can get back. I know you're on the Vineyard, but you can get here faster."

"You mean . . ."

"She's asking for you."

49

CATHERINE

She was still alive. How could she still be alive?

Maril's phone call had been unexpected. Her daughter was giddy with the gossip, that Kate Parker had been shot in her apartment, was in the hospital, and Anna was heading to the city to be with her. The police were looking for Will Stafford. She didn't register her mother's silence, told her she'd call her back later if there was any other news.

Catherine's well-laid plans had come undone. The woman had been shot in the head. Who could survive that? Apparently, one could. Perhaps Catherine should have insisted that this wife die the same way the last one did. There would have been no mistakes that way.

Granted, that was another fine line. Too many headless wives and Hank would become suspect number one, even if he did have an airtight alibi.

She thought about that a few moments. Maybe that wouldn't be so bad. She could visit him in prison, be the one person who would stand by him. Then he would have to realize she was the only woman for him.

Catherine tapped her fingers against the sofa arm as she contemplated the situation. Everything had been going so well. She'd been another step closer to having Hank back. This was what happened when she had to rely on other people.

Catherine had worried about Will Stafford—or John Dudley, if that was really his name—from the start, but he'd come highly recommended. It hadn't been difficult for him to hack in and dismantle the security at Hank's Greenwich home, resulting in the "glitches" Maril told her about. He also had a remarkable lack of conscience that went along with greed. Catherine paid him handsomely, even though he'd insisted on cryptocurrency. She didn't trust it, but she grudgingly admitted it was an easy way to hide the money trail. There was no way anyone could trace it back to her.

He'd been sloppy, though, by being seen at Kate Parker's apartment building. Her anger simmered. She was so close now. But what if more mistakes were made? How much longer would she have to wait for Hank? She'd rarely felt helpless, since she'd been able to orchestrate everything despite her agoraphobia. But at that moment, her world was even more narrow. She needed to take matters into her own hands; there was no one else to rely on. Maybe Maril was right. Maybe she *should* get out of the house. Just the thought of it made her heart beat faster, but she didn't have much time. If she was going to do it, she just had to do it and not think about it, like ripping off a Band-Aid.

Lourdes wasn't coming until after noon; she had a doctor's appointment. Catherine had no excuse.

Catherine went to her bedroom and dressed carefully: a pair of jeans, a white button-down shirt. She pulled her hair back and put on a straw cloche hat and a pair of oversized sunglasses before slipping on a pair of white canvas sneakers. She grabbed a small handbag, putting her wallet and a burner phone inside as she made her way downstairs, stopping in the bathroom to pop a Xanax. She hesitated a moment, then stuck the bottle in her purse. She might have found an inner strength, but it was going to need a bit of a boost. This was more important than worrying about a little agoraphobia. Still, when she stepped into the garage and saw the car—when was the last time she'd driven?—she froze, her heart pounding.

She took a few deep breaths, glad for the yoga she did every morning, and opened the garage door before climbing into the driver's seat of the car. Catherine's knuckles were white as her hands tightened around the steering wheel. The key was in the ignition, but she made no move to start the engine. She looked in the rearview mirror and saw the driveway, the trees, the outdoors.

Would she be able to do this?

Catherine turned the key and the engine turned over. Baby steps, she told herself. Slowly, she put her foot on the gas and backed out, making sure she was keeping the car straight. She watched the garage door close, keeping her out, but the Xanax had started to do its job and she pulled into the street.

It was like riding the proverbial bike. The longer she drove, the more relaxed she became. Maybe she should have ventured out long before this. When Hank came back, he'd need a woman who didn't sequester herself in her house and never go outside.

This last thought bolstered her confidence even further.

The GPS told her to go on the highway, but she wasn't ready for that. Instead, she rerouted on side streets, easy enough to do, and there wouldn't be any cameras, either. The longer she drove, the more comfortable she became—or maybe it was the Xanax. She considered some music but decided she didn't need the distraction.

She knew where to find him. The credit card he had was one she'd provided. It couldn't be traced back to her; it was in the name of an LLC set up years ago and bore the name John Dudley. All she had to do was check the account online to discover he was staying in a motel near Dobbs Ferry and had an afternoon flight scheduled out of Westchester.

It was the old-fashioned sort of motel where people parked in front of their rooms, no indoor access. Lucky for that. Catherine pulled into the parking lot at the motel, scanning the cars, aware that she wouldn't be able to pick out the rental just by sight. No longer did rental car companies advertise on the vehicles.

This area was far from unfamiliar. She and Hank had friends who were members at the Ardsley Country Club on North Mountain Drive, and they'd spent a bit of time there. Hank would play a round of golf, she would have a spa day, and then they'd have cocktails and dinner. Where were those friends now? Did Hank still see them? Or had they dropped him, too, during his succession of wives?

Catherine plucked the burner phone from her bag and texted a message. A response came almost immediately.

Panic began to bubble again in her chest. As she considered another Xanax—would it impair her ability to drive? Most likely, but so, too, could a panic attack—she spotted a man coming out of a room at the end of the building. She squinted and recognized Will Stafford. He put a carryon suitcase into a small, nondescript Nissan, climbed into the driver's seat, and pulled out of the spot.

Catherine inched her car onto the road behind him, far enough away so as not to alert him to being followed. He *was* a military man, after all. Did he know Kate Parker was alive? That he hadn't succeeded in killing her? He certainly drove like a man without a care in the world, so perhaps not.

The road became more twisty as it climbed toward the country club. Catherine's instincts took hold. Hank had indulged her years ago with a defensive driving course at Lime Rock in Litchfield. She'd learned some tricks, yet she couldn't assume Stafford didn't know some himself. But she had the element of surprise.

She spotted a curve up ahead, beyond Stafford's car. She put her foot firmly on the accelerator and the car shot forward. He must have seen her in the rearview mirror, because he sped up, going much faster than he needed to. His car skidded slightly but couldn't regain purchase because another curve came right after the first one. Catherine picked up her foot, her car slowed to a stop, and she watched as Will Stafford's car jumped the guardrail on the opposite side of the road and disappeared over an embankment.

50

Kate hated being in the hospital. All she wanted to do was sleep, but it was the one thing she couldn't do. Too many noises, too many people in and out, checking her vitals, taking blood, making sure she was still alive. Her head was killing her, and she was having a hard time focusing.

All she could do was lie here and listen to the cacophony. She had just closed her eyes again when she sensed someone else had come into the room.

"Kate?"

Her eyes snapped open to see Anna hovering in the doorway. She was surprised how happy she was to see her. "Thank you for coming. They won't let me out unless I've got somewhere to go."

Anna moved closer and covered Kate's hand with hers. It was warm, and Kate struggled to fight back tears.

"Of course I came," Anna said. She didn't ask about Hank, why Kate would ask for her instead of her husband.

"I know you're going through a hard time, so I wasn't sure," Kate said.

Anna took a deep breath. "Gives me something to do other than wait."

Kate felt guilty now. She shouldn't have asked for Anna. But she didn't have anyone else. This time she didn't stop the tears from falling.

Anna stroked her hair, and Kate closed her eyes again.

"Doesn't look too bad," Anna said.

She was talking about the wound. High on her forehead, the doctors had put only a couple of stitches into it. She had a matching one on the back of her head. She had to lie just so against the pillow, but it didn't really hurt that much. The concussion bothered her more. The doctor explained that while she had only superficial wounds, the bullet did hit her hard enough to knock her out. Whoever shot her probably thought she was dead.

All she could remember was her gun in his hand.

"Can you tell us everything that happened?" the police officer had asked.

She'd struggled to put it in order, landing first on the intruder's scent as she was held against the door. The gun. *Her* gun.

She'd shaken her head. "It's fuzzy."

"Do you remember what time it was?"

"No. I didn't look at the clock." Hadn't she? When she closed her eyes, she could only recall the fear, knowing someone was in her apartment and being helpless. The officer had been kind, trying to walk her through what had happened, but it was as though it had been a dream, so vivid at the time but slipping away with each waking moment.

She'd seen the officer getting frustrated. She couldn't remember anything about the intruder: Was he tall, short, heavy, thin? No, she wouldn't be able to describe him for a sketch artist.

Her memory kept landing on the gun. The only thing she knew for certain. She didn't remember getting shot, only that she'd awoken in the emergency room, police and doctors and nurses everywhere.

Was this what amnesia was like?

"When can I get out of here?" she asked Anna.

"They're putting together the discharge papers now."

"Are we going back . . ." Kate couldn't find the words. She knew she'd stayed with Anna somewhere, near Hank's house in Connecticut. What was the name of the town?

"To the inn, yes," Anna said.

"Is it safe there?" Kate wasn't sure she'd ever feel safe again. Her apartment had been her safe place, and she'd never go back there. *Hank would like that, wouldn't he?* The thought startled her.

"It's all being arranged."

Kate might have brain fog, but she still felt annoyed that someone else was arranging things when she had been the one doing the arranging not that long ago. She reached up and touched the wound on her forehead, wincing a little. She wanted to ask about Hank, but she was afraid to. It would open a Pandora's box of emotions—and fears. While she couldn't remember everything that happened the night before, she clearly recalled finding Caitlyn's phone in her husband's carryall and her quick escape to her apartment.

She didn't tell the police officer about that. When he asked why she'd left the penthouse, she'd merely said, "I wanted to be in my own place." He'd seemed to accept that. She'd noted that he wore a wedding ring, so maybe there were times he wanted his own place, too.

A knock on the door, and while she was expecting a nurse, Pawlik came in. He wasn't wearing his usual uniform but a button-down shirt and a pair of jeans, a ball cap on his head instead of the trooper hat. When he moved toward her, she spotted the gun in its holster under his light jacket. He nodded at Anna first: "Ms. Klein," and then at Kate: "Mrs. Tudor." His eyes studied her, landing on the wound on her forehead.

"You're a very lucky woman," he said. "Although it probably has more to do with the fact that you owned a small-caliber pistol. You might consider something a little bigger the next time."

"I'm not sure I need more than one gun."

He cocked his eyebrows, as though she would change her mind. Maybe she would. But the fact that the intruder used her gun didn't give her confidence that owning one would keep her safe, and if she did have a bigger one, the intruder might have actually killed her. She shivered involuntarily at the thought.

The nurse followed Pawlik into the room and handed Kate a pile of papers. "You're all set to leave," she said. "Keep the wound clean and call your doctor for an appointment to take the stitches out in a couple of weeks." She gave a nod at Pawlik and Anna before leaving.

Kate swung her legs over the side of the bed and stood. She was still wearing a johnny, so she held the back together with one hand and took the clothes Anna handed her with the other.

"Do you need help?" Anna asked.

Kate glanced at Pawlik. "Maybe."

Anna followed her into the small bathroom and shut the door after them. Kate turned her back and started dressing, noting that the clothes Anna had given her were not the ones she was wearing last night.

"I went to the penthouse and found some things for you," Anna explained. "I also packed you a bag. They wouldn't let me into your apartment since it's still technically a crime scene."

Kate nodded and quickly pulled on the jeans and T-shirt. A flash of memory—was this the way it was going to be?—of the chaos she'd created in the closet. She lowered her voice and said, "I went a little crazy in the closet before I left. That's why it was a mess."

Anna frowned. "Mess? There was no mess. It was neat as a pin."

Kate froze. Had Hank gone back after she'd left? He would have suspected she'd gone to her apartment. And he might have discovered that she'd found Caitlyn's phone in his carryall.

She slipped on the sneakers Anna had brought. "Thanks," she said, pushing her way back into the hospital room, where Pawlik was pacing. He looked up when they came back in, tucking his phone in his pocket.

He looked at Anna first, then at Kate. "We found Will Stafford." He hesitated a moment, then added, "He's dead."

51

Will Stafford died in a car crash, speeding on a twisty area of road.

"That road is really dangerous, and he must've been driving at a very high speed. The car jumped the guardrail and went down an embankment, rolling over several times before slamming into a tree." Pawlik bit his lip and looked from Anna to Kate. "Your rings, phone, and laptop were in a small suitcase that got thrown from the car."

Kate began to tremble. She'd gone alone into the city with him. She'd suspected that he was the one who told Hank that she met Culpepper at her apartment, despite her attempt to dodge him. He knew where she lived. And then he'd vanished at the same time Joan went missing.

It should make her feel better, right, that he'd died? Instead, she was uneasy; it felt too neat. Kate remembered their conversation in the car when he told her about driving in demolition derbies. She assumed that would make him a better driver, but when she mentioned it to Pawlik, the trooper shrugged it off.

"Different circumstances altogether," he said, but she could tell he was struggling with something.

"What is it?" she pressed.

Pawlik shook his head. "I'm not quite sure how to tell you this, but it'll get out, and you should hear it from me first."

Kate glanced at Anna. "It's not about Joan, is it?"

"A small cooler was found near the wreck." He didn't answer her question.

Kate felt a chill run down her back.

Pawlik bit his lip, his expression grim. "Caitlyn Howard's head was inside."

Anna leaned over and retched. Kate began to shake. A nurse came running into the room.

"Oh my," she clucked, staring at the vomit on the floor, then immediately took Anna's arm and led her out, nodding at Pawlik to do the same with Kate.

As they stepped out toward the nurses' station, Kate heard the nurse instruct someone to go in and clean up as she settled Anna into a curtained area. Someone went past with a small plastic pitcher of water and a handful of crackers.

Kate put her hand on Pawlik's arm just outside the curtain.

"Are you sure?"

He gave a snort. "Yes."

"So Will killed Caitlyn." Kate mulled that over for a few seconds. "Why would he do that? Why would he try to kill me, too?"

"We may never know," he said honestly, "but we aren't finished with our investigation."

"Does his death mean I'm safe now?"

Pawlik nodded. "I would think so."

But Kate was still uncertain. "He was driving his own car?"

"I know what you're getting at," Pawlik said. "Why would he shoot you and then take off in his own vehicle, risking being caught?"

She nodded.

"It wasn't his car. It was a rental. Rented to a John Dudley, who matched Will Stafford's description. And we know that Stafford was using both names."

"Does that mean we might never know what happened to Joan?"

"We're still looking for her," he assured her, but Kate was pessimistic.

Kate settled into the Adirondack chair and looked out over the water on the horizon, the sun's reflection glistening in its ripples. Was it a good idea to return to the inn? Her nerves were on edge. Her brain still felt as though someone had stuffed cotton between her ears. But she had nowhere else to go—and didn't have the energy to make any sort of plan.

Neither Kate nor Anna wanted to talk about what had happened—or about Caitlyn. They were both still trying to wrap their heads around everything. When they'd first gotten back, Kate had sequestered herself in her bedroom, shutting out the rest of the world and crawling between the soft sheets. She'd managed to fall into a fitful sleep but awoke fully at sunrise. She wasn't sure where Anna was, but coffee had been made and was sitting in the French press in the kitchen. She'd poured a cup, wrapped herself in a blanket, and came outside, hoping it would clear her head.

"Kate?"

Hank's voice echoed in her ears. Her husband was standing over her, casting a long shadow across her face. She waited for the familiar excitement at seeing him, but instead her heart began to race with anxiety.

He shifted from foot to foot as though he were a nervous schoolboy, and as she squinted at his face, she could see he didn't know what to do or say.

"You might as well sit," she said, forcing her tone to stay measured. Never let him see weakness, she'd been told before her first interview with the billionaire businessman.

He sank down into the chair next to her and reached over to take her hand. In that moment, she remembered everything about their last conversation, her search of his things in the closet. Caitlyn's phone and the message he'd left for her.

She gently pulled her hand out from under his and placed it in her lap. He stared at the wound on her forehead.

"They said I was lucky," she said.

"I'm lucky," he whispered. "I'm so glad you're okay."

"Well, I'm alive. Not sure I'm okay."

"At least Will Stafford is dead. You don't have to worry about him any longer."

Cold comfort.

"Do you want to talk about it?" he asked.

She shook her head. "Not really." She hesitated a second, then said, "You were at the penthouse. After I left."

He nodded, his eyes narrowing. "It seems there are some trust issues."

"I found her phone. Caitlyn's. In your carryall." She watched his expression closely.

He wasn't surprised. "I don't know how it got there."

Kate snorted. "Seriously? You had her ring, too."

"Kate, I told you about the ring, but on my honor, I don't know how her phone got into the bag."

He reached into his breast pocket and took out a small metal square. The SIM card from the phone. He placed it on the armrest of her chair.

She should have known the penthouse concierge was loyal to Hank and would not have mailed the envelope as instructed.

"What did you think you found? Is this the reason why you left the penthouse?" Hank was asking.

"You left a voicemail for her. About an appointment."

His face grew dark and she could see the anger simmering. She was going too far, but she'd already started down this road and she couldn't stop herself.

"Caitlyn wanted to keep her baby," she said.

Hank sighed. "You know what Caitlyn was like. What kind of mother would she be? A drunk and a drug addict."

"You could have helped her."

"No. No, I couldn't. And you and I, we were just getting started. I wanted *you*, to be with *you*. I didn't want anything to get in the way of that."

Kate felt her heart pounding in her chest. He was going to make Caitlyn get rid of her baby so he could be with her without any ties to his ex-wife. She thought about Anna's description of the girl, hysterical that last night anyone had seen her.

Hank knew she found Caitlyn's phone, knew what she'd heard in the voicemail. How far would he have gone to keep her from telling Pawlik about it? Would he have hired Will Stafford to keep them both quiet?

Kate shifted slightly away from him in her chair, her hands in her lap, clasped to keep him from noticing her tremble.

She didn't want to believe that her husband would try to kill her. Would have his ex-wife killed. And maybe he didn't. But what other explanation was there for what Will Stafford had done? Her husband was a ruthless businessman. Was he capable of murder? And what had really happened to Nan Tudor? Was she dead, like Maggie told Anna? Were her final words in the journal a premonition?

She'd married the man standing before her a little less than three weeks ago and had promised to love him until death. She'd meant every word of her vows, but now they felt like empty promises.

"I asked you a question two days ago, Kate," Hank was saying. He stood, blocking the sun, which illuminated his silhouette. "I do love you, and I want a life with you. But we can't have a life together without trust."

She wanted to be able to tell him she trusted him, but she couldn't.

As though he could read her mind, Hank picked up the SIM card and palmed it before walking away without another glance.

52

CATHERINE

Catherine had been gone barely two hours, but it felt like a lifetime. She left the garage door open to air out the odor of exhaust; it wouldn't do to have Lourdes suspect that she'd actually taken the car out. The moment she stepped back into the house, she took another Xanax, stripped down, and took a hot bath. When she was done, she put the clothes she'd worn earlier back on; again, she didn't want Lourdes to wonder why they would be in the hamper. It wasn't as though they were dirty, she told herself. She'd been careful when she tossed the cooler down the embankment after the Nissan had hit the tree, and she was certain Stafford hadn't survived.

By the time Lourdes came in, the garage was sealed up once again and she was sitting in the library reading the discarded mystery novel from the day before, a cup of tea in front of her. The Xanax hadn't cut the anxiety, but she hadn't wanted to take any more.

"I'm sorry I'm late, Mrs. Catherine," Lourdes said. "The doctor kept me waiting."

She smiled. "No problem, I've been fine here by myself."

And she *was* fine. As fine as she could be. She wasn't sure if she'd go out again anytime soon, but she'd proven to herself that she could, if it was necessary. She wished she could tell Maril about it, so she'd stop harping at her, but of course she couldn't. No one could ever know.

＊

Catherine heard from Maril in the late afternoon. Her daughter was staying at the Vineyard house with the children until their camps started in a week. The other wives had come back to Greenwich, to the inn. Catherine assumed Kate Parker would go back to the city with Hank when he returned from Dubai. She would have to figure out what to do about that later. There had been far too much excitement today to think about it now.

She had just finished her dinner on the patio when she heard the door-bell ring.

"Mrs. Catherine?" Lourdes said, coming out a few moments later. "There's a gentleman here to see you."

Catherine frowned. "Who is it, Lourdes?"

Lourdes didn't get a chance to respond. Tom Cromwell stepped through the French doors, and before she could react, he settled himself in a chair across from her.

Lourdes hovered a moment, but Catherine nodded, indicating that she would handle this unexpected visitor. Lourdes went back into the house and shut the doors after her, giving her employer and her company privacy.

"Good evening, Catherine," Cromwell said when he was sure they were alone.

He was far too familiar. He should never address her so informally.

"I believe I did not invite you here," she said coldly.

"Invitations shouldn't be necessary between friends." He gave her a wide, ugly smile. "And you'll change your mind when I tell you why I've stopped by."

Despite herself, Catherine's imagination considered the possibility that Hank had finally come to his senses. While his wife had not died, he was leaving her, coming back to Catherine, the woman he'd given his heart to so many years ago.

But Cromwell's smile disappeared and a sneer formed instead. He leaned toward her, his elbows on the table between them.

"I understand Caitlyn Howard came to see you."

Catherine's expression didn't change. It wouldn't serve any purpose to lie. "That's right."

"Why?"

"I'm not sure it's any business of yours."

"Any business having to do with Hank is my business. What did she want?"

Catherine waved her hand in the air. "Oh, this and that. I'm not sure why it's relevant now that she's dead."

He sat back, studying her face. "You know they found her head."

"I don't know what that has to do with me," she said.

He gave a short snort. "It was found near the body of a man who worked for Anna Klein. A man named John Dudley, who was using an alias."

"So?"

"His credit card was in the name of an LLC. An LLC that was set up a long time ago."

Catherine willed herself not to show any emotion. "What, exactly, do you want, Mr. Cromwell?" she asked, keeping her tone measured.

Cromwell got up and walked around the patio, surveying the lawn that spread out beyond it. "This is a nice place. You like it here?"

She didn't care for the question. The last time he'd come to see her, she'd ended up at her current house, thrown out of her home she shared with her husband. This house was the consolation prize, but she'd grown to like it. She was comfortable, safe.

She didn't answer him.

Cromwell swung around and stared down at her. "Somehow Caitlyn Howard's phone ended up with Hank. He doesn't know how, but I wonder if John Dudley left it there to frame him."

It was an interesting idea, Catherine had to admit, but if that had been the plan, she wasn't privy to it.

"Nan Tudor kept a journal," he said, startling her. But she wasn't going to show that he'd caught her off guard. "Caitlyn told Alex Culpepper about it, but he said the last he knew, she had it. I wondered if she gave it back to you."

The girl must have told Culpepper where she'd gotten it, but even if Cromwell searched the place, he wouldn't find the safe upstairs. It hadn't been there when they'd banished her here.

Catherine rose and faced him. "I admit that I did have it, and I did give it to the girl. But I don't know where it is now." If pressed, would Kate Parker or Anna Klein tell him she had it? That Kate Parker had seen it in the library? Maybe. But he wouldn't hear it from her.

"If you did have it," Cromwell said, "and it was somehow returned to Hank, he might not be inclined to tell the police about the LLC associated with John Dudley."

She mulled over his proposition. If she agreed, she would be as good as admitting her role in Caitlyn's murder. She kept quiet. Nan Tudor's journal would disappear, and no one would be the wiser. Granted, Kate Parker had taken pictures of its pages, but it would be easy enough to dispute. Let Hank and Cromwell go after *that* wife instead.

"Hank wants to sell this house," Cromwell said then, when he realized his threat hadn't gone far enough.

She almost laughed. What he didn't realize was that she'd anticipated this would happen someday. It was her house. She owned it outright. He hadn't done his homework, surprising her a little, but then again, Tom Cromwell had always underestimated her.

"Let him try," she said. "It's time for you to go." She sat back down and waved her hand, dismissing him.

53

A WEEK LATER

K ate brought her small bag down to the great room, dropping it next to the basket of slippers before going into the kitchen. Anna had made coffee, and the aroma filled the air.

She didn't want to leave. She felt safe at the inn. Ironic, really, since Hank's fifth wife had been found murdered next door and his fourth wife's spouse, who lived here, was missing—probably dead, too, but she wasn't going to say anything like that to Anna. Anna, who was visibly grieving now that days had passed and Pawlik had stopped coming by as frequently. Kate was doing her own grieving—for the marriage she'd been so confident about and the husband she'd loved.

In a perfect world—a world without Hank Tudor and Tom Cromwell—the two women could grieve together, solidify the bond they'd formed.

But it wasn't a perfect world.

It wasn't as though her marriage was being dissolved. Not yet. But Hank had not returned after confronting her with the SIM card. Tom Cromwell had, though.

"He's giving you some time," Cromwell had told her. "Some space. But it would be best if you didn't stay here any longer."

Kate could hear the unspoken message: *No fraternizing between wives.* The more distance between her and Anna, the more comfortable her husband would be. She considered saying no, pushing the envelope even further, but when she thought about it a little longer, she wondered if maybe Hank wasn't right. Maybe she *did* need some space.

Underneath it all, though, she could see his pattern. How when he wanted to end a relationship, he walked away without a look behind him. Was that what he was doing now, under the guise of "giving her some time?" By doing that, he was leaving the decision about their marriage up to her. He didn't have to deal with it.

He hadn't hesitated to take the SIM card, and with it the possible evidence that he may have had something to do with Caitlyn's death. She was sure he'd disposed of the physical phone. He wouldn't be so careless going forward.

Kate could have gone to Pawlik with this, but despite her suspicions, that was all they were: suspicions. And even though Kate was ashamed of it, she still wanted to protect him. She'd been doing it for so long it was second nature.

What did it say about her that part of her wanted to end the marriage—but another part wanted to go back and try to work it out? Despite her doubts. Despite knowing her husband wanted his ex-wife to end a pregnancy so it wouldn't "get in the way" with his new wife? She had no proof that he had gone far enough to kill Caitlyn—or, rather, have her killed. The voicemail wasn't explicit; Caitlyn had said nothing to Anna. Hank told her Caitlyn had given him back the ring. But Caitlyn wasn't alive to ask about any of it.

Could Kate go back to him not knowing for sure he'd had nothing to do with her death?

She had a lot of soul-searching to do.

Kate took the mug of coffee Anna pushed toward her on the island. "Thanks," she said.

"How are you getting to the city?" Anna asked.

"I've ordered a car service." Kate had found a sublet uptown, near Columbia University. A friend was taking a sabbatical in London for a year and offered it to her. She sent a mover to her apartment and put everything in storage except her clothes and some photographs, which she'd had delivered to the sublet. She couldn't bring herself to go back there.

"This doesn't mean we can't see each other," Kate said. "He just doesn't want us living together."

Anna rolled her eyes, then her face grew serious. "Are you okay on your own?"

Kate had been having nightmares about the shooting. She'd reached out to a therapist and had an appointment the next day. "Will Stafford is dead," she said with more confidence than she felt. "I still don't understand why he did what he did, but he can't hurt me anymore."

Anna was quiet a moment before saying, "I trusted him. He'd been nothing but loyal, at least that's what he led me to believe. What's worse, though, is that Joan trusted him, and . . ." Her voice trailed off.

"You said Joan hired him?"

Anna gave her a quizzical look. "That's right."

"Maybe she knew something about him. Or found out something, a secret he had. I wouldn't put it past Joan to confront him about it."

Anna smiled. "Joan doesn't back down from a fight," she conceded, but then her smile disappeared. "What about Caitlyn?"

"What about her?"

"Why would he kill her?"

Kate shrugged as she stared down into her coffee mug, unable to share her fears about Hank's possible involvement. "I don't know. That's for Pawlik to find out." She looked back up at Anna. "We may never know." Immediately she regretted her words, realizing that they probably would never know what happened to Joan. Joan had been gone almost two weeks now, with no sign of her besides that bloody sneaker.

"I'm thinking of closing the inn permanently," Anna said suddenly.

Kate frowned. "But this is your business."

"I'm not good at this, not alone anyway. Joan was the one who made it a success. I mean, Maggie is the one who suggested the slippers." She hesitated a moment, then said, "I might start an online local newspaper."

"There's no money in that," Kate said.

Anna laughed. "No kidding. But I liked being a journalist, running a newspaper. The online thing is different, but it's not like I don't have time to learn how to do it. And maybe at some point, I can figure out how to make some money at it." She didn't have to say that she didn't need the money, that her settlement with Hank was more than enough to support her.

Kate was in the same situation now, and it was uncomfortable. She'd never relied on anyone else before for her livelihood. She and Hank were separated. Should she continue to take his money while their marriage hung in the balance? She had the feeling her parents wouldn't approve.

Kate's cell phone pinged. Her car had arrived. She and Anna both stood awkwardly.

"Well, I guess I'll see you around," Kate said, breaking the silence. She leaned over and they gave each other a quick hug before Anna pulled her into a tighter embrace. When she let her go, Kate felt a tear escape down her cheek.

"It's not goodbye," Anna said. "We'll be talking, and I'll always have a room for you here."

"As long as you're here," Kate said, wiping her eyes and picking up her bag.

"Oh, I'm not going anywhere. I have to stay."

She was going to wait for Joan.

Anna walked her out to the front porch. Kate went down the steps to the waiting car. The driver opened the door for her and put her bag in the trunk. She turned to wave, and guilt rushed through her.

Because Kate was keeping a secret. They'd done a routine test when she was in the hospital.

She was pregnant.

EPILOGUE
NAN

The hardest part had been leaving her daughter behind. It had been pure survival—for both of them. But she had to go—her life depended on it—and despite everything that had happened, she had to believe that he would not hold it against his daughter. If she'd found out that he did, she would have gone back for her, regardless. But so far, it seemed she was well cared for and there was no need to emerge.

She kept tabs on her. Maggie kept her promise. She looked like her father, all that red hair, but she saw the same determination in her eyes and jawline that she saw when she looked in the mirror. The girl was a survivor, too, and she'd do what she had to do. Maybe someday she'd understand. She hoped desperately that she'd understand.

She gave the diary to Maggie. She wanted her daughter to know what life had been like for her, that one day her parents loved each other so much they were willing to risk everything to be together. And then, like that, it was over.

The last words she'd written were imprinted on her memory. Some would say they were melodramatic; she'd been accused of that by him, by Cromwell, by the press. But in the end, she didn't have the courage to risk her life to get her daughter back. If she'd done so, she would have also risked the life of her unborn baby. That was her justification, the only way she could live with herself. Even if he had let her live, he would've taken her son, too, and left her with nothing.

In the end, though, it didn't matter. He still came for her. She saw the shadow cast across the lawn, caught by the light of the moon. She grabbed the bag she'd kept under the bed and made her way down the stairs, creeping out the back and into the night.

The body made it easy to disappear. The headless woman found on the beach, unidentified all these years.

That body was supposed to be her; she wasn't naïve. She knew about the homeless woman who roamed the beach at night. The woman looked somewhat like her, and from a distance and in the dark, they could be mistaken for each other. She saw him attack her, their silhouettes coming together almost like a dance before they disappeared behind the dunes.

They never found her head.

She should feel guilty for not helping her and, in a sense, using her as a decoy. But she didn't. By the time the DNA showed it wasn't her, she was long gone—and she was vulnerable yet again. No, it was easier to stay away, leave the lingering suspicions behind.

Maggie was the only one who knew what had happened. Maggie went to him, said she knew he'd done it, that he was rich enough to cover up the truth, wouldn't the police be interested in his threats—then let herself be bought. It was all part of the plan.

But she'd been wrong all along.

He *hadn't* come after her. Catherine had. Catherine, whose jealousy had simmered and burned until it took over her whole soul.

"We made a mistake," Maggie wrote to her. "We underestimated her."

At first, she chalked it up to Maggie's increasing dementia. Her recent ramblings about a hired killer, a pregnant ex-wife beheaded, blackmail. It sounded like Maggie was repeating her own history—until an internet search revealed facts that she couldn't ignore. The fifth wife was dead. The same way *she* was supposed to die.

And now Maggie was dead, too. Killed in a fire, her house set ablaze.

Maggie had known how to contact her, and she couldn't assume that whoever killed her—and she had no doubt this was no accident—hadn't gotten that information and given it to Catherine.

She was going to have to move them again.

She heard the children's shouts from outside. A glance out the window told her they were playing football in the street, her son quicker and more athletic than the others. Her heart swelled with pride. He was only eight, but he was getting taller every day. He was going to look like his sister, like his father, but they both had her eyes. Someday she hoped he could meet his sister. They were so much alike.

She grabbed her cloth shopping bag. She wanted fresh oranges for her juicer and some cheese and wine for later. She didn't have to work tonight; the restaurant was closed on Mondays. The cobblestone streets were uneven beneath her feet as she headed for the market. The village was small enough and remote enough that she'd been able to stay here longer than anywhere else. Still, she didn't make too many friends. She and her son spent evenings reading; she helped him with his schoolwork. She couldn't begrudge him friends. He didn't know about her life before, only about their life now. He'd gotten used to the frequent moves, but he would soon be old enough to start asking questions. Maybe this next move would be their last. Maggie was gone, after all, and with her, the risk of discovery.

She wandered the market stalls, the scents of flowers and citrus in the air. She was going to miss it here. She nodded and smiled and exchanged pleasantries with her neighbors. Even if they'd seen photographs of her from those years, they wouldn't recognize her. She was no longer the American wife of a billionaire. She was a French cook, a single mother. She was thinner and older, her hair shorter and curlier. She dressed in jeans and T-shirts, no designer clothes now. The stylish wife who'd been envied was gone. Sometimes she missed parties and lively conversations and debates with her husband, but this life was simpler. It was easy to keep her secrets.

There were days when she thought she saw him. When she was certain that he was watching her, waiting for her in dark corners. She sensed his presence, an electricity in the air that always preceded him. In those early days, she'd sense him before she saw him.

Did the others feel it, too? Jeanne, who played the game so well, was the martyr, the one who died before his power could torture her. Even if she hadn't, he would have tossed her aside, eventually. Despite everything, the bitterness still rose in her throat, jealousy overwhelming her. Even after all this time, she hated that woman. She had no reason to hate the others. She'd never known them. They came after. And the one who came before had never been a real threat—until now.

Still, she sometimes woke up in the night with desire so strong that her entire body ached for him.

A woman bumped into her, and she stumbled, dropping her bag, oranges rolling across the cobblestones.

"I'm so sorry," the woman said.

She wasn't going to engage, just wanted to let it go. She stooped down to gather the fruit.

"Let me help you," the woman said, handing her one of the oranges.

She took it, forced a small smile. "Thank you."

"Oh, you speak English."

"Yes."

"Such a relief. I'm still trying to learn the language."

She continued to pick up the oranges. When they were all back in her sack, the woman didn't move on. She stood awkwardly, uncertain what the woman wanted from her.

"I've just arrived here," the woman said. "I'm renting a vacation home in town. Maybe you could show me around? It would be wonderful to have a local guide."

The woman's smile was kind, reaching her eyes, which were a soft shade of green.

What harm could come of it? It would take a few days to make arrangements, and then they'd be gone.

The woman held out her hand.

"I'm Joan."

ACKNOWLEDGMENTS

This book wouldn't exist if I hadn't read Mary M. Luke's *A Crown for Elizabeth* when I was fourteen. That book was the catalyst for my lifelong obsession with everything Tudor. The only fiction about that era that I've read is Hilary Mantel's *Wolf Hall* trilogy and Elizabeth Fremantle's *Queen's Gambit*, preferring the multitude of biographies by historians such as Alison Weir, Antonia Fraser, David Starkey, Joanna Denny, Gareth Russell, Giles Tremlett, Linda Porter, Karen Lindsey, and Hayley Nolan.

I have always wanted to write about the Tudors, but I'm not a historian, and I don't write historical fiction. I wondered what Henry VIII and his wives would be like if they lived today, in the twenty-first century without royal trappings. As I began to sketch out Henry and his wives, I realized it might not be too difficult to bring them into the modern day. All of his wives were, in their individual ways, strong, intelligent, and progressive. I do believe he loved them all—until he didn't. My interpretations of who they would be in the present are, I believe, consistent with who they were in the past.

I've spent a long time with this, trying to strike a perfect balance—and weaving in what I am most familiar with writing: a central crime.

My agent, Josh Getzler, fellow Tudorphile and all-around cheerleader, has been on this book's journey with me almost from the beginning. He's been hearing me talk for years about it—even as I was stalled by a concussion and then Covid and long Covid—reading every version and giving me notes at every turn, each time strengthening the story and the characters. I owe so much to him.

I am grateful to Claiborne Hancock and Jessica Case at Pegasus Crime for taking on my modern version of the Tudors. I am so thrilled to be part of the Pegasus list. My editor, Victoria Wenzel, looked at the manuscript with an eagle eye, and it is better for her careful attention. I'm excited to be working with publicist Meghan Jusczak, and a big thank-you to Maria Fernandez for interior design and Lisa Gilliam for her excellent copy editing. Amanda Hudson at Faceout Studios designed the amazing book cover that perfectly captures the pages inside.

Even before I had a completed draft, Cheryl Violante was encouraging, so I moved forward. Clair Lamb was the first to point out that Catherine had a much larger role to play than I'd even realized. Dorothea Halliday and Danielle D'Orlando gave me a lot to think about—and a lot to work on. I owe more than she might believe to Kristen Weber. She forced me to rethink the book's structure, and it is a lot tighter and more focused than it was before she read it.

Dr. Dave Hart and Jim Born offered their expertise, patiently explaining what might happen if a person is shot in the head with a small-caliber bullet. John Halliday and Ray Tartaglione were invaluable with their suggestions of twisty roads in Westchester County.

Ultimately, this is a book about women. Strong, intelligent women and their relationships with men and with each other. A huge shoutout to those women whose friendship I cherish and with whom I've shared hours of conversation about books, writing, politics, and life in general: Nancy Lyon, Patty Smiley, Kerri Pedersen, Liz Medcalf, Dorothea Halliday, Theresa Braine, Alison Gaylin, Cheryl Violante, Laura Benedict, Eleanor Kohlsaat, Clea Simon, and Clair Lamb. I am also so proud of my daughter, Julia, and the woman she's become.

This book is dedicated to my mother-in-law, Edith Hoffman, an art historian and academic in a profession dominated by men. She was a trailblazer, and I know she would toast this book with her signature Manhattan.

And finally, thank you to my husband, Chris Hoffman, for his support and love. There's no one I'd rather go through life with, and we've been married long enough so I feel fairly confident that I will never be inconvenient.